In M 52

D1295721

A WAY OF
ESCAPE

A NOVEL

SERENA B. MILLER

SB C1

LJ EMORY
PUBLISHING

F
mil

LJ EMORY
PUBLISHING

This book is a work of fiction. Names, characters, places, and incidents are a product of the author's imagination or are used fictitiously. Any resemblance to actual events, locales, or persons, living or dead, is coincidental.

Copyright © 2014 by Serena B. Miller

Find more books by Serena B. Miller at *SerenaBMiller.com*
Find her on Facebook, *FB.com/AuthorSerenaMiller*
Follow her on Twitter, *@SerenaBMiller*

All rights reserved. No part of this publication may be reproduced, stored in a retrieval system, or transmitted in any form or by any means without the prior written permission of the publisher. The only exception is brief quotations in printed reviews.

First L. J. Emory Publishing trade paperback edition November 2014

For information about special discounts for bulk purchases, please contact L. J. Emory Publishing, sales@ljemorypublishing.com

Cover and interior designed by CJ Technics

Printed in the United States of America
10   9   8   7   6   5   4   3   2   1

ISBN 978-1-9402-8314-2
ISBN 978-1-9402-8315-9 (ebook)

To my sister, Vivian Bonzo Woodworth,
for so many years of encouragement.

I want to express my gratitude to:

Connie Troyer for helping make this a stronger book.

Sergeant Roger L. Cooper, OSHP Retired, for searching the unfinished manuscript for procedural errors.

Dr. William Ellis, for sharing his personal Appalachian Trail journal with me.

Kerri Davis for agreeing to be my cover model.

My immediate family who help with every aspect of creating these stories, and I'm especially grateful to my readers who—to my unfailing amazement—continue to ask, "When is that next book coming out, Serena?"

I lift up my eyes to the mountains.
Where does my help come from?
My help comes from the LORD, the Maker
of heaven and earth.
He will not let your foot slip . . . The LORD
will keep you from all harm. He will watch
over your life . . . your coming and going
both now and forevermore.

—Psalm 121 (NIV)

PROLOGUE

Blake Ramsey was in over his head and he knew it. He shoved the kilo of cocaine deep within his desk and slammed the drawer shut. This was the unadulterated stuff, worth well over a hundred grand on the street—a heady number for a small-town lawyer.

After locking the desk drawer, he strode over to his law office's large front window, slit the blinds, and stared out at the dark, rain-slicked streets of Fallen Oak, Tennessee. It was April, his favorite time of year—rain or no rain. This was his home, his Mayberry, the county to which he had devoted his life

This was also where he had taught an adult Sunday school class for the past eight years and won the office of county prosecutor by running on a zero-drug-tolerance platform.

His wife, Erin, would be shocked and upset when she discovered what he had gotten himself into. He longed to call her and explain, but no cell phone service was available in the remote area of Honduras where she and their teenage daughter were on a mission trip with their church.

He couldn't have told her the truth anyway, at least not over the phone. He had begun to suspect that his telephones

1

might be bugged. It wasn't as though he had training in such things so he wasn't sure. All he knew was that he needed to be careful.

Still, it would be nice to hear Erin's voice.

Tonight he wished with all his heart that he had become a plumber, a mechanic, an accountant, or anything at all except a county prosecutor. As much as he had once loved the law, tonight he wished he had chosen a profession that didn't constantly pit him against the worst elements and temptations in the county.

A car came to a stop in the alley behind his office. That was strange. It was long after office hours, and there were seldom any emergencies requiring the need for a lawyer at this time of night. At least not in this small town. He glanced out the back window and saw three men quietly getting out of a car. Only one of them was familiar to him. What he didn't understand was why they were here, why they were together, and why they were approaching his office from the alleyway. All the parking spaces directly in front of his office were open.

Their very furtiveness put him on high alert.

Suddenly his brain solved the puzzle he'd been mulling for the past twenty-four hours and everything became clear. He knew exactly why they were there. For the first time in his life he regretted ignoring Erin's pleas for him to keep a loaded handgun in his desk.

He also knew that if anything happened to him tonight, Erin needed to be warned that this town was no longer safe. Not for her, and not for their daughter. Probably not safe for anyone. He could send her an e-mail, except he had already shut his computer down for the night. It had been getting slower lately. He'd been planning to have someone who knew about computer viruses to take a look at it, but hadn't gotten around to it. It would take several minutes for it to boot up—minutes he didn't have.

Thinking fast, he scribbled a line on a scratch pad and dated it—a line he knew only Erin would understand. He ripped the page off and stuck it inside the Bible he kept on his desk. Knowing Erin, if anything happened to him, the first thing she would take from his office would be his study Bible—the one she had given him for their first anniversary. When she opened it, the first thing she would see would be the lone yellow page within. It was all he could do for now. It would have to be enough.

As he opened the door, he tried to convince himself that he was being paranoid. He tried to convince himself that there was no threat, no danger, and that this hasty message to his wife would not be necessary. He tried to convince himself that he would be meeting her and their daughter at the airport tomorrow night with nothing more earthshaking to discuss than their trip to Honduras. He tried to convince himself that he would live through the night.

CHAPTER ONE

"Buying a horse is out of the question." Erin Ramsey felt a headache starting behind her eyes. "I'm sorry, but it just is. You should be able to understand that."

Thirteen-year-old Lindsey whipped the yellow dish towel off her shoulder and dried the antique blue-and-white serving bowl with such force that Erin was afraid she would rub the pattern off.

"But that's just it. I *don't* understand." Lindsey was so agitated, her strawberry blonde ponytail flipped back and forth with every jerky movement.

"We can't afford it, for one thing." Erin tried to lay a comforting hand on her daughter's shoulder, but Lindsey shrugged it off.

"Since Dad died, all you can think about is money and how much things cost!" Lindsey said. "The trip to Honduras cost a lot more than Doc is charging for the horse, and I didn't even want to go. You aren't being fair."

Erin took the bowl from Lindsey and placed it safely away in the cabinet. She longed for the old days when washing and drying the dishes together had been a pleasant mother/daughter task—a time when they would talk and laugh.

They were talking now, all right, but neither of them was in the mood for laughter. This was escalating into one of the worst arguments they'd ever had, and she didn't know what to do about it.

She felt like she barely knew her daughter any more. Lindsey was wearing those raggedy jeans again, the ones with so many rips and holes in them that Erin wanted to throw them in the trash. That faded t-shirt Lindsey had on needed to go away, too. Why couldn't the child wear any of the nice clothes Erin bought for her? Why must her beautiful daughter have to walk around looking like a street person? The headache intensified.

She tried reasoning with her daughter. "I care deeply about you and what you want, but I cannot justify buying a horse. Not right now. The last thing we need is a two-ton animal to buy feed for. Things are tough enough around here the way it is."

It was true. Since Blake's death two months ago, she found it hard to even crawl out of bed in the mornings, let alone care for an animal in which she was certain Lindsey would lose interest within a few weeks. Her teacher's salary barely stretched to meet their living expenses as it was. The last thing she needed was another living creature for which she would be responsible.

"But, Mom, you don't understand. Snowball is the best, sweetest, smartest horse Doc's ever owned. He's only selling her because she's getting too old for the children to ride. He says it takes too much money to feed her. If someone else gets her, they might mistreat her or even worse, take her to a slaughterhouse."

"That's not my problem, Lindsey."

Her daughter's face crumbled. "But why *can't* we take her?

She wouldn't be that much trouble. We already have a barn and pasture that we're not using. You can take the expenses for her out of my allowance. What's the big deal, Mom? Why do you keep saying no?"

Erin's headache was growing worse by the second. All she wanted to do was crawl back into bed, pull the covers over her head, and let someone else deal with Lindsey . . . and life in general.

Unfortunately, there was no one else. Not anymore.

"I'm sorry about Snowball. Really. I care about animals too. But we can't take her on as our responsibility. I've given you my answer. If you want me to continue allowing you to work at Doc's horse farm, you need to quit nagging me about that horse."

"But, Mom . . ." Lindsey's voice rose on a note that was a near wail.

"Not one more word. I mean it."

She knew other mothers and daughters sometimes fought, but there was an underlying tone of grief to Lindsey's desperation for this horse that worried her. Blake's death had devastated them both, but instead of comforting one another, it seemed as if she and her daughter had grown further apart. Erin had no idea what to do about it.

Lindsey muttered something under her breath.

"What did you say, young lady?"

"I *said* if *Dad* were alive, *he would* let me have Snowball." Lindsey whirled on her, eyes blazing. "I wish he were here instead of you!"

Erin did not believe in physical punishment for children. Not even the slightest spanking. Lindsey, an only child, had been raised with much praise, gentle reprimands, and rare time-outs.

Neither she nor Blake had ever lifted their hands against

their daughter and she had no intention of doing so now, but Lindsey's words were so deliberately hurtful that her right hand seemed to develop a mind of its own. She slapped Lindsey so hard that her hand stung.

As the sound of that slap echoed in Erin's ears, they stood looking at each other, stunned at what had just happened. Then tears welled up in Lindsey's big blue eyes and Erin knew that her action was unthinkable and unforgivable and she hated herself for it already.

Unfortunately, her head was now hurting so badly that it was hard for her to think clearly, let alone apologize. If only she could go lay down for a few minutes, maybe she could pull herself together. After she recuperated a little, maybe she could deal with this mess, but first she had to drive her daughter to Doc's place where Lindsey doggedly clung to her volunteer work at the Little Acorn Horse Farm. It was one of the few positive things in her daughter's life right now. In spite of her angry words, Erin had no intention of taking it away from her.

"Go wait for me in the car, Lindsey."

Sobbing, her daughter ran out of the house, slamming the door so hard that the windows rattled. Erin reached for a bottle of Tylenol. It had been full only a few days ago; now it was nearly empty. She washed down two capsules with a cup of tepid, leftover tea and grabbed her car keys, hoping her headache would diminish on the way to the horse farm.

She locked the door and slung her purse strap over her shoulder. Her hand still stung from the slap, and she would apologize for that as soon as she got into the SUV. Overall, she was grateful that Lindsey had the job at Doc's. She and her daughter periodically needed to get away from each other and have time to cool off.

Stepping onto the back porch, she stopped and took several deep breaths while gazing out over their peaceful eastern

Tennessee property—the twenty-acre hobby farm that Blake had loved. The view of fields and mountains in the distance usually helped calm her when she was upset, but not today.

It wasn't her father's death alone that was causing Lindsey's attitude. Nor was it the horse. Her daughter had been angry ever since they left for that disastrous short-term mission trip that Erin had forced her to go on, hoping the trip would bring them closer. For the last year, Lindsey's teenage moodiness had been prying them further and further apart.

Lindsey had reluctantly agreed to go to Honduras, but once there the girl had picked at her cuticles and been utterly miserable. Who knew she would react to passing out sandwiches to street children by withdrawing into a silent, morose shell? The trip had only made things worse between them.

They were barely speaking by the time they arrived home, only to discover that while they had waited in stony silence at the Honduras airport, Blake had died alone in his office from a cocaine overdose.

No matter how hard she tried, she simply could not wrap her mind around it. Blake, her brilliant, disciplined, run-five-miles-a-day attorney husband, had died from an accidental overdose. The irony was *not* lost on the local news or the people who had voted him into office on the basis of his zero-tolerance drug platform.

It was hard to hold her head up these days and even harder for Lindsey who had idolized her father.

She sighed, squared her shoulders, and headed toward their detached garage, hitting the button on her keychain remote to start her car as she walked. Her carefully constructed life was in a shambles and Lindsey seemed determined to make things harder for her. If that child didn't straighten up and straighten up soon, Erin didn't know what she would do.

Two seconds later, an explosion rocked their garage as her

dependable, soccer-mom SUV burst into a ball of flame. She staggered backward, shielding her eyes with her forearm, as the heat of the blast hit her full in the face. The explosion was deafening.

Her ears ringing, she lowered her arm and stared at the garage in dumbfounded shock. Then a wild realization hit her.

"Lindsey!" she screamed, sprinting toward the garage.

CHAPTER TWO

Cole Brady watched the countryside race past. It seemed so strange to be looking at the fields and mountains through a squad-car window instead of from an eight-by-thirteen prison cell. He wondered if he would ever get over the miracle of getting out of prison after so many years and so little hope.

"How long are you staying around?" The sheriff drew deeply on his cigarette and slowly blew a stream of smoke between pursed lips. The man had put on at least sixty pounds in the fourteen years since Cole had last seen him.

Cole rolled his window down a crack. Riding with Sheriff Dempsey had its drawbacks but he did appreciate the man coming to pick him up. Not all released prisoners had that luxury. Most were given nothing more than bus fare, a hundred dollars, and no place to go.

Prisoners like Cole who had been exonerated didn't even get the bus fare or the hundred dollars. Unless a prisoner sued, the state preferred to pretend that the mistake had never happened. Cole had chosen not to bring suit, mainly because he never wanted to see the inside of a courtroom again.

"Josiah and Marie say I can stay with them until I can figure out what to do next."

"The Newmans are good people." Dempsey pushed his sunglasses onto his forehead and rubbed the bridge of his nose. "They wanted to pick you up, but I told them I was headed over toward Pikeville anyway." He lowered his sunglasses and flicked ash into the car's overflowing ashtray. "How long did you live with them?"

"From the sixth grade on. They kept about a dozen other foster kids over the years—all teenagers. The ones who got to go to the Newmans' were the lucky ones."

"Brave folks."

"*I'll* say!" Cole choked out a laugh, remembering some of the trouble he'd gotten into before he realized that the Newmans actually did care about him.

The sheriff took another drag on his cigarette. Cole rolled the window down all the way. Cigarette smoke made his chest hurt. It always had. Dempsey didn't seem to notice.

"I'm sorry about what we did to you, Cole. In fact, pretty much everyone in this county is sorry about what happened to you."

Cole didn't know how to respond. What was he supposed to say to the people who had put him, an innocent nineteen-year-old, behind bars? Did they think he was going to tell them not to worry about it? Was he supposed to make a joke about being wrongfully incarcerated? Was he supposed to say that everyone made mistakes and that he forgave them?

He was a Christian, but he wasn't *that* good of a Christian. Being in prison had been a living hell. At the moment, he had a well of bitterness in his soul deep enough to drown in. His life was ruined and the odds of finding a decent job were slim.

He had rehearsed the scene a million times while lying on his steel bunk in the Southeastern Tennessee State Regional

Correctional Facility—the fancy name someone had given the penitentiary where he had been imprisoned. It was every innocent man's fantasy, to be able to look into the faces of the people who had misjudged him and say, "See? I told you I didn't do it. I *told* you I was innocent!"

Yet now that he was outside the miles of looped razor-wire fencing, away from the stares of bored tower guards armed with rifles and attitude, the only thing he felt was . . . overwhelmed.

He was even having trouble absorbing the shock of so many different colors rushing past. Tennessee in June wasn't just green; it was a thousand shades of green. The vibrant hills practically shouted at him with color.

"You okay?" the sheriff asked.

"Yes. It's just that everything is so . . . bright."

"Yeah. I bet it is." The sheriff reached into the glove compartment and dug out a second pair of sunglasses. "Try these."

"Thanks."

"No problem. Keep 'em."

Cole put on the sunglasses and closed his eyes. Behind his lids, embedded there forever, was the image of the prison bars he had stared at for one hundred seventy-four months, three weeks, two days, and six hours. Over half of his life.

He opened his eyes, took off the sunglasses, and drank in the colors again. A barn with peeling red paint. A white house with sun glinting off a blue tin roof. A black trampoline with two little boys in denim shorts and white T-shirts, jumping up and down. A farmer on a green-and-yellow John Deere tractor, plowing up brown earth.

Normalcy.

Cole wished he could tell the sheriff to stop the car so he could walk out into the middle of the field. He craved the feel of reaching into that rich, loose earth with his bare hands.

He wanted to touch it, smell it, and wash his hands in it. He wanted to rub off the stink of prison with the aroma of God's clean, fertile soil.

He had lived for a while with his grandfather, an elderly widower who tended a big vegetable garden each year and taught his little grandson how to plant the young seedlings. Those few years before his grandfather passed away had been a tender time. He'd loved the feel of digging in the earth and helping his grandpa. It was a memory he cherished. He had learned the value of often revisiting good memories in prison. Doing so had helped him keep his sanity.

Someone who had not watched life draining away inside a gray prison cell, day by endless day, couldn't possibly understand the desire to simply run their fingers through freshly plowed earth.

Instead of asking the sheriff to stop the car, he sat quietly which was something he had learned to do well in prison. He had practiced the art of becoming nearly motionless in order to make himself practically invisible. Even in his stillness, though, he couldn't help but gaze at the countryside as it whizzed past—a quiet, starving man gobbling up the scenery with insatiable eyes.

"I checked your records, Cole. I saw that you had some carpentry training while you were in prison. Vance Patterson says he'd like to hire you."

Now, *that* was interesting. He glanced sideways to see if Dempsey was joking. The man's face was serious. Cole remembered Vance well, a decent man who had built his construction business from the ground up, and the hardworking father of the girl Cole had been wrongly convicted of murdering.

"Vance says he'll pay you well," the sheriff said.

"That . . . that's good of him. I would like that."

The sheriff's gun holster creaked as he shifted in his seat and retrieved a thick envelope from his pants pocket.

"Vance wanted you to have some walking-around money. It's a gift. He doesn't want it back. If you're interested in a job, he says he'll get you set up as soon as you're ready to come to work."

Cole glanced inside the envelope. After working years in prison for less than fifty cents an hour, the thick stash of crisp new twenty-dollar bills looked like a fortune.

"I appreciate it."

There was a time when Cole would have rejected Vance Patterson's pitiful gesture to make up for his imprisonment, but not anymore. He had endured too much to laugh at anyone's attempt at kindness. Compassion had been rare in his world. At thirty-three, he felt like sixty. At thirty-three, he would take Vance's money and job with gratitude and somehow try to build a life out of the years he had left.

He filled his lungs with the fresh, clean air blowing in through the open window. It was heady, this scent of country air not tainted with the acrid sweat of hundreds of hopeless, angry men held against their will.

DNA evidence was not only a scientific breakthrough, it was a miraculous answer to Cole's fervent prayers. He was exonerated. Truly, unequivocally, permanently exonerated. The man who had killed Terri had been executed one year earlier for seven similar crimes. It had taken the justice system awhile to catch up and come to the conclusion that Cole had nothing whatsoever to do with her death, but he wasn't complaining. Not now. He had decided not to waste his time with complaints.

He was free.

"You want to stop and get something to eat when we get to town?" the sheriff said. "We're almost there."

A long time ago the sheriff had made a terrible mistake, but

Dempsey wasn't really a bad guy. Cole had *met* bad guys—the worst Tennessee had to offer. Dempsey had simply done what he knew best: played by the book. Now he was trying to undo the past with a car ride and food. Cole appreciated the attempt, as meager as it was. Many men would have avoided any contact with him at all after what Dempsey had done.

"Thanks, but no." Cole said. "Marie's making my favorite meal."

"And what would that be?"

"Chicken and dumplings. Turnip greens with ham. Candied baby carrots. Apple pie."

"Now that's a meal to come home to."

Cole forced himself to look directly at the sheriff. He was going to have to train himself to do that again. For too long he had avoided looking anyone in the eyes. In prison, it was best to avoid eye contact until it was unavoidable, and usually only then because you were fighting for your life.

He looked straight at the sheriff, making certain his eyes didn't waver. "Marie and Josiah came to see me twice a month, every month, for fourteen years."

The sheriff nodded. "Good people."

Dempsey's radio squawked with a garbled, unintelligible voice. The sheriff interpreted for Cole's benefit. "A neighbor lady just reported a fire out at the Ramsey place. Black Hollow Road. A mile away. Mind if we check it out?"

He shrugged. What were a few more minutes?

Sheriff Dempsey lowered his window, flicked his cigarette out and did an expert U-turn in the middle of the gravel road.

He replayed the sheriff's words and a chill swept over him. "Are you talking about Blake Ramsey's place?"

"Yeah. You probably remember him, don't you?"

It was a rhetorical question. Cole knew exactly who Blake Ramsey was. How could he ever forget? He flashed back to

Blake's expert, slice-and-dice questioning while his own wet-behind-the-ears court-appointed attorney looked on in awe.

"I heard Blake died of a cocaine overdose. Is that true?" he asked.

"Yeah." The squad car fishtailed on the loose graveled road and the sheriff brought it under control. "A couple months ago. I know it's hard to believe, him being so squeaky clean and all."

Cole found it hard to feel sympathy for the man who had put him behind bars. "What happened?"

"I checked in with him at his office on the night he died. He'd been working really long hours, practically living there while Erin and their daughter were away on some kind of a church trip. I found him the next morning. Drug paraphernalia on his desk, a packet of pure coke opened beside it. He was already gone."

"Sounds rough."

"It was. He was a good friend of mine. Breaking the news to Erin was the second hardest thing I've ever had to do as sheriff of this county."

"What was the first?"

Dempsey glanced at him and then back at the road. "Seeing the look on Marie's face the morning we came to the house and arrested you."

CHAPTER THREE

Strong arms grabbed Erin around the waist and dragged her, clawing and scratching, out of the broken window in the back of the garage. The flames and smoke were simply too intense near the garage door. The window was her only remaining option to get to her daughter.

It had been a struggle to lever her body up and into the opening. She had barely managed to get halfway inside before some idiot pulled her out. The frustration of being thwarted from reaching Lindsey infuriated her and she fought back like an animal protecting its young.

"Let go of me!"

"Hold onto her." It was Sheriff Dempsey's voice. "Let me see if I can get to her little girl."

She bit the first thing she could sink her teeth into—a shoulder that smelled of harsh detergent and tasted of sweat. The man's arms loosened momentarily but he didn't let her go.

"I'm sorry, ma'am." The man's voice was calm. "But you'll die if you go in there."

She kicked, scratched, and howled. The man turned her away from him and pinned her arms around herself in a sort of self-hug, holding her so tightly against him that she had no choice but to stop struggling. There was no use. His arms felt like iron bands.

"Do you see her?" The voice behind her asked.

Her eyes were too blinded by smoke and panic to see anything.

"No. And I can't go in," Sheriff Dempsey said. "It's a death trap."

"I heard her screaming!" Erin yelled at the men. "Lindsey's *in* there!" She kicked back against her tormentor, trying once more to extricate herself. He immobilized her legs with one of his.

A fire truck siren wailed.

"Thank God," she heard her captor whisper to himself.

Slowly, her vision began to clear. She saw firemen running toward them with a fire hose and extinguishers. They began spraying water and foam into the garage.

The building was not large. The fire was over in minutes once the firemen arrived. They stood back with hoses dripping, and then one went inside. She held her breath. Waiting. Waiting. Against her back she felt the heartbeat of the man who held her. His arms no longer felt like a trap. He had relaxed his grip just enough that it felt almost like an embrace as she waited for word of her daughter.

The fire chief, Jeff Hammond, emerged. He wiped his eyes with one hand and shook his head. "She's gone."

Erin's mind went blank.

~~~

Cole felt Erin's body go limp as she lost consciousness. He eased her to the ground, noting the cosmic irony that the first woman he had held in his arms in fourteen years was the very woman who had helped put him behind bars.

"What did I say?" Jeff took off his helmet, scratched his head, and stared down at Erin. "Her daughter's not in there. She's gone. No body. No *nothing* except a smoking hunk of metal no one will ever drive again."

There were deep cuts on the palms of her hands. She wore a black T-shirt and jeans with blood seeping through from more lacerations from trying to climb through that broken window. Her shoulder-length honey blonde hair was tangled and her face was smudged with smoke. The only jewelry she wore was silver hoops and a thin, silver crucifix necklace.

She had always been a beautiful woman and Cole supposed plenty of men would find her attractive in spite of the cuts and trauma, but this woman had caused him so much suffering that he could hardly bear to look at her.

"I'll get the first-aid kit," Jeff said. "She's torn up pretty bad. She must have really thought her daughter was in there."

"She said she heard her daughter screaming," Cole volunteered.

Sheriff Dempsey knelt down on one knee and gently brushed the disheveled hair away from her face. "I think she was hearing her own screams and thought they were coming from her daughter."

It sounded plausible. Erin had been screaming like a banshee when he'd dragged her from the garage window. So where was the daughter? Why had Erin been so convinced that she was inside the garage?

"People do strange things when there's a fire." Jeff opened a first-aid kit and began to pick glass slivers from her hands as the others looked on.

Watching, Cole remembered the first time he had seen Erin. It had been the day she started teaching at the school where he had worked as a janitor's assistant. She had been, at twenty-two, the most perfect woman he had ever seen. Stunningly beautiful, smart, and classy. Too good for him, of course—he knew that—but it didn't keep him from quietly admiring her from afar.

These past fourteen years, he'd spent a lot of time fervently wishing he had never laid eyes on her.

Jeff finished picking the glass out of Erin's palms and then pulled out a pair of scissors. He cut a slit in her jeans from the cuff to above her knee, revealing multiple cuts, before he began extracting more shards with tweezers. "She sure was determined to save her daughter. Where do you suppose the girl is?"

Her eyes fluttered open and Erin came to. She sat up so quickly that she almost knocked Jeff over.

"Where's Lindsey?" Her eyes darted to each of the faces of the men circling her. She spoke louder, as though they were hard of hearing. "Where is my *daughter*?"

The sheriff helped her to her feet. "We don't know, but she's not in the garage."

"Not in the garage?" Her voice sounded almost childlike with wonder. "My daughter is not in the garage?"

"There's no one in there, ma'am." Jeff tucked the bottle of antiseptic he had been using back into his first-aid kit. "I promise. I looked real good."

Cole grudgingly admired the speed with which Erin pulled herself together.

"Will you gentlemen please help me find her?" she said.

~~~

The men scattered. One went into the barn, one headed toward the creek, and another searched her house. Sheriff

Dempsey called in a report for his deputies to be on the lookout for a thirteen-year-old with long strawberry-blonde hair. Then he left in his squad car to check with the nearest neighbor, Gerta Brame, whose house was a half mile away.

Erin was left standing beside the man who had pulled her out of the burning garage. She turned to thank him, assuming he was one of Sheriff Dempsey's deputies. Because of her husband's job, she knew each deputy by name.

The man was a complete stranger. Instead of a uniform, he wore jeans and a gray T-shirt that stretched across his muscular chest. His hair was short and coal-black. Dark sunglasses covered his eyes.

A rivulet of blood trickled from a scratch on his left cheek, put there, no doubt, when she had clawed at him with her nails. A damp place on his shoulder reminded her, to her shame, that she had bitten him. But the thing that struck her most was his nearly unearthly stillness. He stood motionless, silent, watching her.

"I am so sorry for the way I acted," she said. "I lost my head. I . . ."

He slowly removed his sunglasses.

It took her a moment to recognize him, but when she did she gasped and took two steps backward, pressing the back of her hand hard against her lips.

It was Cole Brady. She'd had recurring nightmares about him for years. His appearance had changed since the last time she saw him. He'd gone from a tall, skinny kid pushing a broom in the school hallways, into a tall, hardened man. The lines around his mouth were much deeper than they should have been for someone who would only be in his early thirties. His eyes, so dark brown that they were nearly black, were impenetrable. There were multiple tattoos on his arms that had not been there before.

She had heard rumors that he was getting out of prison, but Blake's death had put Cole's impending release well beneath her personal radar screen.

For as long as she lived, she would never forget that moment in the courtroom after the judge had read the "guilty" verdict. Cole had erupted with a wild fury and was dragged away while shouting that he was innocent, shouting threats that someday he would pay Blake and her back for what they had done to him.

Under the circumstances, that outburst was not the smartest thing for him to do. Even though Cole had been an exemplary prisoner with no prior convictions and could possibly have eventually qualified for a parole, Blake had shown up at every hearing thereafter, making certain the man stayed in prison.

Even considering all his good behavior, Cole had never stood a chance at release with Blake making certain to keep him behind bars. That is, not until DNA evidence found him to be absolutely innocent—just as he had said.

Her mind boggled with the reality of coming face-to-face with a man against whom she had mistakenly testified. He had endured years of prison based primarily on her testimony.

In trying to become a wife that an up-and-coming attorney could be proud of, Erin had secretly read up on etiquette, but there was nothing in any book of etiquette that could have prepared her for a moment like this. What could she possibly say to a man who'd lost half his life because of a mistake she had made? What words could make the injustice she had helped create to go away?

The innocent man she had helped put behind bars was standing in front of her and Lord help her—she didn't know whether to apologize or run.

CHAPTER FOUR

"**M**om!" Lindsey leaped out of the squad car and barreled straight into Erin's waiting arms. "Are you okay?"

Erin could only nod and cling to her daughter in gratitude. Reassured that Lindsey was truly alive she pushed her daughter's hair behind her ears, grabbed her slender shoulders, and gave her a shake.

"Where *were* you?"

"Down at Mrs. Brame's."

"Why did you go there instead of to the car?"

Lindsey scuffed the toe of one tennis shoe into the dirt. "I was really mad at you."

"Both of us were mad." The fight seemed so trivial now. "I'm so sorry I slapped you."

"It's okay." Lindsey shrugged. "Me and Mrs. Brame heard the explosion and saw the smoke. I wanted to run back right then, but she told me to stay put while she called 911. She can be really bossy for an old lady."

Gerta Brame was past eighty and lived alone. Erin hoped she had not been too traumatized by all that had happened.

"Is Gerta all right?" Erin asked the sheriff.

"I'd guess making that phone call was the most excitement she's had in weeks," Dempsey said. "She'll be talking about it for months, but she's fine. I thanked her for you, by the way."

A garbled crackling from the fire truck's radio started the firemen rushing to gather hoses and paraphernalia.

"Someone let a trash fire get out of control over near Ken Seaman's dairy farm," Jeff Hammond informed the sheriff. "Now his back pasture is afire. We need to get over there. I'll let you finish up here."

"Ma'am," Jeff nodded to Erin. "Remember to take care of those cuts."

"Thank you!" she called. "For everything."

Sheriff Dempsey, Cole, Lindsey, and Erin watched in silence as the fire truck sped away.

She was uncomfortably aware that Cole was standing right beside her. They'd been interrupted by Lindsey before she could even acknowledge the past, let alone address it. There was so much she wanted to say to him, so much for which she wanted to apologize, but not now, not here, and not in front of the others. Instead, she focused on the matter at hand—the explosion.

"What do you think happened, Sheriff?"

He stared at the garage, pondering her question. "I'll have to talk to the fire chief about it, but was your gas tank full?"

"I filled up yesterday. Why?"

"It's nearly ninety-eight degrees out. A dark tin roof like what's on that garage of yours soaks up heat like a sponge. It had to be boiling inside."

"Cars don't blow up from sheer heat, Sheriff."

"No, but I am thinking that maybe a combination of heat, a full tank of gas, and an electrical spark from that remote I saw lying on the ground could have triggered an explosion."

"I think it was a bomb." Lindsey jammed her hands into her pockets. "It sounded like a bomb."

"This isn't Baghdad, sugar." The sheriff smiled and shook his head. "This is just good old Stark County, Tennessee. There's probably no one within a hundred miles of here who would have any idea how to set a car bomb, let alone want to hurt you and your mom."

Erin saw moisture beading his forehead and wondered if he was sweating from the heat or the effort, for Lindsey's sake, of pretending that the explosion was an accident.

"The two of you are upset." There was real concern in the sheriff's voice. "I know how hard things have been for you recently. I'll call Hank when I get back to town and have him bring his tow truck over. I'm sorry this happened, Erin, especially after everything you've been through."

Erin hesitated, then patted Lindsey's arm. "Go on inside, sweetheart. I'll be in presently."

Lindsey cocked an eyebrow. "Why?"

"Please.

Lindsey shrugged and plodded off toward the house. Erin watched until she was safely out of earshot before asking the sheriff the question that had been on her mind ever since finding out that Lindsey was safe.

"I know you say that Blake's death was an accident, Sheriff, and I've been trying to accept your investigation, but I still can't believe Blake would have voluntarily taken cocaine. Is there *any* possibility—any at all—that this explosion and his death are somehow connected?"

"Ah, Erin, don't break my heart like this." He put his arm around her shoulder. She respected Sheriff Dempsey, but she felt a wave of nausea as the smell of sweat, coffee, and too many cigarettes rolled off him. "You have to give up on that idea and concentrate on raising your daughter. Blake died from too much coke, plain and simple. It wasn't your fault. The sooner you accept that, the sooner you can get on with your life."

"But Blake *hated* drugs." She eased away from the sheriff. "I *know* him." She corrected herself and used the past tense— something she kept forgetting to do. "I knew him. He would never have done such a thing."

"Erin, I was there. I was the one who found him, remember? There's no way it could have been anything but an accidental overdose. No sign of forced entry. No sign of foul play. No sign of a struggle. Not even any fingerprints except Blake's on the drug paraphernalia."

This was not what she wanted to hear. She stared at the ground, blocking out the sheriff's words, as hope drained from her yet again. It was so very hard to accept the fact that her husband had not been the decent, disciplined man she'd thought.

"Erin, look at me." Dempsey took her chin in his hand and forced her to meet his eyes. "You have to face the facts. Both doors were locked from the inside. No one but he and his secretary had a key and she was in Florida with her grandkids. That's good enough for me and good enough for the rest of the people in this county. I wish I could change the facts and paint you a prettier picture, but I can't. No wife ever knows her husband completely. Trust me, I know. I've seen too much."

She closed her eyes. Maybe the sheriff was right. Maybe no wife ever really knew her husband. That certainly seemed to be the opinion of every law official from the state attorney general's office to the FBI. She had contacted all of them this past week, hoping that someone with more training and resources than Sheriff Dempsey would come and review the evidence. Their local law-enforcement tried hard, but the county couldn't exactly afford a trained CSI unit.

Unfortunately, every official she contacted had acted as though she was just a grieving widow who couldn't accept the fact of her husband's drug problem.

"Like I said, I'll contact Hank's tow truck service. He'll get that vehicle out of here so you and Lindsey won't have to look at it. Now, why don't you go on inside and lie down a spell? Maybe you should call a friend to come over. I'll take care of everything."

Erin suddenly felt too tired to argue. She had no evidence to combat the irrefutable. She had nothing to base anything on except her faith in Blake—which everyone seemed determined to dismiss as naïve.

Dempsey nodded to Cole. "Let's go, Brady. Time to get you home. We've kept you here long enough."

Erin turned toward Cole, determined to say at least *something* to the man who'd just saved her life. "Cole, I . . ."

The ice in his dark eyes when he looked at her froze her speech on her lips before she could say another word.

~⚊✕⚊~

Cole's right hand gripped the squad car armrest so tightly that his knuckles turned white. He forced himself to loosen his hold because he didn't want Dempsey to know how profoundly he had been shaken by seeing Erin again.

Fortunately, the sheriff wasn't paying attention.

"What did you make out of that mess back at the Ramsey's?" the sheriff said.

He chose not to reply. In his opinion, the explanation the sheriff had given Erin was ludicrous. If cars exploded from heat that easily, the South would look like a war zone.

"I know that story I told her was a load of bull," Dempsey said, "but I didn't want to spook her or the girl any more

than they already are. I need to get to the bottom of this." He
steered with his knee and lit another cigarette. "It doesn't make
sense."

"Won't the insurance company investigate?"

"We take care of our own problems in this county. In
my experience, it's never been a good thing to let outsiders
become involved. Hank owes me a favor. He'll have that SUV
in his crusher within the hour. I'll write up the report for
the insurance company. That will be the end of it, but I'll be
keeping a sharp eye on the Ramsey place. That road is going
to be on my personal patrol route."

Cole nodded. The sheriff could set up a tent in Erin's front
yard and live there, for all he cared, or do nothing whatsoever.
Erin Ramsey and her daughter was none of his concern.

"So," Dempsey said, "what did you think of Blake's widow?"

Cole didn't answer, but he didn't need to. Dempsey had
plenty to say about Erin.

"That woman was quite a looker when she first moved here.
She's put on a few pounds since then." The sheriff scratched
his protruding stomach. "I hate it when a pretty woman lets
herself go."

Pretty? Erin was magnificent. Always had been. As much
as he despised her, it was impossible not to notice that she
had definitely not "let herself go." If anything, she was more
beautiful than she had been fourteen years ago. But the woman
was a stone-cold liar. If it weren't for her, he wouldn't be sitting
here in this squad car wondering what he was going to do with
his life. He would already *have* a life. Maybe he'd even have a
wife and a couple of kids by now.

He'd been dreaming of a good life the night he'd gone out
with Terri Patterson—the night she was killed. It had been
nothing more than an innocent trip to the movies. He'd dug

deep into his pockets for enough change to pay for two tickets *and* popcorn.

He had misjudged the cost and was almost a dollar short. Terri had quickly reached into her purse and quietly stuffed a dollar into his hand.

The girl had been an eighteen-year-old sweetheart with kind eyes, a lilting laugh, a full scholarship to Lipscomb University in Nashville, and aspirations to be a kindergarten teacher.

Generations of five-year-olds had lost an incredible teacher when Terri was killed.

They had been friends. That's all. He had tried to tell Sheriff Dempsey, Blake Ramsey, Vance Patterson, and everyone else in that courtroom that Terri and he were just friends. He'd never so much as kissed her. Their movie date had turned into a long walk afterward as they talked about their big plans for their lives—back when they still had plans. He had dropped her off at her parents' doorstep, well within her curfew, said good night, and walked home happier than he'd ever been in his life.

He still remembered the peace he had felt that night after his date with Terri. He had drifted off to sleep in a loving home where no one fought or drank, feeling safe in God's grace and his future rich with promise, a sweet evening with a good girl tucked into his heart.

The next morning the sheriff and two deputies had stormed into his bedroom, read him his rights before he was fully awake, handcuffed him, and marched him out into the living room in front of a horrified Marie and Josiah.

The scene was so clear in his mind that he had to force himself to stop replaying it in order to pay attention to what the sheriff was currently saying.

"A lot of men around here are going to be interested in Blake's widow in a few months. I wouldn't mind asking her out, myself, if I wasn't married."

For the first time in a long time, Cole stifled the desire to laugh. Dempsey thought he might have a shot at Erin if he weren't already married? He seriously doubted it.

Against his will, Cole's mind went back again to the first time he had ever laid eyes on Erin. The ink on her teaching certificate had barely dried. Everyone in town was impressed with the lovely new English teacher, especially Blake Ramsey, who was eight years her senior and already rumored to be one of the best attorneys in the state.

Marie, a long-time school cook, had managed to wrangle a job for Cole as a janitor's assistant, in spite of the chip-on-the-shoulder attitude he had worn like armor back then. Even with Josiah's and Marie's love and acceptance, for several years he had carried a bellyful of anger from the wreck that had taken his parents' lives. It had been a drunk driver who had caused the wreck. The worst part of it all was that the drunk driver was his own father.

Somehow Erin had always had a smile and a kind word for him at a time in his life when he had needed kindness almost more than oxygen.

Cole had privately made certain that her trash cans were always the first to be emptied, her wooden desk polished weekly until it gleamed, her floors always the first to be mopped and waxed.

She had never known the extra effort he had gone to, each task a quiet labor of love. But she *had* noticed how he had guarded her when she worked too late—carefully watching as she walked from her classroom out to the parking lot. He had not gone home until he knew she was safe. Not once.

He had felt gallant, imagining himself her secret, self-appointed knight, ready to fight anyone who might dare lay a hand on her.

A *knight*. Of all things! Had he ever been that young?

She had seen it differently. She had called it stalking.

The jury had believed her. Who would not? She was so perfect.

He, on the other hand, already had a reputation of getting into trouble. It didn't take much convincing. Blake had thrown Erin's testimony into his face. The jury had listened, took a good hard look at him, and had seen nothing but a former foster kid with an attitude and no alibi.

Erin would be thirty-six now. Three years older than him. She had put on maybe twenty pounds, but those pounds looked good on her.

It was infuriating to find himself physically attracted—even if it was only momentarily—to a woman he had spent years wishing he'd never met.

"It's a real shame that Blake died of an overdose," the sheriff said. "It's lowered the morale of the whole county."

Again, Cole remained silent. He certainly had no love for Blake Ramsey but he couldn't imagine him indulging in recreational drug use. He might have hated Blake but he never doubted that the man was as straight as an arrow. To him, the idea of that determined county prosecutor snorting cocaine was unthinkable.

CHAPTER FIVE

Erin closed the hood on the old blue '78 Dodge farm truck that had been in the barn when they bought their property. It ran after a fashion, as long as it was filled with motor oil which it guzzled like soda pop. Because of that, Blake had always kept a case of Valvoline in the barn near where the truck was parked.

In her mind, a hundred things shouted for her attention but she couldn't bear to examine any of them right now. She shoved aside her fear of facing the future alone with an unhappy daughter. She fought to not replay the horrific moment when the garage exploded and she thought she'd lost Lindsey forever. She chose not to reexamine who or what might have been behind that explosion.

Instead, she focused on one thing and one thing only: getting this old truck to start. If she could manage that, some small portion of her life would feel under control.

Apart from using the battered vehicle to haul mulch or an occasional antique, she seldom drove it. The tailgate was honeycombed with rust and the front fender had a huge dent. The upholstery was tattered. The old truck definitely wasn't pretty, but as far as she knew, it still ran and it would get them where they needed to go for a couple of days until she could make other arrangements. She wished she hadn't sold Blake's car last month, but it had felt like the right decision at the time.

She climbed into the cab and turned the ignition key. The motor ground three times and stopped. She pumped the accelerator and tried again. The motor growled twice . . . and stopped.

The huge barn door slid open and her daughter wandered in. "I need to get to work, Mom. I'm really, really late."

"Just give me a minute." Erin said.

Lindsey left while Erin worked with the truck. In a few moments, she reappeared. "I called Marie. She said she would come over and take me."

"You called the preacher's wife?"

"Now that she's retired she says she has a lot of time on her hands. She told us girls in the teen class to call her if we ever needed her."

"Please don't do that again without telling me." Erin said. "I'm sure Marie has better things to do with her time than to be our chauffeur."

She turned the ignition key yet again and jammed her foot onto the accelerator, but it still didn't start. She pressed her forehead against the steering wheel and blew out a breath of frustration—not only because of the truck, but because Lindsey was so doggedly determined to get to the Little Acorn, in spite of everything they'd been through today.

It amazed her how her daughter lived and breathed for the opportunity to curry horses, muck out stalls, and untangle the special-made harnesses and saddles for the handicapped children who came to the Little Acorn for riding therapy. All this from a girl who usually couldn't be persuaded to clean her own room.

Lindsey leaned her chin on the open window near Erin's elbow. "Marie said she didn't mind, honest."

Erin surreptitiously wiped away tears of anger and frustration.

Lindsey didn't notice her mother's tears. "I think I hear Marie coming down the road now. I need to go get my stuff." She ran back to the house.

Erin climbed out of the truck and threw an empty oil container into a trash barrel just as Marie skidded to a stop in the middle of the driveway and bolted from the car. She was wearing a shapeless, loose-fitting housedress decorated with an old-fashioned cabbage rose print. Her hair was a disconcerting mass of wet, gray ringlets.

"Lindsey told me what happened." Marie gave Erin a hug. "Are you okay?"

"I'm a little shaken up, but . . ." Erin took a deep breath. "I'm okay."

Marie glanced down at Erin's bandaged hands. "I hate to break this to you, sweetie, but you don't exactly *look* okay. What happened to your poor little hands?"

Erin held out her hands and gazed at them. "I cut myself trying to climb through a broken window. I thought Lindsey was in the garage when it . . . caught fire."

"Thank God you and Lindsey weren't hurt any worse than you were."

"Amen to that."

"Do you have any idea what happened? What caused it?"

"No. I wish I did. Sheriff Dempsey said he'd investigate and not to worry about it for now."

In spite of the seriousness of their conversation, Erin couldn't help but wonder about the dripping ringlets that had replaced Marie's normally sedate hairstyle.

"Marie, I apologize for asking, but what's going on with your hair?"

"Oh." Marie put a hand on top of her head. "Josiah was finishing giving me a home permanent when Lindsey called."

"Our preacher gives perms?"

"Only under extreme duress."

"I would have given you a home perm, Marie. Josiah didn't have to."

"I know," Marie said. "For that matter, I could have gone to Shirley's Beauty Shoppe in town, but it is payback time today, Erin. I'm still mad at him for telling that story about me during Sunday's sermon. There are few things he hates more than the smell of a permanent wave solution."

"You're punishing him?" Erin asked.

"I most certainly am." Marie put her hands on her hips. "And he deserves it."

In spite of all she'd been through, Erin couldn't help but smile at Marie's indignation. "Was it the story about you borrowing his underwear because you'd run out of your own clean ones?"

Marie's left eyebrow shot up, a sign that she was not amused. "That's the one."

"It *was* sort of funny, Marie."

"Oh, yeah, the church really got a big kick out of it—at my expense—I heard the laughter. But does anyone remember the point he was making?"

"Sure. He was talking about how it is unwise to force ourselves into roles we weren't meant to fit into."

"So, someone *did* manage to retain something other than the mental image of me standing around in Josiah's too tight BVD's." Marie huffed. "What he failed to mention is that we had three funerals and one wedding that week, my kids were having finals at school, and *his* third cousin decided to drop in unannounced for a week's visit from out-of-town. Plus I was working full-time. There was a very good reason I hadn't kept up with the laundry. He didn't have to go telling the whole world about it. I felt like a fool."

"No one thinks you're a fool," Erin soothed. "That story only caused us to love you more."

The screen door slammed and Lindsey came running out. "Hi, Marie. Thanks for picking me up." As Lindsey gave Marie a hug, an impish grin stole over her face. "Are you wearing the preacher's underwear today?"

"One time! It was *one* time!" Marie's eyes narrowed. "See? Now even the kids are going to remember it. That man is going to scrub the kitchen floor when I get back. On his hands and knees. With a toothbrush."

"He's a good man, Marie. Don't be too hard on him."

"I'll try, but if I've told him once, I've told him a zillion times—*ask* before you use stories about me in a sermon!"

Lindsey climbed into the front seat of Marie's '98 Buick. "I'm already really late, Marie. Please?"

"I'll be right there, pumpkin." She turned back to Erin. "You go on inside now. Make yourself some tea. Put plenty of honey in it, and lie down for a while. Don't worry about a thing. You've had a bad shock today and you need to let yourself recuperate a bit."

"I might just do that." Erin walked Marie to the car where Lindsey waited impatiently.

"I'll bring her home too." Marie said. "You just relax."

"I don't know . . ."

Lindsey interrupted. "Doc's going to bring me home after the Little Acorn closes therapy sessions this afternoon. I already called him."

"I guess that's settled," Marie said.

Erin said a quick prayer as Marie's car careened out of

sight. The woman had not had a wreck yet, but it wasn't, in Erin's opinion, for lack of trying. As much as she liked Marie, she wasn't entirely comfortable with Lindsey riding with her.

At least there was no need to get the truck started right this minute. If the old truck was flooded, which she suspected it was, it needed to sit awhile anyway. Besides, the initial shock had worn off and she was starting to realize how badly her entire body ached from the events of this morning. She wanted nothing as much as to sink into a hot tub, soak for a while, and try to forget that this day had ever happened.

She went inside to the kitchen and put on a kettle of water for tea and honey which was Marie's prescription for everything from a sore throat to heartbreak. As she waited, there was a loud clanking noise in her driveway. She turned off the tea kettle and hurried outside. Hank Toliver's tow truck had backed into her driveway.

"Doesn't someone need to investigate this before you take it away?" she asked.

"Don't know about that." Hank was flat on his back, hooking a cable beneath her still-smoking vehicle. "All I know is Sheriff Dempsey told me to come get it."

"Okay, but . . ."

"No need to worry your pretty little head, Mrs. Ramsey. We'll take care of it." Hank climbed into his tow truck, started the motor, and slowly pulled the hulk of her SUV away, leaving her standing beside an empty, charred garage.

Not once did Hank look her in the eyes.

She seemed to be getting a lot of that lately. It was as though Blake's death had left some sort of mark on her. Most people had no idea what to say, so they avoided saying anything. In many cases they wouldn't even look directly at her.

After Hank left, Erin realized that she had lost her desire for tea. All she really wanted was to wash away this day. She went inside, filled the bathtub, dropped her ripped clothes into the trash, and soaked her wounds until the water turned tepid.

She dried off, slathered her cuts with fresh antibiotic ointment, used up half a box of Band-Aids, and then pulled on a pair of Blake's soft jogging pants and one of his T-shirts. They still smelled faintly of his cologne, which was comforting.

Contrary to Marie's and the sheriff's instructions, she did not rest. Instead, she dug into a project that she had intended to start ever since the funeral: sorting through Blake's personal files. Somewhere in his papers there might be a clue to his death. The problem was she had no idea what she was looking for. All she knew was that she had to do *something*.

⊰⋈⊱

Dempsey dropped him off in front of Marie and Josiah's house. The garage was open, and he could see Josiah working on something as he walked over.

"Need some help?" Cole asked.

"Cole!" Josiah, a tall, thin man in his early sixties, stood up from where he'd been down on one knee jerking the cord on a push lawn mower. Josiah wiped his hands on the old black dress pants he wore before pulling Cole into his arms. Cole closed his eyes and savored the feel of being hugged by the man who'd helped raise him. Although Josiah and Marie had faithfully come to see him every month, they'd never been allowed to touch him . . . until now.

"So *good* to see you, son!" Josiah's face was alight with joy. "I hope you didn't mind riding with Dempsey today. Marie and I wanted to come get you, but he flat-out insisted."

"It was fine that he came."

"Good. Good." He stepped back from Cole and looked him up and down. "You are a sight for sore eyes, boy."

"You too. Thanks for the clothes you sent with Dempsey."

"Marie thought you'd want to change out of whatever they gave you. She has several new outfits put away in your old room. Ever since she found out you were coming home, she's been shopping for you."

Cole glanced at the house. "Where is she?"

Josiah looked around, distracted, as though he had accidentally misplaced his wife. Then he snapped his fingers. "Oh, now I remember. She left to drive one of the teenagers from church to the girl's job. We didn't expect you quite this soon. She'll be back shortly. I'm warning you, she's been fussing around in that kitchen since yesterday morning. I hope you're hungry!"

"I'm looking forward to Marie's cooking."

"It will be so good to have you with us at the table again." Josiah put both hands on the small of his back and stretched.

"Back hurting?" Cole asked.

"A little."

"Having trouble with the mower?"

"I think we need a new one."

Cole squatted to examine the mower. It had been a long time since he had gotten to tinker with a piece of machinery.

"Marie tells me I have to mow this yard before I can go back inside the house." Josiah sounded genuinely worried. "She's a little upset with me."

"Why?" Cole screwed off the lid of the gas tank.

"Oh . . . just something I said about her in my sermon last Sunday."

He peered inside the dry-as-a-bone tank. Just as he had thought—Josiah had forgotten to fill it. Some things never changed.

"Frankly, Cole, after all these years, I still don't understand women. I thought the story made a memorable illustration for an important spiritual point." Josiah grumbled. "I had no idea she would take it this way." Then he brightened. "The story *did* get a big laugh though."

Cole stood up. "You're out of gas."

"Again? I just filled it up last week. Or maybe it was a couple weeks ago." Josiah polished his glasses on the tail of the old, white dress shirt he was wearing. "Maybe it was last month."

"Why don't you go back inside and work on your sermon?" Cole grabbed the red gas can sitting nearby and swished it. There was enough gasoline to get the job done. "I'll take care of the yard for you."

"Are you sure? You just got home. Don't you want to rest up or something?"

"I've had a bellyful of rest, Josiah. There's nothing I'd rather do right now than yard work."

"I appreciate your help." Understanding was written all over Josiah's face. He seemed to know how badly Cole needed to do something manual and normal—like mow a yard. "Welcome home, son."

Welcome home, son.

It was all Cole could do not to break down hearing that simple phrase. Words came hard for him after all these years. Instead of telling Josiah how their support had sometimes been the only thing keeping him from despair, he tried to make a joke around the lump in his throat. "It might be best to leave Marie out of this Sunday's sermon."

"You think?" Josiah grimaced, leaned in, and whispered, "She made me give her a pedicure last night in penance. Today it was a home perm. I had to bring her coffee in bed this morning and she sent me back twice because I didn't put enough cream in it. I don't know how much more of this I can take, Cole. The woman is vicious."

Cole smiled as Josiah left. Marie might be many things, but
vicious was not a word he would use to describe her. Staying
here with these two gentle people for a while was going to be
heaven after what he'd been through.

He looked around at the familiar farmhouse parsonage with
its huge yard shaded by two ancient oak trees. There were a
few bare spots peeping through the grass. He noticed an old
bag of fertilizer lying in the corner of the garage along with a
half-empty sack of grass seed. He would fertilize the bare spots
and sow the grass seed after he finished mowing. It would feel
good to make this small landscaping improvement. He took off
his T-shirt, hung it on a nail, and got started. He wondered
if anyone who had not been incarcerated could ever begin to
understand the joy and anticipation he felt in simply mowing
a yard.

CHAPTER SIX

"Sheriff Dempsey said *what*?" Marie peered at Cole over the half-glasses she used for sewing. An unfinished quilt top lay temporarily forgotten in her lap. They had just finished dinner, and Josiah was making a great deal of racket in the kitchen.

"Break as many as you want, dear," Marie called, winking at Cole.

They could hear Josiah muttering overtop of the sound of running water. Cole heard something coming from the kitchen that sounded like "Elpidzo!"

"Is he okay, Marie?" Cole asked.

"Elpidzeis." *Splash.* "Elpedzeis!"

"Don't you remember? Josiah doesn't cuss when he's upset," Marie explained. "He conjugates Greek verbs."

Splash. "Elpidzei!"

Crash. Slosh. "Elpidzomen!"

"Sometimes it sounds a little like cussing," Marie admitted. "Now tell me what Dempsey said."

"Um, I could go in and help him, Marie."

"ELPIDZETE!" *Slosh, splash, crash! CRASH! CRASH!*

43

"Oh, my." Marie looked worried. "I may have pushed this penance thing a bit too far."

Josiah appeared in the doorway with a look of supreme satisfaction on his face. He held a large, black garbage bag in front of him.

"The dishes are finished!" He gave the bag a shake. The sound of broken china rattled from within.

"Thank you, dear," Marie said. "You are forgiven now."

Cole thought she was acting awfully calm for a woman who'd just had most of her dishes destroyed.

"Finally!" Josiah marched over and planted a kiss on the top of her head. "Sunday's sermon will be about the faith of Abraham. I want you to know that you are absolutely *not* in it, Marie."

"That's very wise of you, Josiah." Marie picked up her needle and quilt top.

Josiah went outside and Cole heard the heavy garbage bag hit the bottom of the tin trash can with a loud crash. Then Josiah walked back past them, disappeared into his study, and firmly closed the door.

"He broke your dinner dishes. You're okay with that?"

Marie smiled. "I hope he broke *all* of them."

"Why?"

"Bertha Saunders gave me that set because she was tired of them. I didn't like them and didn't want them, but I couldn't refuse, or she would talk about me. That woman never misses an opportunity to criticize. Now I can truthfully, and regretfully, say, in case it ever comes up, that Josiah accidentally broke them while he was washing the dishes."

"And he knew all this?"

"Of course he did, that sweetheart!" Marie smiled happily. "Now I get to go shopping for new dishes."

Cole shook his head. Good marriages and what made them tick were a mystery to him.

At that moment, he heard a roar overhead as an aircraft landed at the county airport directly behind Josiah's and Marie's house.

"Was that a jet?"

"I believe so," Marie said.

"I don't remember jets landing here when I was growing up. There were just a few smaller planes that people flew as a hobby."

"I know. I mentioned it to Sheriff Dempsey. He said a commercial flight school has started using our airstrip as a safe place to practice night landings. There's not a whole lot for a plane to crash into with all these cornfields around us."

"But the airport closes down at night."

"The sheriff said the runway lights can be activated remotely by the pilot."

"You don't mind the noise?"

"It doesn't happen all the time. I think it's a small price to pay for pilots who know how to land safely, don't you?" Marie fluffed the pillow behind her back. "Now," she said, "back to what Sheriff Dempsey said about Erin. I *do* want to hear this."

∽∝∾

Looking through Blake's personal files was proving to be a painful and slow-going process. Some things were written in legalese and were difficult for her to understand. Other things were much more private. He had saved her love letters from before they were married and their daughter's crayon drawings. There were birthday cards, clippings, and articles about the vegetables and fruit trees Blake had intended to grow but was always working so hard he never quite found the time. Going through these things was emotionally draining.

Nothing she found had anything to do with his death, of course, but since she had no idea what she was looking for, she figured it was best to work her way through the four-drawer file cabinet one piece at a time. After several hours, she'd only managed to finish a fourth of one file drawer.

She had already gone through the whole house, looking for something—anything that might shed light on what had happened. She'd gone through all of Blake's bureau drawers, suit pockets, garage, even the barn. Anything she could find that would be a clue as to who her husband really was—the fine man she had always thought him to be, someone with a secret addiction, or . . . was there something else going on? It was the 'something else' that consumed her.

Sheriff Dempsey said he and his staff had gone over Blake's office with a fine tooth comb and found nothing at all amiss except for the evil powder that had killed her husband. Erin had not yet had the courage to go into his office. It was all still too new, too raw. She'd talked at length with Evelyn, his middle-aged secretary after the woman got back from Florida. Evelyn was also shocked and mystified by what had happened.

Blake had tried to be disciplined about their budget, and she supported that. He always wrote down every expenditure. It was a habit he had acquired while working his way through law school. She had taken pride in the fact that they were one of the few couples she knew who had no credit card debt and lived within their means. Their frugality had been a necessity. They had also taken on the extra responsibility of supporting his widowed mother until she passed away, which had used up most of their excess for the first ten years of their marriage. Erin took care of the bills and balanced their checkbook. What this meant now was that she had no idea where Blake could have found the money to even fund an addiction. Cocaine was expensive.

On the other hand, as the sheriff said, could a person ever really know what was going on in the life of another person? She'd certainly been mistaken fourteen years ago.

Even though she had tried desperately to shut him out all afternoon, Cole Brady filtered into her mind again. If she lived a hundred years, she would never forget the way he had looked at her this morning with such a mixture of sadness and anger in his eyes. How badly did he hate her? And what horrors had he experienced within those prison walls?

There was nothing she could do that would make it up to him, of course, and yet it had been an honest mistake. Anyone could have made it. She had been so *certain* of what she'd seen and yet she had been so terribly, terribly wrong.

She could not allow herself to think about that right now, though. There were only so many things the human brain could take in and deal with in so short a time. Her mind was already crammed to overflowing with Blake's death, the explosion this morning, Lindsey's rebellion and anger. There was no room left for Cole Brady.

Having slept poorly last night and all previous nights since returning from Honduras, she laid her head on the desk and closed her eyes.

Someone lurked in the deep shadows of the school portico. Erin felt his eyes on her as she tried to fit her key into the lock of her car. Her hands shook so badly that she dropped the key—twice. As she stooped to pick it up a second time, she glanced over her shoulder.

He had not moved, thank goodness. He wasn't approaching

her, but a security light fell across his face and she could see those eyes watching her.

Cole Brady. Always watching.

She had tried to be nice to him, had tried to talk to him, but he had barely said two words to her. He just watched. Every night. It was creepy.

As she tore out of the school parking lot, she checked her rearview mirror. The shadowy figure finally moved away.

Safe once again. She wished she could stop staying so late in her classroom. The problem was, there were so many papers to grade—back in college she had never dreamed there would be so much after-hours work for a teacher—and the furnished one bedroom apartment she was renting was tiny and cramped. There wasn't even a desk to work at. If she could just make it through the next few weeks, school would be out and she would become Blake Ramsey's wife. Her life would be perfect then. Cole Brady would have to leave her alone once she became Blake's wife.

"Mom? Mom?"

Someone was shaking her. Erin swam upward through the inky blackness of her dream toward her daughter.

"Wake up, Mom."

The shaking got more intense. Lindsey's voice took on an edge of panic. "Mom!"

Erin opened her eyes and lifted her head. What was she doing here in their home office? Oh, the files. She had been trying to work her way through them before she had dropped off.

Old Doc Wilson's face hovered above her. The good doctor's expert fingers were already on her wrist, taking her pulse. He laid a cool hand on her forehead. She closed her eyes and leaned into it. It was a comforting gesture, taking her back to early childhood, her mother checking her for fever—the mother she barely remembered.

"Pulse and temp are normal." The doctor peered into her eyes, concern written all over his face. "Erin, are you ill?"

"No, I'm fine." Erin felt disoriented, and her mouth was dry. "I've not been sleeping well, Doc. I must have been more worn out than I realized."

"Lindsey told me about the fire," he said. "That kind of scare is enough to zap anyone's strength."

A fire. That's what it was. An explosion. That was the cause of the sick feeling in the pit of her stomach.

Everything came sharply into focus as Lindsey watched her with concern.

"Did you two have a good day?" Erin said, feigning normalcy. "Did things go well with the children and horses?"

"Great, really great," Lindsey said with false enthusiasm. "If you're okay, I'm going up to my room now."

Her daughter ran up the stairs as fast as her thirteen-year-old legs would take her.

"She's having a tough time," the doctor observed.

"We both are. Do you have any advice?" Erin asked. "We're not doing so well with this grief thing."

Dr. Wilson sank down into the armchair opposite Blake's desk. He looked so weary and no wonder! He was past seventy, a widower, and still managing a medical practice along with running the horse farm that had been his wife's dream and her life's work.

"There's no shortcuts to grief," he said. "If I knew any, I'd tell you. Lindsey's acting pretty normal for her age. Especially under the circumstances."

What a nice way of putting it. *Under the circumstances.*

"You'll figure it out." He rose and patted her hand. "I need to be getting back. The vet's with one of my mares right now. She's having a difficult birth. Will you be all right?"

"Sure." She managed a smile. "Thanks for bringing Lindsey home."

His eyes swept over her. "You need to come in for a checkup, Erin. It's been awhile. I could prescribe something that would at least help you sleep."

"Thanks, Doc. I'll be in soon."

She saw him to the door and watched him make his way back to his car. He had started to fail this past year. She feared that everything was getting to be too much for him. The town would be bereft when Doc could no longer practice medicine.

She loved the old man. Everyone did, but one thing worried her. Blake had told her that Doc had explained to him once that he held no belief in God or in heaven or hell—that his religion consisted simply of doing as much good for as many people for as long as possible.

There was nothing wrong with doing good but Erin did not believe it could take the place of faith. How did the man get up in the morning and face life without a belief in a loving God?

She decided it might be wise to go upstairs to check on Lindsey. Something had felt a little off about her daughter when she'd come home.

The bedroom door was ajar, so Erin pushed it open. Her daughter was sitting cross-legged on the bed. Her head jerked up the second Erin entered.

"Stay *out*, Mom!"

Too late.

She saw Lindsey quickly hide something beneath the covers of her unmade bed. Erin's heart nearly stopped. Had her daughter gotten involved with drugs?

"What's that?" Erin strode over to the bed and plucked a

package from beneath the bedspread. Lindsey lunged for it, but Erin held it out of reach.

"I have *no* privacy!" Lindsey shouted, crossing her arms across her chest and falling back against a pile of pillows.

Erin checked the label on the box. "Hair dye?" She could hardly believe her eyes. "Black? You were going to dye your beautiful hair *black*? Why?"

"It's *my* hair, Mom."

Relieved, Erin reached to tuck her daughter's strawberry-blond hair behind her ears. Hair dye. That was a far cry from drugs. But . . . black?

Lindsey jerked her head away when Erin's hand touched her face. The motion made her hair flip, and Erin gasped at what she saw. There was a huge bruise on her baby girl's left cheek.

"What on earth happened? Did you fall?"

"No."

"Okay." She tried again. "So what happened?"

"Someone hit me," Lindsey said. "But I punched them first!"

"You were fighting?"

Lindsey shrugged and stared at the bedspread.

Erin grasped Lindsey's chin and made her turn her head so that their eyes met.

"I want to know the truth, and I want to know it now. Why were you fighting?"

Lindsey heaved an exaggerated sigh, but her blue eyes filled with tears. "It was about Dad."

"You were fighting about your father?"

Lindsey nodded. "One of the boys who volunteers out at Doc's farm said my dad was a junkie."

Erin's heart sank. She had hoped that people would at least be a little sensitive to Lindsey's feelings—but kids could be so cruel.

"What did you say?"

"Nothing."

"Nothing?"

"What could I say?" Lindsey picked at a hangnail. "It's true. I couldn't deny it. So I hit him."

"You attacked one of the boys at the farm?" Just when she had thought things couldn't get any worse. "How old is he?"

"Sixteen. He's a lot bigger than me too."

"So this older, bigger boy hit you? That's how you got this bruise?"

"Yeah." There was a small light of battle in Lindsey's eyes. "But he looked a whole lot worse than me when we were finished. I got him *good*, Mom."

Erin had quite a collection of parenting books. She'd thought she had some answers about how to raise a child, but nothing she had ever read in them had ever prepared her for dealing with a situation like this.

"Dying your hair black won't change anything. It won't bring your dad back."

Lindsey's shoulders drooped. "I know. It's just that . . . it's just that I hurt so *bad*, Mom! I feel dark and sad on the inside, so I figured why not on the outside too? Can't we just move away from here? Go someplace no one ever knew about Dad and what he did?"

Erin's heart ached for her daughter. She knew how hard it was to be ashamed of a father. Her own dad, Bill Emory, was a Vietnam veteran who had become a reclusive survivalist after the war. He had a nickname back home in the mountains of Virginia. The name "Wild Bill" in the mouths of her classmates was *not* a compliment.

This time when Erin reached for her, Lindsey fell, sobbing, into her arms. As she rocked her daughter, silent tears spilled over onto Lindsey's sun-streaked hair.

"Come on, Cole. I want details. What did the sheriff say, again?"

Cole knew Marie tried to not be a gossip, but the woman did love a bit of news.

"Dempsey said he just hated it when a pretty woman like Erin Ramsey let herself go."

Marie's laughter started from deep inside her belly, rumbling upward until it erupted from her mouth. Cole loved the way his former foster mother laughed. She held nothing back. No polite tittering for Marie. She threw her whole body into it, kicking her feet, tossing her head back, pounding the arms of her chair, roaring with laughter.

Cole savored the sound. Her laughter washed over him like a favorite song.

She slowly settled down, wiped her eyes, giggled a couple more times, and picked up her sewing. A few more chuckles escaped before she could talk normally.

"Oh, that man!" she said. "Has he looked at himself in a mirror lately? It's been a few years since he was a football hero in this town."

"Once a jock, always a jock."

"Isn't that the truth!" She picked up two squares of fabric from her lap, fitted them together and began sewing with uneven stitches. "Take Josiah for example. He's never quite gotten over the fact that he was a wrestler in high school."

"Josiah was a *wrestler*? He never told me that."

"He was quite good, actually. State champion his senior year," she said proudly. "Of course that was back in '62." She sighed. "He was *so* handsome." Her eyes twinkled. "And that man still has some moves!"

Well, *that* was a subject Cole did not want to explore.

She bit off a thread and held up the squares to inspect them. They were a half inch off. "So you don't buy Dempsey's explanation about the explosion?"

"*He* doesn't buy it," Cole said. "Mainly, he seemed unhappy that something this big had happened in the county without his knowledge."

Marie digested this information while Cole listened to the familiar sound of the old wind-up wall clock ticking in the background. The *tick-tock* was like a lullaby to him. He'd always loved the homey sound of it. He could feel the muscles in his shoulders completely relaxing for the first time in years as he sat in Marie and Josiah's comfortable living room listening to that old clock tick.

His hair was still wet from the long, hot shower he'd taken after coming in from mowing the lawn. A shower with privacy. A shower with soap that smelled like lilacs. A shower that felt like a new birth.

Marie, mother hen that she was, had insisted he take a nap after his shower while she finished dinner. He had obediently crawled between sheets that smelled like sunshine, sunk onto a bed that felt like a cloud, and listened to the happy sound of Marie rattling pots and pans. He had not napped. He was too geared up to sleep—but he had lain between those pristine sheets, his body alive from outdoor labor, savoring every new sensation.

The meal Marie had prepared with such love and that Josiah blessed with such sincerity was food for his body *and* his soul. He had silently thanked God for every morsel.

"Did Erin recognize you, Cole?"

"She did."

"I didn't tell her you were getting out. She's had so much to deal with lately—I didn't know how she would take it." Marie held up her misshapen quilt, sighed, and shook her head. "This quilt is even worse than I thought."

"Why did you take up quilting? You always said you and sewing needles were not a good combination."

She arched an eyebrow. "For your information, I am practicing up to be a good old lady. Quilting is what old women do around here. They either quilt, raise gardens, or crochet. The overachievers do all three."

Cole smiled. "I love you, Marie."

"I love you too." She dumped the offending quilt top, along with her needle, thimble, and scissors, into a large basket beside the sofa. "Okay. I give up. I am done with that mess. I can buy me a quilt at Big Lots for thirty-five dollars and I'm gonna."

"You told me that they aren't as nice as handmade ones."

"They're nicer than *my* handmade ones." She gave a sigh of relief. "I never wanted to be a quilter anyway, but what am I supposed to do, Cole? Ever since I retired from my job as a cook at the school, I don't know what to do with myself. I thought it would be great not to have to get up and go to work every day. But I miss being in the middle of all that school hustle-and-bustle. I loved the kids and loved trying to sneak some nutrition into those picky little eaters."

"Which would explain this town's aversion to meatballs."

"There's nothing wrong with mixing some brown rice and zucchini into a vat of hamburger meat."

"True, but it's a little disconcerting when you're a first grader."

"At least I tried."

"Yes, you did. Personally, I love your meatballs, zucchini and all." Cole looked out the picture window at the dark night. "What really happened to Blake Ramsey, Marie?"

Marie smoothed her flowered dress over her knees. "What do you mean?"

"As much as I hated the man, I'm still having trouble getting my mind around the image of Blake snorting coke."

"You aren't the only one." She shook her head. "He wasn't perfect, but in my estimation someone could have dumped a truckload of cocaine into Blake Ramsey's backyard and all he would have done was wade through it to get the license plate number of the truck."

"The sheriff seems to think the case is cut-and-dried."

"I know that." Marie took off her glasses and rubbed her eyes. "I don't know what to make of it. I feel so sorry for Erin. She still wants to believe her husband hung the moon but if enough people tell you that you're crazy, you start to believe it."

"How well I know," Cole said.

She leaned forward and laid a hand on his arm. "Oh, honey, I'm sorry. I didn't mean . . ."

"I know you didn't. Trust me, Marie, there's nothing you or Josiah could ever say that would offend me. I'm simply stating a fact. It's hard to have faith in yourself or in someone you love when the whole world is telling you that you're wrong."

"That's very true."

He'd never asked what it had cost her and Josiah to buck the rest of the county and believe in him for so long. He didn't ask because he knew they would never acknowledge that there had ever been any hardship attached to their love for him.

Marie grabbed a paring knife and an apple off a side table and started to peel the fruit. "I think Dempsey is in way over his head on this one."

"Why?"

"You want a piece?" She held a slice out to him.

Fresh fruit. It had been a luxury in prison. Now he could have it every day if he wanted. Amazing. "Thanks."

"Two years ago there was a rumor that some kind of drug

cartel had hired someone to kill Blake. Nothing ever happened to him and the rumor eventually died. Lately, I've been wondering whether maybe it was true after all and the cartel simply decided it was time to take him out."

"That might be a possibility."

She handed him another slice of the apple and ate one herself. "I don't think Blake Ramsey killed himself with an overdose—accidental or otherwise. I think someone wanted him out of the way. I have no idea who or how they did it, but I do know that there are some dangerous men in this world, Cole, and some of them may be right here in this county. I want you to be careful."

"I know all about dangerous men." Cole bit into an apple slice. "I survived these past fourteen years by becoming one of them."

CHAPTER SEVEN

"Have you made any progress figuring out what happened to my car, Sheriff?" she asked. "Lindsey is still insisting it sounded like a bomb. I think so, too."

It was the third time she had tried to get through to the man today. Finally he'd answered. She had a strong suspicion that he was avoiding her calls and she didn't know why.

"If it was a bomb, it wasn't a very good one," he said. "Only the back half was destroyed. I'm thinking it might have been a faulty primary fuel pump. It could have ignited the gas tank when you started the car. It's rare, but I've heard of it happening. Thank God you weren't in the car."

"But you looked?"

"Of course I looked." There was a hesitation in his voice. "Besides, who would want to hurt you? It just doesn't make sense."

That was true. It didn't make sense. She had no enemies—at least none she knew about. None except maybe Cole, but he'd been with the sheriff.

"Sometimes things just happen," Dempsey said. "It really

was very hot in that garage. Lots of things could have ignited that blaze."

"The car insurance people will want some kind of a report," she said.

"And I'll be happy to give it to them," he said. "Tell me what company you're with."

Erin gave him the name and they hung up.

She had never realized how much paperwork and phone calls were involved in the aftermath of a spouse's death. It didn't help that she had always relied on Blake to deal with anything remotely legal. She'd attacked this morning with a firm resolve to get everything finished but there was much to do. Dealing with insurance companies was one more mountain to climb. She'd been putting it off for far too long.

She rolled her shoulders trying to relieve some of the tenseness. It was late afternoon and most insurance agencies were starting to close. She was tired and needed a break. Tomorrow she'd start in again. Perhaps later on tonight she'd try to work through more of Blake's files to see if there were any clues to the circumstances of his death.

At that moment, she heard Lindsey stumble down the stairs and wander into the kitchen. Her daughter had slept most of the day away. Lindsey had been so dead asleep, Erin had checked on her a few times to make certain she was breathing. No doubt it was another growth spurt. She often found herself wishing she could flip a switch that would make Lindsey's headlong rush into adulthood halt temporarily until they could both catch their breath and regroup. Or it could be the fatigue that grief brought. Either way, sleep was healing and so she'd left her daughter alone.

When Erin went into the kitchen, Lindsey's head and shoulders were buried inside the refrigerator. An open package of Oreo cookies lay on the table.

"Where's the milk?" Lindsey asked.

"We're out. I'll pick some up tomorrow."

"We're out?" Lindsey wailed. "I'm *starved*. I wanted milk and cookies and we don't have any *milk*?"

"I'm sorry." Erin checked the clock and was surprised to discover that it was already six o'clock. "I forgot to go to the store today."

Lindsey slammed the refrigerator door. "There's nothing good to eat and I'm really, really hungry."

She sounded so irritated that Erin chose not to break it to her that not only did they not have milk in the house, she didn't have a clue as to what they were going to have for dinner. Guilt washed over her. There had been a time when she was so organized that she had menus and shopping lists planned two weeks in advance. She offered the quickest solution she could think of.

"How about we go have dinner at the Brown Betty Restaurant tonight? Thursdays are Lasagna Night, remember?"

"Wow. Lasagna sounds really, really good." A shadow suddenly passed over Lindsey's face. "But how will we get there?"

"Good point. I didn't make much headway today with the insurance company so I guess we'll have to depend on that old truck of your dad's for a while," Erin said. "I think I flooded it yesterday, but maybe it'll run now."

Her drama-queen daughter's eyes grew wide. "I'll *die* if anyone from my school sees us in that ratty old thing."

"I'll park a couple blocks away from the restaurant."

"Well . . ." Lindsey shrugged, which seemed to be her favorite body language these days. "I suppose if it means getting something to eat . . ."

"Don't you want to change clothes first?" she asked. Her daughter was wearing a white tank top with pajama bottoms.

Lindsey's eyes narrowed. "I'm fine."

Erin realized she'd seen quite a few girls Lindsey's age wearing something that looked like pajama bottoms in public recently. She decided that this was not an issue that was important enough to fight over. At least Lindsey hadn't started piercing or tattooing anything yet.

Lindsey slipped on her flip-flops, Erin found her purse, and together they went out to the barn. As a precaution against what happened to the SUV, Erin had been keeping the barn padlocked. Lindsey waited while she unlocked the door, then together they slid the barn door open, climbed into the vehicle, and Erin turned the ignition. It took some creative work with the clutch and gas pedal, not to mention a lot of heartfelt prayer, but the engine finally started and they lurched out of the barn. Lindsey held onto the frame of the window to keep from bouncing out of her seat.

"Sorry," Erin said, once they made it to high gear and headed into town. "Are you okay over there?"

"Not too skilled with a standard shift, huh, Mom?"

"No, but we're moving."

"If you can call this moving." Lindsey laughed. The note of frustration had left her voice. Evidently the anticipation of real food had sweetened her disposition considerably.

Erin patted her daughter's leg. "I'll get us there, kiddo. Just hang on."

She was grateful for the crotchety old truck. This was the first half-way lighthearted conversation they'd had in weeks.

⁂

"I'm so tired of my own cooking." Marie stood in the doorway of her walk-in pantry, perusing the shelves.

"You're a great cook, Marie," Cole said.

"I know, but I still think we should go out to dinner tonight."

Cole stood at the kitchen sink savoring a glass of lemonade. He'd just showered and changed clothes after trimming all the overgrown hedges at the back of the yard along with doing several repairs around the house.

"I'd like that." He finished draining the glass. "Where's Josiah?"

"He's making hospital visits and won't be back until late. I could bring him something home, though. He loves the lasagna at the Brown Betty."

"Sounds good."

"But I can't go out to dinner in this old house dress." Her brow creased. "And my hair is every which way."

"If you want to go change, Marie, that's fine. I'm in no hurry."

"Great! I'll just be a minute."

As Marie rushed off, Cole absent-mindedly leafed through the church directory that was lying beside the phone. There were so many changes in the directory, so many people he did not recognize. He ran his finger down the names and addresses until he came to Ramsey—Blake, Erin, and Lindsey. He wondered if Erin's faith was helping her through her grief, although he reminded himself that he didn't actually care. As far as he was concerned, the woman could dress in black and grieve for the rest of her life. He felt sorry for her young daughter, though. It had to be hard on the girl right now.

His own faith had kept him from losing his mind. If it hadn't been for Josiah and Marie, as well as the courageous prison-ministry volunteers who came every Sunday, he wasn't sure he could have held onto his sanity.

"I'm ready!" Marie emerged from her bedroom and turned in a circle so he could admire her. She wore a flowered, purple dress and had indulged in a liberal use of pink lipstick. Her beaming face was framed by a halo of gray frizz from Josiah's home perm.

"You look beautiful, Marie." He meant it. There were so many different ways to measure beauty. The pride and love he saw in her eyes every time she looked at him, the kindness in her voice, her enthusiasm for life and the people around her . . . by these things measured against Cole's inner yardstick, Marie was a knockout. He kissed her cheek.

"You look pretty good, yourself," Marie said. "Do you like the clothes we bought you? Josiah helped picked them out. He hates to shop, but he went anyway."

"Yes, I do." He was surprised at how well they'd judged his size and taste, although probably anything would have been his taste after being locked up for years with men who were all forced to wear orange.

This evening, after his shower, he'd reveled in the luxury of having a selection of clothes from which to choose. He had pulled on a pair of tan slacks and a dark-blue polo shirt. There was even a nice pair of brown leather loafers on the floor of his closet that fit him. It felt wonderful to get to choose his clothing again.

The only setback he had was when he went to the door of his bedroom. He had stood there in front of it for a couple of beats before he realized he had to open it on his own. For fourteen years, he had had to wait for a guard with keys or one in the control room to push a button for the door to open. He would have been embarrassed if anyone had seen him pause like that, but it felt good to put his hand on the cool doorknob and twist it open.

"It's going to take a lifetime for me to pay you back for all your kindnesses, Marie."

She looked up at him from checking in her purse for the car

keys. "Do you have any idea how much pleasure it gave Josiah and me to do that little bit of shopping for you? Now, quit standing there and let's go get something to eat. I'm starved."

The Brown Betty was housed in an old Victorian mansion built by a coal baron and inherited by his spinster daughter who willed it to the town in the form of a museum dedicated to her father. When the town lost interest in funding a museum in memory of a man no one had liked much except his daughter, the coal baron's great-niece had been allowed to buy it. She had since turned it into a mildly eccentric restaurant serving up dinner and dinner alone to grateful townspeople.

It was a bright and cheerful place, although outrageous with its turrets and gingerbread trim. The new owner, whose name came as no shock, was Betty Brown. She presided over the kitchen and dished out a different comfort food every night. From the number of cars Cole saw parked outside the restaurant, Lasagna Thursday appeared to be a huge hit.

"Don't you think it's pretty?" Marie said as they entered the dining room, decorated in busy rose-patterned wallpaper. "Every time I come here, I want to redecorate our house!"

"How does Josiah feel about that?"

"Josiah? He wouldn't care if I painted the whole place fire-engine red. That's one of the many things I appreciate about him. The man has no interest in decor, so I can do whatever I like." She glanced around, distracted. "I need to visit the ladies' room."

"I'll save you a place."

Cole chose a corner booth where his back was to the wall and he had a good view of the entire dining room—yet another habit acquired in prison. He watched as people filled the room. Several families were there, many with small children, along with older couples who were enjoying a night out. A buzz of friendly conversation filled the room punctuated from time to time by a baby's cry. It was all so normal, so different from what he was used to.

He was enjoying the rich smells coming out of the kitchen and thinking about the flavorless meals he'd eaten in prison when he saw Erin and Lindsey being seated.

Erin glanced up and their eyes locked. He watched as various emotions chased across her face: surprise, guilt, fear, regret. It was a veritable rainbow of feelings. It was oddly satisfying to know that his presence could cause such an emotional storm in her.

The moment Erin saw Cole Brady she wished she had talked Lindsey into settling for a peanut butter sandwich. It took all her willpower not to get up and leave the restaurant. She wasn't sure she could swallow her dinner with Cole's eyes on her. Like Scarlett O'Hara, she didn't want to think about Cole today. She would think about him tomorrow. Or better yet, never.

She knew she had to face him though. Avoiding him completely, pretending she didn't see him would be cowardly. Besides, he had saved her life or at the very least kept her from being badly injured. If they were going to live in the same town together, she couldn't pretend not to see him each time their paths crossed.

"I need to speak to someone," she told Lindsey.

Then she forced herself to rise and walk toward him.

CHAPTER EIGHT

C ole saw Erin lean over and speak to her daughter. The girl's head popped up from behind the menu and she stared at him with bright, curious eyes.

He had hardened himself to the challenge of living with murderers, psychopaths, and other serious bad guys, but to his surprise, watching Erin approach reduced him to a nineteen-year-old dropout—and that was frustrating. He didn't want to talk to her. Not yet. He wanted time to regain his equilibrium in this new world before he said the things to her that he'd been rehearsing.

She wore an emerald-colored blouse with loose-fitting black pants and carried herself with poise except for slightly favoring her right leg, which he figured was brought on by the numerous cuts and abrasions she'd sustained from trying to rescue her daughter yesterday.

As she neared, heads turned and several people whispered to one another. He realized what Blake's death must have cost Erin—not only a widow's grief—but all the innuendoes and whispers about how her husband died.

Of course some of those whispers might be because of him.

Small towns had long memories. No doubt many of the people in the room knew all about the life-and-death drama in which he and Erin had once participated.

As he'd walked around town today, the people who recognized and remembered him didn't quite know how to act with him. Some apologized for the town in general. Some simply avoided eye contact and pretended they didn't see him. Some spoke to him and pretended that nothing had ever happened.

"Hello, Cole." She reached out to shake his hand. "I don't believe I properly thanked you for helping me yesterday."

He dropped his napkin on the table and stood, taking her hand in his. Knowing all eyes were on him made him determined to show the town that he could be polite and civilized in spite of being incarcerated for all those years.

He caught a whiff of perfume and as their hands touched, he was surprised to discover that in spite of her calm appearance, her entire body was trembling. Up close, he could see the dark circles beneath her blue eyes.

She was tired, grief-stricken, no doubt plagued by the humiliation of the cause behind her husband's death, and obviously either frightened or nervous about speaking to him. This should have given him pleasure, but it didn't.

Her eyes looked into his, searching, waiting for him to say something. What did she expect him to say? He had been angry with this woman for over a decade. Now, with a stab of annoyance, he realized that what she thought of him still mattered.

"Would you . . ." He could hear the tightness in his voice and cleared his throat. "Would you and your daughter care to join us for dinner?"

Was that the right thing to say? Had he used the right words? It had been years since he had lived under normal circumstances. Less than three days ago, saying something as simple as "Would you care to join us for dinner" in the wrong tone of voice to the wrong person could have been an invitation to get a shank between his ribs.

Erin looked uneasy. "Thank you, but no. Lindsey's having a difficult time these days. I think I should concentrate on her tonight."

"Of course." He had kept his emotions so deeply buried for so long that even though he had not wanted for her to accept his invitation, he was surprised to find that her refusal stung.

At that moment, a waitress came bustling up and edged her way between him and Erin. She wore a low-cut red blouse, tight white capris, jangling bracelets, and a mass of blond curls.

"Whatcha havin', darlin'?" Her pencil hovered over the pad as she eyed him. "The special tonight is our world-famous lasagna—or, if you're interested, me!"

She brayed with raucous laughter at her joke. Erin hastily excused herself and rejoined her daughter.

"I'm back." Marie plumped herself down across from him. "Are you having the lasagna? I'm having the lasagna."

"Sure." Cole was still distracted by Erin. Why did it still matter to him what she thought? This was ridiculous. He had every reason in the world to hate the woman.

The waitress was chewing gum and she blew a bubble while she wrote down their order. "My name is Dinah. Anything else you want, you just call, you hear?"

Marie noticed Erin and Lindsey over at their table and waved. Erin raised her hand in brief acknowledgment and then buried her head in her menu. Lindsey acted as though she was eager to come over, but she glanced at her mother and stayed where she was.

Marie took a sip of water, put both elbows on the table,

and leaned toward Cole. "Now, tell me about your day. *I want details.*"

I want details. That was Marie. She loved hearing about other people's lives and found her friends and family endlessly fascinating.

"There's not much to tell. Before I started in on those repairs and the yard, I walked into town to see Vance Patterson."

"Vance? What happened?"

"I can start working for him on Monday. He said that I could have a job with him for as long as I wanted."

"That's wonderful! And what did *you* say?"

"I asked him if he would take me to his daughter's grave."

"Oh, Cole." She covered his hand with her own. "How did that go?"

"We stopped at the florist's on the way to the cemetery so I could get some flowers. Vance told me that Terri's favorite was daisies. I hadn't known that. We stood at her grave for a long time. I finally got to tell him all about that night—the movie we watched, how I'd driven her home, how we'd then walked down to the school playground. I told him that if I'd been him, I'd have probably jumped to the same conclusions he did."

"How did he take it?"

"Frankly, we were both pretty choked up."

Marie shook out her dinner napkin and dabbed at her eyes. "So many people would be bitter after what you've been through."

"I am bitter, but not against him. Vance was just a grieving father."

Dinah brought their food, and they suspended conversation until after she had sashayed off.

"What about Erin?" Marie asked. "Are you still angry with her?"

"Angry?" He gave a disparaging laugh. "That's not a strong

enough word for what she and Blake did to me . . . but on
Monday I start a new job and a new life. I won't let her steal
one more second of my life. She's already taken enough. I wish
I never had to see her again."

"Well, it won't be possible to live so close and not run in
to her." Marie spread her napkin on her lap and gave him a
long, measuring look. "I can see I'm going to have to double
up on my prayer time. The Lord needs to drain this anger out
of you and give you a measure of peace. Not for Erin's sake,
but for yours. If anyone deserves happiness, son, it's you—but
it won't happen if you allow memories of how unfairly you've
been treated eat you alive."

～≍～

Her stomach full, Lindsey was quiet all the way home. Erin
was okay with this. Her own mind was preoccupied with that
awkward meeting with Cole. She had walked over to him this
evening, intending not only to thank him for his help yesterday
morning, but to apologize for, well, everything—the scratch
down his cheek, the bite on his shoulder, fourteen years of his
life.

His polite invitation to join him and Marie at dinner had
thrown her. That was not how she had expected him to act.
So what had she expected? A man who growled and ate with
his fingers?

She had spent her entire life trying to do the right thing,
the kind thing. But ever since she had learned that the DNA
evidence was not a match to Cole, she could hardly bear to live
with herself. How could she and Blake have been so wrong?

Erin could still see the scene clearly—the testimony she
had given with such assurance. Terri had worn a yellow-striped
top and white slacks, which made her especially visible against

the shadows of the school building. The light from a full moon had revealed the gunmetal-black hair and lanky profile of Cole Brady. The two were easily identifiable.

Terri and Cole had been sitting on the school playground swings the night Erin drove by the first time. She'd been going to Blake's house to measure his kitchen windows. She would be living there after their wedding, and she had stars in her eyes thinking about how much fun it would be to shop for her very own window curtains.

On her way home from Blake's she had seen Cole and Terri again, only this time he'd been crossing the school yard, carrying Terri in his arms. She had slowed down, but nothing seemed to be amiss.

She had wondered at the time if Terri knew what she was doing in going out with Cole. He'd had an episode four months earlier that had nearly cost him his job. He had broken into the local car dealership owner's home two days before Christmas, gotten drunk on the man's liquor, taken the son's motorcycle out for a joyride, and wrapped it around a telephone pole.

The fact that the car dealership owner's son had been a jerk who continuously taunted Cole about being a foster kid had helped Josiah and Marie understand Cole's uncharacteristic actions that night. Cole had done community service, and everyone had given him the benefit of the doubt when he appeared to be truly contrite over his actions.

However, the morning after seeing Cole carrying Terri away from the playground, when she learned that Terri's lifeless body had been found in the bushes beside the school yard, Erin was convinced that she had witnessed the prelude to a murder.

She had gone straight to Blake who had insisted she come forward with her "evidence." He said that other girls' lives could be at stake—including her own. Memories of Cole watching her from the shadows of the same school building had convinced Erin that it could easily have been *her* body discarded in the bushes instead of Terri.

She was totally sincere in front of the jury, telling her story while looking straight into Cole's unflinching eyes. He had not made a sound until the moment the jury found him guilty and then all the rage he had been carrying erupted into an explosion of emotion that had stunned everyone in the courtroom. That display of anger had further convinced her that she had been right in testifying against him.

Now she would have to carry that burden of guilt forever.

CHAPTER NINE

"This is Brenda Thomas. I'm out of the office, but I'll get back to you as soon as . . ."

Erin slammed the phone down in disgust. She had heard the same recording five times from her car insurance representative yesterday, on Friday, and was tired of leaving messages.

The phone rang the minute she hung up, but it wasn't from the insurance agency. It was her Realtor saying that someone had contacted her about leasing Blake's office.

Although this was good news financially, it meant that cleaning out Blake's things could no longer be avoided. She hadn't been inside his law office since before she and Lindsey had left on their disastrous mission trip. Somehow it had seemed that as long as she didn't go in there she could continue to pretend, at least for a while, that he was still there. Now even that small pretense that she'd clung to would be gone.

Lindsey was happily tucked away among her horses at the Little Acorn for the rest of the day, so this was as good a time as any to do this job she'd dreaded. She changed into work clothes and tried not to think too much about what was ahead of her.

The truck engine was down a full quart of oil. No surprise there. She filled it and lurched into town, stopping at the grocery store first to pick up empty packing boxes. Using a standard shift was becoming a little easier for her—the truck didn't rabbit-hop quite as much as when she'd first started trying to drive it.

She managed to back into the parking spot in the alley behind Blake's office and then walked around to the front. The shiny brass plate above the dark green door read:

BLAKE RAMSEY
ATTORNEY-AT-LAW
COUNTY PROSECUTOR

Her husband's life, summed up in seven words.

Grasping the key so tightly it cut into the palm of her hand, she swallowed hard and shoved the piece of metal into the lock. This office, even more than the home they'd shared, was his turf, his territory.

The lock grudgingly clicked open and she entered. The smell of old law books and lemon furniture polish assaulted her which was a scent she had always associated with Blake.

It was a cloudy day and the front office felt gloomy. She carried in the supplies she'd brought with her and then opened the blinds in the large windows that faced the sidewalk.

Her plan was to empty his desk drawers as quickly as possible and then attack the books in the back room. Unlike Blake's personal files at home, the ones he kept in the office were now officially county property. She would call someone from the courthouse to come and get them after she finished loading his personal possessions.

She planned to store Blake's private law library in their attic. There was an outside chance that Lindsey might want to go to law school when she grew up. Perhaps Blake's daughter would someday have need of those books.

The thought of Lindsey in front of a jury made Erin smile. No doubt her daughter would argue her point of view with vehemence and precision, just like her father.

Erin set thoughts about Lindsey aside as she sat down at her husband's desk. This was where the sheriff had found him slumped over his desk. There was no lingering indication of what had happened here, thank goodness. Sheriff Dempsey, bless him, had seen to that.

She glanced through the venetian blinds to the tree-lined street. This was the view he had seen nearly every day of their entire married life. He had loved presiding over this small law office and had even loved it when people walked in off the street to ask advice or just to shoot the breeze.

"What happened to you, Blake?" Erin whispered.

When she pulled open the top drawer of his desk, three unopened packages of whole wheat crackers and a bag of peanuts slid to the front. He'd kept snacks there because of the long hours he worked. She had always purchased a few nutritious things for him to bring with him to the office.

In the weeks before his death, he had pushed himself way too hard, and she didn't know why. She had stopped asking questions about his work years ago. Blake didn't share information with her until his cases were over. He said he had once watched an associate's wife destroy her husband's career by talking when she should have kept quiet.

Blake kept his own council until a case was closed. Then, after keeping her in the dark for weeks, he would do a sort of "ta-da!" routine and explain the whole thing in detail. She had not minded this small vanity of his and been quick to applaud his successes.

Still, he had been wrong about her. She would not have

told anyone. Maybe if he had trusted her more, she would have a clue as to why this had happened. Maybe if he had trusted her more, it wouldn't have happened at all.

One by one she emptied each desk drawer into a box to take home with her without stopping to look through the papers and books she found there. She was afraid that if she stopped to sort through anything, she'd never finish her task in the few hours she had before it was time to pick up Lindsey.

Finally, she pulled at the bottom right hand drawer. Something had been shoved inside making the drawer jam. She worked at it until it finally came unstuck. Blake's study Bible was the culprit. She gently lifted it out. It was well-thumbed, the pages multicolored from his incessant underlining.

There had been a time, before she met him, when he had spent a year in seminary studying to be a minister. After much prayer, he had decided that the Lord had different plans for him and instead entered law school, but he was still a disciplined student of the Bible. She knew no one who had memorized more of it.

She laid it on the top of the table and ran her hands over the brown leather. Of all the possessions he'd owned, this Bible seemed the thing most stamped with Blake's personality. She gathered the book to her chest. In the privacy and stillness of her husband's office, the sobs she had fought against for so long finally racked her body.

Cole had been cleaning a winter's worth of leaves out of Marie and Josiah's gutters when he leaned too far, nearly lost his balance, caught himself and managed to put a gash in the underside of his arm from a sharp edge on the gutter. Marie was serving at a funeral dinner at the church that Josiah was preaching, so Cole cleaned the wound the best he could. It was deeper than he'd realized, so he walked into town to see Doc Wilson—his doctor from when he'd lived there years before.

The day was muggy and hot and most of the community had chosen to stay indoors. In fact, there was only one other person on the sidewalk except for him. From a couple blocks away, he saw Erin Ramsey pause in front of the red brick office building. After what looked like a short struggle with the lock, she entered her husband's office.

He fully intended to pass by without even glancing inside Blake's office. Unfortunately, his eyes couldn't help straying as he passed the plate-glass window—and his feet stopped moving.

Erin sat behind her husband's massive desk, a cardboard box at her feet. She was hugging what appeared to be a large Bible. And she wasn't just weeping—the woman was sobbing so hard that her shoulders were shaking.

He tried to harden himself against her obvious emotional pain, but his natural compassion got the better of him.

He knocked once. When she didn't answer, he opened the door.

Erin whirled when she heard him enter. "What are *you* doing here?" She swiped at both eyes as though ashamed to have been caught crying.

Her hair was tied back in a ponytail, and she was devoid of makeup. She was wearing faded jeans with an oversized red shirt. A bag of cleaning rags, a broom, and a mop were propped against the desk. She had obviously come planning to do some serious cleaning. It struck him that even dressed like a cleaning lady and wearing no makeup, Erin was classy enough to turn any man's head.

"Are you all right?" he asked.

She swallowed. "I'm fine."

"I only came in to see if you were . . ."

"I said I'm fine." Her shaky voice and red eyes contradicted her words.

She was trembling again, just like last night at the restaurant. Evidently his presence had an extremely negative effect on her. He didn't know how to feel about this. He had done nothing wrong. *Nothing.* Was the woman actually afraid of him?

"I only stopped in because you were upset." He inadvertently took a step toward her. She jumped up from the chair, ready to bolt. Her eyes darted to the door.

Coming in here was a mistake. He instantly regretted the impulse. The last thing he needed was for this woman to start accusing him of something *else* he hadn't done.

"I didn't mean to upset you." He backed away. "I'll leave."

"I'm sorry." She reached out a hand as though to stop him, but then snatched it back. "Except that saying I'm sorry just isn't enough. It won't ever be enough and . . . I don't know what to do about it."

He let out a deep breath, a breath he felt like he'd held in for fourteen years.

Her voice trembled. "Was it really awful in prison? Did they treat you badly?"

Awful? He had no idea how to reply. *Awful?* Such an anemic word to describe what he'd endured. Memories of brutalities poured through his mind that he could only pray to forget someday.

"It was an honest mistake, Cole. I *did* see you with Terri in your arms that night. You *were* carrying her."

"She'd broken the strap on her sandal," he said. "I carried her home to show off. Didn't you notice that she was laughing? We both were."

"I didn't register anything except that Terri was in your arms. When I tried to remember, it seemed to me like she was struggling. I was too wrapped up in measuring the windows at

Blake's house to process anything clearly. He and I were going to be married in a few weeks and I was excited about ordering new curtains."

Curtains. He had endured all those years of prison because she was concerned about curtains.

She jammed her fists deep into her jeans pockets and stared at the floor. "I—I know it sounds silly, but that's why I was driving past that night. The only reason I even remembered that I'd seen you two together was that I had wondered at the time whether Terri knew what she was doing, going out with you."

"What was wrong with Terri going out with me?"

"Well . . . you know, she was a top student and . . ."

"And I was a dropout."

"It wasn't that. It was . . ."

"Because you saw me carrying Terri, you were *so* certain I was a murderer that you managed to help convince a jury. Why? I'd done nothing to you. I *cared* about you. I'd stayed late at work each night trying to watch over you."

"Watch over me?"

"Yes."

"What are you talking about, Cole? You barely said two words to me the whole time you worked there. Instead, you stared at me from the shadows every night when I went out to the parking lot. It was creepy. Blake thought so too, when I told him."

"What exactly did you tell him? That I was stalking you? No wonder he was so determined to put me behind bars and keep me there!" Cole raked his fingers through his hair in frustration. "There were a couple of senior boys at that high school who were troublemakers with police records. I'd overheard them saying some pretty suggestive things about you. I didn't trust them. You were always working late in your classroom. I thought someone ought to be keeping an eye out in case they tried something when no one was around to protect you."

"Why didn't you tell me?"

"You were something so fine in my eyes—you seemed so innocent. I wanted to protect that. I couldn't have looked you in the face and repeated the words they'd said."

"I wish I had known. It might have made a difference."

He groaned inwardly. Back then, he had been so ignorant that up until the moment she gave her testimony, he thought she was mounting the witness stand in his defense.

Instead, lovely, sweet Erin Emory managed to make him sound like some sort of monster that she'd seen dragging Terri off into the bushes.

How badly he had wanted to testify on his own behalf! Set the record straight. Explain what happened. His court-appointed attorney said it would be a mistake. He should have insisted.

Even after all this time he discovered that he desperately wanted Erin to finally understand *exactly* what had happened that night.

"The movie let out earlier than we expected," he said. "We drove back to Terri's house, but it was still an hour before her curfew. The elementary school playground was only a block away, so we walked there, sat on the swings, and talked. When it came time to leave, she realized that the strap on one of her sandals had broken. Terri was such a little thing, and I knew I was strong. She laughed the whole way, swinging her sandal by its broken strap. I didn't set her down until we got to her porch and once we got there I waited until she was safe inside before I drove home."

"How did she end up back at the playground?"

"I've given that a lot of thought. She had her purse with

her that night and she laid it on the ground when we sat down on the swings. Neither of us thought to grab it when I carried her back to her house. My guess is that, once she got inside the house, she remembered that she'd left her purse behind and went back to get it. She probably never thought she could be in danger in her own hometown."

"It's so strange that there just happened to be a killer there at the playground," Erin said. "I know that you're telling the truth but back then it seemed like too much of a coincidence that someone else could have been waiting to prey on her."

"No doubt that's exactly what the jury thought too. Did you hear what the man who killed Terri said when the DNA evidence linked him to her death?"

"No."

"He had developed an almost-foolproof method of getting by with murder and he was proud of it. Boasted about it once he knew he had no hope of ever getting out of prison. He would target a pretty girl in one random town—one per state. Just one. He would study her, watch for his chance and then move on after he was finished. He had a fifty-state plan . . . like it was a hobby or something."

"I don't even know what to say." She dropped down onto the oak desk chair as though her legs could no longer hold her. "I wish I could give you back those lost years. I wish I could go back and undo everything I said on that witness stand. I wish . . ."

"And what I wish is that I'd never laid eyes on you."

She flinched. "I deserved that."

"Yes, you did," he said.

"You're bleeding." She noticed the awkward bandage he had applied. "You hurt yourself."

"I was on my way to Doc's."

"A couple months ago he started working only half days," she said. "You'll need to hurry or you'll miss him."

"Thanks." As he left, he felt just a little . . . lighter. The weight of prison was still with him, but at least the woman who'd put him behind bars had apologized. It wasn't much but at least it was something.

Prison had permanently changed his viewpoint about life in general. In order to survive, he had studied and evaluated the other prisoners. He knew it was imperative that he understand everything possible about them. Lying on his bunk with nothing to do but think for hours at a time, he evaluated every nuance about the criminals with whom he lived. He memorized what set them off, how they reacted when angry, and he sorted out the pecking order of the prison. There had been serious talk of a riot for a while, and he had a plan in place to survive if it happened. It never did.

Surviving prison was a lot like playing a high-stakes chess game. He had to have everything well planned several moves in advance and know all the possible variables and alternatives.

It wasn't just the other prisoners he had to figure out. He also studied the various guards, their flaws, their weaknesses, their humanity or lack of it.

He had seen some sadistic guards, people who weren't all that different from the men they guarded except for the fact that they were allowed to go home at the end of their shift. He'd also known decent family men who were guards, simply trying to survive the best they could while working a soul-sucking job until they could retire with a pension.

As he had lain there hour after hour on his bunk, he'd come to the conclusion that there were basically two kinds of people in the world—the predatory animals and the human beings. What people chose to become had little to do with their station in life or upbringing. He'd seen a handful of guards over the years that he knew to be predators because they enjoyed making others suffer. Although a great many of his fellow prisoners were predators, which he avoided the best he could, he had also experienced many small kindnesses from fellow prisoners who he discovered to be human beings.

He decided that whether to become an animal or a human being was a choice a person made, and he decided that no matter what had happened to him, no matter how unfair his life had been, or how brutal the situation in which he lived, that he would choose to be a human being. He would not allow prison to destroy his soul.

CHAPTER TEN

Doc Wilson's office was a half block down the street. The doctor was just preparing to leave when Cole walked in. Doc was a distinguished gray-haired man in his early seventies.

"Do I know you?" Doc asked.

"I'm Cole Brady. I cut my arm. I was hoping you could take a look at it."

"Aren't you Marie and Josiah's boy?"

"Yes, sir." It felt good to be referred to as Marie and Josiah's boy. He'd been a number for far too long.

"I heard you were back." The doctor glanced at the cut. "Let's go into my examining room so I can take a closer look at that."

Cole was struck by how the doctor and the office looked as though they'd been painted by Norman Rockwell. Heavy, wooden furniture graced the small waiting room. Striped wallpaper covered the walls. Framed photographs of horses and young riders were everywhere.

"My nurse and receptionist have already gone home," the doctor said. "I'm closing up earlier these days. Just can't work the long hours I used to."

While Dr. Wilson unlocked the inner door to his private office, Cole examined the photographs. He noticed that beneath the protective riding hats, some of the riders had the unmistakable signs of Down syndrome. Others appeared to have cerebral palsy. All were handicapped in some way and yet all bore the wide grin of someone having the time of their life.

"Do you like the pictures of my kids?" Dr. Wilson looked over Cole's shoulder. "We've had dozens . . . though we weren't able to have any children of our own. My wife loved horses and with her work in special education, it was a natural progression to blend the two together. Our Little Acorn Farm became her life after she retired twelve years ago. You'd be surprised what being able to ride a horse—even with help—can do for the self-esteem of a special-needs child."

"It looks like a truly great work." Cole said.

"It was my wife's doing." Dr. Wilson chuckled, fondly. "I was just the money man. I made it and Carol spent it all on the kids. The small fees we charge at the farm have never really covered the expenses."

Cole saw the doctor with a new respect. "I'm impressed."

"Come on into my examining room and I'll fix you up," the doctor said. "Have you had a tetanus shot recently?"

"Yes." Cole thought back to the knife wound a year earlier that had barely missed his kidney.

"Good." Doc Wilson began cleansing the cut and spreading ointment on it. "We won't bother with stitches. There have been so many improvements since I graduated from medical school. The butterfly bandage is just one of hundreds."

Cole was tough, but getting stitched up was low on his list of favorite things to do. Butterfly bandages sounded like a good deal to him. As the doctor worked, the subject of Blake Ramsey came up.

"Wasn't it Blake who helped put you in prison?" Doc asked. "It sounds like you got a pretty raw deal."

"It was, and I did," Cole said.

"Blake was a good friend to me," the doctor said. "What happened to him was hard to take." Dr. Wilson put a final piece of tape on Cole's arm. "I'm especially worried about Lindsey. She was always so proud of her father. It isn't easy being thirteen under any circumstances, but having the whole world know that your father was a secret drug addict is hard for a kid to face."

"Is there any chance it might not have been accidental, Doc?"

Dr. Wilson drew off his latex gloves and dropped them into the trash. "I know Erin's having trouble accepting what happened. She's talked to me about it, but that's wishful thinking on her part. Blake died of an accidental cocaine overdose, pure and simple. Why do you ask?"

"It doesn't matter to me how the man died," Cole said, as he inspected his bandage. "But Marie seems to have doubts."

"I should have been more aware and maybe I could have prevented what happened. Blake had been going without sleep for quite a while and he appeared to be losing weight. I never dreamed that he was developing a drug habit. The sheriff called me as soon as he found Blake. I was there within minutes of the phone call. It was very apparent what Blake had been doing. He was facedown at his desk with drug paraphernalia and cocaine beside him on the desk." The doctor shook his head. "He was a good man, and I miss him. I wish I could have helped him."

"The death scene you describe sounds awfully neat," Cole said. "We had a couple cocaine overdoses while I was in prison. A guard had been paid to bring in the stuff. Those guys had convulsions and seizures before they died."

"They usually do." Doc paused. "But not always."

"Well, you're the expert." Cole got off the table, anxious to get back outside. The room was small and close—not much larger than his cell. "Where do you think he got the stuff?"

"There's always accessibility with the kind of business Blake was in."

"I suppose that's true." Cole reached for the billfold Marie had included as part of his new clothes. "What do I owe you?"

"My receptionist isn't here to deal with the billing so don't worry about it. How about we let this one be on the house? My personal apology for what this town did to you."

"Thank you, but . . ." Cole took a twenty-dollar bill from his billfold and held it out. "Could I make a donation to your farm?"

It felt good to have money to give to a good cause. For so long, he had worked for pennies an hour, hoarding dimes and nickels to buy a few essentials.

Dr. Wilson put the money into his breast pocket. "I never turn down a donation for my kids. You ought to come out and see the place."

"I will and I'll look forward to it," Cole said.

—————

Erin felt grimy as she drove home after handling Blake's old law books all day. She wanted to grab a quick shower before heading over to the Little Acorn to pick up Lindsey. She topped a small rise in her old truck then dipped down to her home—the twenty-acre hobby farm she and Blake had purchased several years ago.

Until yesterday their home had always felt like a haven. The closest neighbor was a half mile away and hidden behind a copse of oak trees. She and Blake had loved the peace and quiet and privacy. Now, the house simply seemed lonely and vulnerable.

It was definitely a relief to know that, at the very least, Cole meant her no harm.

She was in the process of unloading boxes of books when Marie's Buick pulled into the driveway.

"Hey, Mom!" Lindsey sprang out of the car as Marie waved from inside.

"You didn't have to do that, Marie," Erin said. "I was planning on picking her up."

"No need," Marie said. "I was over there anyway. Doc's been looking kind of peaked to me, so I took him some of my chicken soup. Guaranteed to heal what ails you. Lindsey was ready to come home early, so I just brought her."

"That was kind of you, but . . ."

"No buts about it!" Marie yelled as she backed her car out of the driveway barely missing the ditch. "See you tomorrow at church."

"I didn't ask her," Lindsey said defensively. "Marie volunteered."

"No, baby, it's fine." She put her arm around her daughter's shoulders. "I got Dad's things out of his office today, and I could use some help unloading them."

"Sure. I'll be *happy* to help."

Erin glanced at her daughter's face to check for sarcasm. It was not like Lindsey these days to acquiesce so cheerfully.

"The boxes are heavy."

"I'm getting a lot stronger, working out at Doc's."

Evidently Lindsey had had a *really* good day.

Erin backed the truck to the back door, and Lindsey let down the tailgate. Together, they lifted the first box of books.

Even though the boxes were heavy, by continuing to work together, they eventually got the entire truck unloaded and carried up to the attic. Lindsey kept up a great attitude the whole time. When the job was finished and Erin had let down her guard, Lindsey dropped the bomb she had been holding inside.

"Doc says he'll come down on the price for Snowball if we buy her. No one else has asked about her yet."

"Oh?" Erin knew exactly where this conversation was headed. Her daughter was nothing if not tenacious.

"She's a really good horse, Mom. We have a good, fenced pasture and a big barn. I'll take care of her and feed her. I give you my solemn promise that you won't even know she's here."

"Lindsey, you're practically living with those horses of Doc's as it is. How much more 'horse' do you need in your life?"

"I need Snowball. She's a really good horse, Mom. She likes me better than she does anyone else. If Doc sells her to someone besides me, they might be mean to her. I couldn't stand it if they were mean to her."

"Doc isn't going to sell Snowball to someone who will abuse her. Now, how about I go in and make us some dinner?" She forced enthusiasm into her voice. "What about grilled cheese sandwiches? That's your favorite."

Lindsey was silent.

"I'm sorry, honey. I simply can't deal with a horse right now."

Lindsey turned accusing blue eyes on her, as though Erin— all by herself—was bent on destroying the life of a horse.

"I'll go fix the sandwiches right now." Erin chose to ignore those eyes. "You go ahead and wash up for supper."

Grilled cheese and tomato soup: they had cured nearly everything in Lindsey's life since she'd started eating solid foods. Erin hurried into the kitchen and started slicing cheese and buttering bread. After she had the meal ready, she garnished their plates with pickles.

"Lindsey?" she called. "It's ready. Come and eat."

There was no answer.

"Lindsey?"

She went up to her daughter's room, but Lindsey wasn't there or in the bathroom. Lindsey was not in the barn or the empty hay loft, either. She wasn't in her room or the attic or the basement or any of the other rooms in the house. She wasn't in the abandoned corn crib or the field behind the house.

Her child had run away. Again.

Erin jumped into the truck and ground the key into the ignition. It coughed several times before it caught. Lindsey was probably just down at Gerta Brame's again, where she'd gone the day of the explosion. There was no need to panic. Nevertheless, Erin spun gravel as she gunned the truck and tore out of the driveway.

***

Saying good-bye to Doc took much longer than Cole expected. Once they got back to the waiting area, the old man wanted to tell Cole long, meandering stories about his "kids." Each picture on the wall held a story Doc felt compelled to tell.

Finally, he was free to start walking the two miles back to Marie and Josiah's. The Newmans had offered to take him wherever he wanted to go, but after all those years of pacing the miserly few square feet of his prison cell, he loved the heady freedom of walking—and walking as far and to wherever he wanted. Two miles didn't feel like a chore; it felt like recreation.

Still, come Monday after his first day of work, he would look into getting his driver's license. With a steady job, he should qualify for a car loan in a few weeks. Or maybe he would get a motorcycle! Now *that* would be something he'd enjoy.

A horn sounded behind him. He jumped and whirled. He was hardwired to respond to a loud horn signaling an attempted prison break which always resulted in immediate and total lockdown. It took him a moment to realize that it was only Marie—waving at him happily. She had no clue how hard his pulse was pounding.

"You want a lift?" Marie said.

"Where are we going?"

"Lindsey left her backpack in my car. I need to take it to her."

"Sure." He climbed into the passenger seat. "What have you been up to today, Marie?"

"I made a huge pot of chicken noodle soup after we got home from the funeral. I took some of it over to old Charlotte Esham—she just got out of the hospital. No cancer by the way, thank the Lord. Then I ran another quart of soup out to Doc's. That's going to be yours and Josiah's supper too, in case you're wondering. The reason I have Lindsey's backpack is because I took her home after she got off work at Doc's."

"You've done all that just since this morning?"

"There's more. I stopped by Big Lots and picked up some china I've had my eye on. It wasn't on the shelves anymore and I thought I'd waited too long but then I found it on the clearance shelf! Seventy-five percent off, thank you very much." Marie patted herself on the back. "I saved so much money that I splurged and bought myself a new quilt for our bed. Then I went home and caught a soap opera while I starched and ironed Josiah's shirt for Sunday. Then Lindsey called my cell phone and said she had forgotten her backpack in my car, so I told her I'd bring it out to her—and now I get to pick you up and have company while I ride out to Erin's farm. I think I'm starting to get the hang of not having a job." She sighed with satisfaction. "I just love being retired."

He grinned at her innocent enthusiasm. "Glad you're enjoying not having to work anymore."

"Me too!" Marie missed the irony. "So, now tell me what *you* did today."

"Well, first I—wait, isn't that Lindsey?"

Marie shaded her eyes and squinted. "That sure is."

A solitary figure walked toward them—a slender girl with long strawberry-blond hair. Definitely Lindsey. It was over a mile to her house, but she was walking in the opposite direction. Marie pulled up beside her and rolled down the window. "Where are you headed, punkin'?"

Lindsey kept her head down and kept walking. Marie drove past then stopped.

"Erin will kill me if I don't make her come home. Go talk to her, Cole. Please? I don't back up so good."

He got out of the car and caught up to Lindsey. "Marie wants me to ask you where you're going. Can we take you someplace? Are you okay?"

She stopped and peeked at him through long bangs. She was close enough that he could see her tear-streaked face. Her shoulders began to heave and then she began to wail with an opened mouth, like the child she was, standing right there in the middle of the gravel road.

He wasn't sure what to do. His first instinct was to put his arms around her, but she wasn't all that little and he was a man only two days out of prison. It could be misconstrued—by her or by anyone else who might pass by.

"Can we take you home?" he asked.

She shook her head.

"Is there someplace else you want to go?"

She nodded and wiped her nose on the tail of her T-shirt.

"Then how about you get inside Marie's car and tell us? It isn't safe for you to be out here by yourself."

Lindsey thought it over for a moment then turned around and walked back to Marie's car with him. She climbed in the backseat and fastened her seat belt. "I'm sorry, but do you mind taking me back to the Little Acorn, Marie?"

"Sure don't." Marie reached into her open purse, grabbed her cell phone, and handed it to the girl while Cole got in. "Why don't you call your mom and tell her where you are?"

"She doesn't care." Lindsey said.

Cole turned around to look at her. "Of course she does."

Blazing blue eyes pinned him. "If she cared, she would let me have Snowball."

He was lost here. Was Snowball a doll? A dog? A boyfriend?

"Who's Snowball?" he asked as Marie put the car in gear and headed toward the Little Acorn.

"The best horse there ever was, and Doc has to sell her," Lindsey answered. "Just because she's old."

"Ah." Everything started to make a little more sense.

"You want to buy a horse and your mom won't let you, so you ran away?"

"I didn't run away."

"Correction. You walked away."

"Uh-huh." *Sniff.*

"Does your mom know you're gone?" Marie asked.

Lindsey shrugged.

He knew Erin must be frantic. In that moment, he was very glad he wasn't a parent.

"I sure have been seeing a lot of this place," Marie said, pulling into the Little Acorn's driveway. "Where are you going now that you're here?"

"I want to see Snowball."

"May I see her too?" he asked. "I like horses."

Her eyes brightened. "If you really want to."

"I do."

"Go ahead," Marie said. "I'm a little tired. I think I'll stay here with the car."

She touched her cell phone, and Cole knew she would be calling Erin as soon as they were out of earshot. That's exactly what he had intended.

He followed Lindsey through a maze of stables and sheds. There didn't seem to be anyone else around. At one point they passed a heavily timbered outbuilding that was secured with a giant padlock. It struck him as a little odd. None of the other buildings had padlocks.

"What does Doc keep in there, Lindsey?" He pointed to the padlocked shed.

"His wife's special saddles and tack, some of her trophies. She used to show horses. He loved her a lot and said he couldn't stand it if someone stole her things."

"Why doesn't he keep them in the house?"

"He says it hurts to see them, but he doesn't want anything to happen to them."

That made sense. He admired the old man—the fact that he still had the heart to pour his life into his patients and those sweet children.

An elderly white horse stood in the back stall of the largest barn. Lindsey climbed over the stall gate and began to pet and stroke the animal.

"This is Snowball," the girl said. "She's been here longer than any of the others. She's so gentle that Doc can put his most fragile child on her back. It's like she can sense that she has to be careful. All those years of helping others, I guess. She deserves more than to be sold to just anyone. If I had her, I would love her and take good care of her."

Cole watched the horse nuzzle Lindsey. It was as though the mare could sense that she'd been crying. There was no doubt in his mind that Erin's refusal to allow Lindsey to have this animal was breaking the child's heart.

Lindsey pressed her face into Snowball's mane and seemed to forget that Cole was even there.

"Before I go, do you need anything?" he asked.

"No." She shook her head. "I'm okay now. But thanks."

He walked away as she began to murmur to the horse. He smiled as he overheard the words "doesn't understand" and "not fair." Typical words from a kid her age when they didn't get their way.

He stopped and stood still as she began to cry again. Thinking he was gone, she began to talk louder. What he overheard broke his heart. The girl was confessing to her favorite horse that maybe if she had been a better girl and made better grades, her daddy wouldn't have turned to cocaine and her mom wouldn't upset all the time.

She was blaming herself for her father's death. That was surely one heavy load she was carrying.

Kids always thought the world revolved around them. If something went wrong, even in the lives of the adults around them, they automatically internalized the blame. He was well aware of the syndrome. He had done exactly the same thing as a kid.

He considered going back and talking to Lindsey about it, explaining that her behavior, whatever it had been, had nothing to do with her father's death. But words, as he well knew, had little effect. He found himself wishing he could do something to prove that Blake had *not* died of an accidental overdose.

For Lindsey.

Maybe for Erin, too.

CHAPTER ELEVEN

"**D**id you get hold of Erin?" Cole asked Marie as he slid into the car.

"No." Marie looked distraught. "She's not answering."

"She's probably out hunting for her daughter."

"I know." Marie bit her lip, thinking. "Is Lindsey okay?"

"When I left her, she was busy telling all her troubles to a horse."

"She'll be fine if we leave her here for a few more minutes. Let's drive over to Erin's and see if she's out searching. I hate to think of her worried half to death when Lindsey's fine."

"Should I stay here?"

Marie considered the thought. "I know you're an innocent man, Cole, but it probably would be best if you didn't. Lindsey's a young girl who is upset and might say things later that could be misconstrued."

"Got it." Cole said as he climbed into the car. "And you're right."

As they drove toward Erin's, they kept a watch out for her truck. A quarter mile from her house, they saw her pulled over to the side of the road. The hood of the truck was up and she was staring at the motor.

Marie parked behind her and they both got out. As Erin turned toward them, Cole noticed that her eyes were haunted and weary. The woman looked as if she'd been through a personal war.

"Lindsey's run away," she said. "I can't find her anywhere. Not even down at Gerta's. *And* I think my truck just died on me permanently." She gave the old blue truck a kick.

Marie bustled over and laid a comforting hand on Erin's shoulder. "We found Lindsey walking along the road and took her where she was headed, out to Doc's."

"Maybe I should rent a stall for her out there." Erin's voice was bitter. "My daughter would rather live in a barn with those horses than with me."

"She's thirteen," Marie said. "They all lose their good sense at that age. Someday you'll be friends again. You're a good mom. You always have been."

Erin slumped back against the truck and closed her eyes, as though to gain strength from Marie's encouragement. Then she straightened again. "I'd better go get her. I am so sorry about all this fuss. We've become such a burden to you, Marie . . . and Cole."

Marie put her arm around Erin's waist and walked her over to her car. "I don't have one thing better to do right now than take you to your daughter. Cole? You coming?"

He was already beneath the truck's hood. He could see that it was only a water hose that had blown—a simple repair. He thought he could patch up the truck enough to make it run a while longer.

"You go on without me. I want to see if I can get this vehicle fixed," he said.

"Blake's tools are in the garage," Erin slid in beside Marie. "If any of them are still usable, feel free."

The garage still reeked of smoke and ashes, but the back part of it was still standing. There was a relatively undamaged metal toolbox beneath the workbench. He sat it on the charred top and opened it. Inside was a nice assortment of Stanley tools. He sorted through them to find what he needed, trying to ignore the unwelcome feeling of intimacy with Blake that handling the man's things gave him.

Small town or not, this was the last time he planned on having any personal contact with Erin or her daughter. He had enough problems of his own. He had no intention of getting sucked any deeper into this family's struggles.

~~~

Cole was wiping off the tools he'd used when Marie brought Erin and Lindsey home. It was obvious he'd managed to repair the truck, since it was parked beside her house when they arrived.

"You fixed it?" Erin asked as she and Lindsey climbed out of Marie's car.

"After a fashion." Cole dropped a wrench into the metal box sitting on the opened tailgate. "You need to make some other arrangements soon. It isn't going to last much longer without some major repairs.

"Thanks for getting it off the road."

"I was afraid someone would plow into it and hurt themselves."

Erin noticed that he didn't bother to say she was welcome. She didn't blame him.

"I think we had better be going, Cole," Marie said. "Erin and Lindsey have a lot to talk about. We'll see you later."

Cole returned the toolbox to the garage and then he and Marie drove away—leaving her and Lindsey alone.

Lindsey had offered no explanations when Erin had found her in the stall with the horse she wanted to rescue and Erin had not asked for any. She was so angry at her daughter at that point that she was afraid if she opened her mouth, she would start screaming and not stop. The ride home in Marie's car had been thick with unspoken, angry words.

Why did her daughter have to give her so much grief at the very time she had so little strength to deal with it?

"You smell like a horse barn," Erin said. "Go upstairs and shower. We'll talk after you finish."

Lindsey whirled and disappeared into the house. Erin followed more slowly, shaking with anger.

Unable to sit still, she paced around, nervously putting things to rights. She straightened couch pillows, centered lamps, refolded an afghan Lindsey had tossed onto a chair. The paperwork she'd been working on the day before lay scattered on the roll top desk in the small alcove office off the living room. She went over and stacked the papers in one corner and then shut the roll top. The file drawer she'd been going through was hanging open. She closed and locked the cabinet and then tossed the key back into the small candy dish on top. The file cabinet was yet one more annoyance in her life. Unless she kept it locked, there always seemed to be a file drawer hanging open.

Having expended some of her anger by putting everything to rights, she sat on the living room couch to wait for her daughter. A home-decorating magazine had arrived in the mail the day before and was lying on the coffee table. Under normal circumstances, she would be tempted to read it the moment it arrived. She loved seeing new ways to decorate her home, but currently she had no desire to even flip through the glossy pages. The last thing she needed right now was the hottest new plan to make her house more attractive. What she needed was an idea on how to make her *life* more attractive.

Several other women's magazines were fanned beside it, all unread. She stared at the titles of articles emblazoned on the fronts. Every one revolved around dieting, exercise, sex, or organizing the clutter in one's life.

Organizing the clutter. Her eyes snagged on that. She wished it were possible to buy little plastic boxes and place all the clutter of her life inside. She could put neat labels on each one like "ANGRY TEENAGER," or "DECEASED HUSBAND," or "ESTRANGED CRAZY FATHER." Then she could put them on a closet shelf, up high, and only take down one box at a time, dealing only with what was in that one box when she needed to.

Life was never that neat. Right now it was coming at her like the waves of a violent ocean, knocking her to her knees again and again, sucking her down with an almost vicious joy. The only thing she knew to do was struggle to her feet and fight to reach shallower water before the next big wave knocked her down again.

She had never been a big fan of the ocean.

The upstairs shower ran on and on. The hot water tank would soon be depleted, at this rate. Lindsey was probably putting off coming downstairs and facing her again, especially without anyone else around to cushion the fireworks they both knew were going to take place.

Erin leaned her head back against the couch and sent up a silent plea.

She's run away twice now, Lord. What am I to do? What sort of punishment can I use that will be harsh enough to keep her from running away ever again?

Her mind darted this way and that, trying to come up with

something big enough and bad enough. The obvious answer was not allowing her to work at Doc's farm for a while, but taking one of the most positive things in her daughter's life away from her seemed unwise. Doc had told her more than once that not only did Lindsey have a knack with the horses, she was unusually patient with the special-needs children who depended on her as well.

It was hard for Erin to imagine a patient Lindsey. It was even harder for her to understand Lindsey's desire to care for horses.

Erin had been raised around horses and mules and every possible farm animal during her young life on the mountain in Virginia where she and her father had lived. He had expected her to work like a man beside him from the time she was eight. She had mucked out tons of manure. It had never struck her as recreation. By the age of fifteen, she couldn't wait to escape her father's log fortress. By eighteen, she was gone.

Unlike Lindsey, she had not run away. Instead, she had worked toward a full scholarship, left home, and never looked back. Her father had never quite forgiven her, nor had she forgiven him for the absurdly paranoid and strange childhood he had given her.

Living alone with Wild Bill on that mountain top had had some good moments. There was great beauty and peace to be found in the mountains of Virginia, but it had been a lonely and embarrassing existence. Her dad trusted no one but with only a GED, he did feel strongly about the necessity of education for his daughter. He had taken her to school every morning and was waiting outside every afternoon—along with the mule he used to transport her up the mountainside. Worst of all, he always came armed. Her dad didn't believe in carrying concealed—he believed in carrying. Period.

That would have gone over fine maybe a century earlier,

but not when she was growing up. Having a little girlfriend come to spend the night was impossible. None of the parents would have allowed one of their children to leave with her and her bearded, suspicious, gun-toting father. Wild Bill would never have allowed her to go to another child's home. She knew better than to even ask.

Instead, she dreamed of creating a normal life when she grew up and Blake had helped make that dream come true. At least for a while. Now, yet once again, everything in her life was abnormal.

Her upbringing did nothing to equip her to know how to deal with her own, rebellious daughter. She simply didn't understand her. She had given Lindsey everything that she herself had longed for as a child. Nothing had been spared in making certain Lindsey had the perfect childhood.

She'd created a beautiful girl's bedroom for her daughter. The walls were painted creamy white with light pink accessories and a princess bed—instead of the log walls she had stared at when she was growing up.

There was the piano and piano lessons. Ballet lessons, too, even though she had to drive an hour one way to get Lindsey there. She'd made certain there were routine hair appointments and manicures. Lovely dresses. Perfect birthday parties.

And all Lindsey seemed to want to do was dress and act like a stable hand.

It was hard for Erin not to resent her daughter for rejecting the very things she had fantasized about when she was growing up.

Lindsey tiptoed down the stairs, looking apprehensive but wrapped in the fuzzy pink bathrobe Erin had bought her and that Lindsey hated.

"I love you, Lindsey." It was the first thing that popped into her head to say, but it was true and so she said it. "I love you more than I love myself."

Lindsey's eyes narrowed.

How long had it been since she had told her daughter she loved her? She couldn't remember.

"What are you going to do to punish me, Mom? Take away my TV? My computer? Ground me to my room? Just tell me what you're going to do and get it over with."

"We're not doing so well, are we, Lindsey?"

"What do you mean?" Her daughter continued to look at her through suspicious eyes, as though Erin was asking her a trick question.

"We've been through too much. We've been in so much pain that we're turning on each other. But if we don't take care of each other, no one is going to do it for us. God gave us each other. For better or worse—we're all we have."

Lindsey still looked wary, seemingly waiting for the other shoe to drop.

Erin didn't know if what she was about to suggest was good parenting or bad. All she knew was what she'd been trying to do wasn't working.

"I'd like to propose a compromise about Snowball."

Lindsey's blue eyes filled with reluctant hope. "A compromise?"

"You're afraid something bad is going to happen to that old horse if Doc sells it, right?"

Lindsey nodded.

"I don't think I can deal with one more thing. There's so much that Dad used to do, and now it's ours to tend to."

She saw Lindsey stiffen.

"But what if I approach Doc with a deal? I'll buy Snowball from him and pay for her food and vet bills, but she'll have to stay at the farm for now—until we get on our feet and stabilize a little more."

Her daughter turned into a blur of fuzzy pink bathrobe and slippers, diving onto the couch beside her, throwing her arms around her, and hugging her hard. Erin held onto her daughter, inhaling the scent of young girl, wet hair, and citrus shampoo. It felt so good to hold her little girl again.

"Thank you, Mom. I'll never forget this."

Neither would Erin. She should have realized sooner how important saving the old horse was to Lindsey. Instead, she had allowed her daughter's heartfelt pleas to be nothing more than an irritation.

She couldn't put her daughter in a neatly labeled box and shove her onto a shelf until she could deal with her. It had to be here, now. She had to somehow be present—in spite of her own confusion and pain. This young life was too important to mess up.

And this moment was too sweet to let go of quickly. Erin thought it would be good to celebrate somehow. She kissed the top of her daughter's head. "Would you like to go to the Brown Betty tonight? Again? I still haven't shopped for groceries."

"What's Betty fixing tonight?"

"I think I saw that this is Shrimp Saturday."

"I love shrimp! Just let me go blow-dry my hair and put on some clothes."

"You got it, sweetheart. No big hurry. I need to grab a shower, too. It's been a long day."

The sound of Lindsey's footsteps practically dancing up to her room was sweet, indeed. As a mother, Erin felt like she'd actually had one of those moments where maybe she'd finally done something right.

Before she went upstairs to get ready, Erin's eyes fell on the magazines again. She was going to cancel the subscriptions. All of them. She didn't know when she would have the heart to read any of them ever again.

Besides, it appeared she was going to have a horse to support.

CHAPTER TWELVE

C ole came in at dusk from weeding Marie's overgrown vegetable garden and found her sitting at the kitchen table, surrounded by stacks of papers and books, clad in a blue-flowered housecoat with glasses perched on the tip of her nose, and a laptop computer in front of her.

"What are you up to now, Marie?"

"I've taken up a new hobby." She beamed.

"I'm assuming you have given up on raising organic vegetables?"

"I had such good intentions when I planted this spring," she said, sheepishly. "Then, with you coming home and everything else going on, I kinda forgot it was there."

"That's okay," Cole washed his hands off in the sink. "I'll take care of it for you. Now tell me about your new hobby."

"Well . . . it doesn't involve sewing or gardening or cooking."

He couldn't help but grin at her never-ending enthusiasm for her inevitably discarded projects. "And what would it be?"

"Genealogy!" she announced.

"What brought this on?"

"I forgot to tell you that I also went to the library this

morning to see if I could find a book on a hobby I could actually *do*, and I talked to the librarian while I was there and I told her I was retired and didn't like to sew or garden or crochet or even cook all that much anymore and she said 'Have you tried genealogy?' I told her my ancestors hadn't amounted to much and she said sometimes people find out that their family actually used to own castles and be royalty. I told her it was more likely that I was descended from horse thieves and stowaways but I'd give it a try."

"That's nice, Marie." He went to the refrigerator and poured himself some iced tea.

"You sound down." Marie took off her glasses, folded them, and placed them on her lap. "What's wrong?"

Cole drained the glass of iced tea, placed the glass in the sink, and then sat down at the kitchen table across from her.

"I talked to Erin today for a few minutes while she was cleaning out Blake's office."

"Oh?" A look of worry flashed across Marie's face. "I *think* I'm glad to hear that. I'm not sure. What happened?"

"I went to see Doc Wilson this morning,"

"Are you sick?"

"I accidentally cut myself while you and Josiah were at the funeral. Doc fixed me up. It's nothing to worry about."

"Are you sure?"

"I'm fine. Anyway, I was walking down the sidewalk this morning, minding my own business, and checking out some of the changes that have taken place since I . . . left. The last thing on my agenda was going into Blake's office, but when I walked past and saw Erin sitting at his desk, crying her eyes out, something made me go inside. We talked about that night with Terri. She apologized. Told me how sorry she was. Then this afternoon I helped you rescue her daughter . . . and then I fixed that rattletrap of a truck so she had something to drive."

"There's nothing wrong in what you've done."

"Yes there is. I can't do this. I can't get involved in that woman's life again."

"Why not?"

"Because." Cole dropped his head into his hands. "The last time I got involved in her life, she just about destroyed me. If something like that happens again I can't guarantee that I'll be able to walk away. I wasn't exaggerating when I told you that I'd had to become a dangerous man in order to survive. I did things in prison I'll never be able to forget. Sometimes I wonder if I should even be staying here with you and Josiah."

Marie's voice was soft. "Why?"

"Because you two are such gentle good people, and I'm . . ."

"You're our son." Marie covered his big hand with her small, plump one. "We know your heart. There is nothing you could ever do that would make us stop loving you."

He looked into Marie's eyes and knew that she spoke the truth. He also knew that he would do practically anything to keep from hurting them again—even if it meant forcing himself to make peace with himself about Erin.

Erin drove home on automatic pilot. Tonight had been a very good night for the two of them. No fights. No sharp words. Shrimp Saturday at the Brown Betty had been a success, but Lindsey was so tired from her day that she had fallen asleep almost as soon as Erin pulled out of the restaurant's parking lot.

Erin had been in such a hurry to make it to the restaurant in time for supper that she had forgotten to put oil in the motor before they left home. Something else Blake had always taken care of for her. The truck began to buck just past Gerta Brame's and Erin feared they would not make it home. Again.

She pulled into her driveway, cut the lights, and the truck shuddered to a stop. Heaving a sigh, she glanced at the house and froze. Neither the porch nor the living room lights were on. That was odd. She hated coming home to a dark house and always made sure the lights were on before she left. She distinctly remembered turning them on before she and Lindsey left. At least she *thought* she had left the lights on. On the other hand, it had been an extremely upsetting day. She told herself that she'd probably forgotten.

"Wake up, sweetie." She gently nudged her daughter.

Lindsey stirred and opened sleep-drugged eyes. "Are we home?"

"We are, and you can go straight to bed as soon as we're inside."

With their arms around each other they walked to the front door, Lindsey groggy and leaning on her, half-asleep. Erin had her keys in her hand, ready to unlock the front door . . . except she didn't need to. When she went to insert the key, the door was already ajar.

"Lindsey." Her voice quavered. "Did we forget to lock up?"

Lindsey was immediately wide awake. "No, Mom. I checked. I'm as creeped out about coming home late at night without Dad as you are. The porch light was on when we left too."

Erin looked at Lindsey and Lindsey looked at Erin. Then, without saying another word, they sprinted back to the truck, jumped in, and simultaneously locked their doors.

"Are you going to call the police?" Lindsey asked.

Erin considered. Call Sheriff Dempsey? She hated to bother the man. She felt like she had been nothing but a burden to everyone around her. She started reasoning with herself. It was only an unlocked door.

"I think we're overreacting," she said. "I really don't think there's anything to be afraid of. We probably just forgot to lock it. I think we should go in. We can't spend the rest of our lives afraid."

Lindsey unearthed a tire iron from beneath the seat. "Okay, but if we go in, I'm taking this. I'm a good hitter."

That was true enough. Lindsey was a key player on the middle school softball team.

Erin pulled a can of pepper spray from her purse. Now armed, they climbed out of the truck and crept up to the house.

The living room light was a medium-sized chandelier. The control for it was directly inside the door on the right-hand side. Erin knew exactly where to reach to flip it on, and she did. Suddenly the entire living room was illuminated. She pushed the door open wide. Nothing there.

She scooted inside with Lindsey so close behind her that they were practically stepping in unison. She turned on the light in the kitchen. Nothing there.

Downstairs bathroom, family room, den. All clear. The door leading to the basement was still latched. Definitely no one down there.

She had become so used to the sound over the years that she'd forgotten how badly the stairs creaked, but each one groaned as they mounted them to the second floor. Nothing in the master bedroom, nothing in the guest bedroom. No one hiding under Lindsey's bed or in any of the closets.

Breathing a sigh of relief, she stuffed the pepper spray into her pocket. "Now, aren't we glad we didn't call the sheriff? No one's in here and nothing's been disturbed. We must have forgotten to lock up after all."

At that moment, from directly beneath them, they heard the front door close.

Lindsey jumped and clenched the tire iron with both fists while they looked at each other, wild-eyed.

"Maybe the wind blew it shut," Erin whispered.

"There wasn't any wind," Lindsey said.

An engine started from behind the barn and a car tore out of their driveway.

Erin locked the bedroom door and shoved a heavy armchair in front of it. Then, holding her shivering daughter, she hit "recent calls" on her cell phone to contact Sheriff Dempsey. At least she thought she'd dialed the sheriff's office. She didn't realize she had accidentally hit Marie's number until she heard Cole's voice answering.

CHAPTER THIRTEEN

C ole had never seen Josiah drive so fast.

"That house is so isolated anyone could do anything to those two women and there would be no one to hear or know." Josiah said as he wheeled into the driveway and skidded to a stop.

They jumped out of the car and ran to the front porch. Erin answered the door holding a black canister of pepper spray. The pepper spray seemed incongruent against the backdrop of her pink blouse, dark dress jeans, slip-on shoes, and pearl earrings. Behind her was Lindsey in khaki shorts, a blue Titans T-shirt, and tennis shoes. She had accessorized with a tire iron that she gripped with both hands.

"Thank God you're all right!" Josiah stepped through the door and gathered Erin and Lindsey into his arms.

Cole, still on the porch holding the screen door open, noticed that Lindsey clung to Josiah long after her mother had stepped away. The child was obviously hungry for a father's touch. He was glad Erin had called them—even if it had been accidental. Josiah was the perfect person to be there with them.

The circles beneath Erin's eyes had gotten darker since this morning. In his opinion, someone needed to tuck that woman into bed for about a month and let her get some rest.

She motioned him inside as Lindsey released Josiah. "Sorry we bothered you again, Cole. I was shaking so badly, I really had no idea I was calling your house instead of Sheriff Dempsey. I'm sure you have better things to do with your time than getting us out of scrapes. Is Marie in the car?"

"She was in the shower," Cole said. "We didn't want to wait. We came without her."

All of them stiffened at the sound of a car pulling into the driveway. A spotlight played over the house and yard.

"I called Sheriff Dempsey right after talking with you," Erin explained.

The short walk from the patrol car into the house had winded the overweight sheriff, but he tried to mask it. "Have you found anything out of order?" He stopped to catch his breath. "Anything taken?"

"No. Not that I can tell," Erin said.

"Tell me everything that happened." He lowered himself onto Erin's couch and pulled out a leather notebook.

Erin sat in an armchair while she outlined the details of the evening. Lindsey took up a position beside her mother, still grasping the tire iron. Josiah sat forward in the other chair. Cole leaned against the wall, taking it all in.

"I'll need to inspect the house." The sheriff snapped his notebook shut after he had listened to Erin's description of what had taken place.

"Of course," Erin said.

She led the sheriff into the kitchen as Cole, Josiah, and Lindsey followed. As a group, they surveyed the kitchen. Dempsey opened a broom closet, found nothing except a mop and a broom, and closed the door. Cole wondered if he had actually expected to find a burglar hiding in the tiny space.

Together they continued the tour through each room. It was interesting to Cole to see how the Ramseys had lived. Although it was a nice home, the furnishings were not nearly as elaborate or as expensive as he would have expected.

Dempsey opened the closet of the master bedroom and seemed surprised to find Blake's suits and shirts still lined up in a neat row.

"It might be a good idea to clear these things out and donate them to charity, Erin," the sheriff said. "Hanging onto a spouse's clothing too long just makes the grieving worse."

It was an innocuous thing to say, but to Cole's surprise, Erin exploded.

"In the past two months," she said, her eyes flashing and her voice deadly. "I've buried a husband, escaped a car explosion, hunted for a lost child, tried to keep a crippled vehicle running, *and* had a break-in. And you're concerned because Blake's clothes are still hanging in my *closet?*"

"Now, Erin," Dempsey said. "No need to get upset. I was just giving you a little advice."

Cole had been impressed with her strength and self-control the times he had seen her recently, but now that facade crumbled and he saw the frustrated, angry woman beneath.

"For your information, Sheriff, I've been wading through Blake's files, trying to find something that would explain why and how he died. The *real* reason. That's something no one else seems to have the least bit of interest in. At least not in this godforsaken place. I don't care how many times you describe the scene to me; I *know* there's something else going on here. I can feel it in my bones. I see it every time I walk past that burned garage."

"Now, Erin," Dempsey said, "Everyone has their weaknesses. Even your husband. Blake was no saint."

If Cole thought Erin was angry before, he was mistaken.

He would not want to face the woman he saw grab Dempsey's shirt as she looked him straight in the eyes.

"Sixteen years ago my husband held his own brother in his arms in the emergency room minutes after he died of an overdose. His brother's buddies had dumped him there and fled. Let me tell you something, Sheriff. There was no person on the face of this earth who hated illegal drugs more than Blake. You worked with him. You knew him. He may not have been a saint, but the idea of him using cocaine is ludicrous, and you know it."

"You *don't* know that." Dempsey's face grew red, and a vein on his forehead visibly throbbed. He removed her hand from his shirt. "You don't know *what* your husband was doing. No wife does. I could tell you a lot about what wives don't know about their husbands in this county."

"Not Blake." Erin crossed her arms over her chest. "I knew my husband."

"Really? You think you knew Blake? Then you must have known about that affair he was having with Dinah. You know— that cute little waitress that works for Betty Brown?"

"How *dare* you say something like that in front of my daughter!" Erin's face went pale. "I'm sorry I called you. Blake always said that the law in this county was a joke, and now I can see why."

The sheriff's chin went up and his fists clenched. "You can say what you want but . . . I'm not a joke."

Cole tensed and took a step forward. He did not want to have to manhandle Sheriff Dempsey, but there was no way he would allow him to strike Erin.

"I think everyone's said enough," Josiah said in a soothing voice. "It's been a trying day, and everyone needs to calm down. There's no need to . . ."

"Go home!" Lindsey burst out. "Just go home, Sheriff. My

dad wasn't having an affair. He would not cheat on my mom. He wouldn't cheat on *us*. He loved us!"

Cole had to admire the girl. Tears were streaming down her face, but she was standing in a loose baseball stance, as though she would like to send the sheriff's head whizzing into the next county.

"I apologize." Dempsey relaxed his fists. "I shouldn't have said that, but all this is getting pretty hard to take. I know you've been calling all over the country this past week trying to get someone else to come here. I've had some phone calls from state and federal authorities asking what happened. None of them have seen any reason to investigate. If you think someone from the outside can do my job better than me, you're wrong."

"Then what you said about Blake and that waitress was a lie to get back at me?" Erin asked.

"No, ma'am." It sounded as though there was genuine regret in the sheriff's voice. "I shouldn't have brought it up. Not now, not after he's gone, and especially not in front of your daughter, but I did see Blake and Dinah holding hands over in Gatlinburg awhile back. I'm sorry—but it's true . . . and there's something else I've been debating whether to tell you about."

"If it's something else about Blake I'm not sure I want to know right now." Erin glanced at her daughter.

"I don't know if Blake has anything to do with this or not," Sheriff Dempsey said. "But you and Lindsey were right about the garage. It wasn't a faulty fuel pump. I came over today to take a better look. There's some C-4 residue."

Erin shook her head. "I don't understand."

"C-4 is an explosive," the sheriff said. "About the consistency of modeling clay. There are some splatters of it on the walls."

"I had a cellmate who about drove me nuts talking about

setting fires and blowing things up," Cole said. "I learned enough from him that I know there had to be a trigger."

"I've been thinking about that," the sheriff said. "All it would take would be some wires attached to a back tail light. Take the bulb out, wire it to a detonation cap, have the C-4 near the gas tank. Whoever planted it must have been expecting the car to be started from the inside. Instead, when Erin used the remote, the lights still went on . . ." He shrugged.

"But *why*?" Erin asked. "Why target me and my daughter?"

"My first guess is that Blake was involved with some people pretty high up in the business. That coke was extremely pure. If it were regular street quality, it would have been cut. This wasn't. Let's say if for some reason Blake couldn't pay, it's pretty common for drug dealers to target family members."

"Again," Erin said. "Why?"

"To make an example."

"I don't understand."

"Drugs are a big business, Erin," the sheriff said. "Dealers buy the pure stuff—sometimes straight from Columbia. Then they cut it and sell it to smaller dealers. Many dealers support their families with their income. Sometimes if things go wrong, families are killed. It's nothing personal to these people. It's just an object lesson to keep other dealers in line . . . or sometimes to warn the families to keep quiet."

"You're saying that you think Blake was a dealer?"

"I think it's a strong possibility."

"My dad?" Lindsey said. "No way. He wouldn't *do* something like that."

Erin ignored her. "What can I do, Sheriff?"

Cole could hear the panic in her voice.

"It might be wise to stop calling every law enforcement agency in the country you can think of—asking them to come here and investigate," the sheriff said. "You don't know who might be involved in this. In the meantime, I'll find out what I can and try to keep you safe." He glanced around. "You might want to hire someone to install a security system for your house."

⁓⊙⊱⁓

They stood in complete, shocked, silence while the squad car backed out of the driveway.

"Well, *that* was fun," Erin said.

"Mom?" Lindsey's voice was plaintive. "That wasn't true about Dad having an affair with that waitress, was it?"

"Oh, Lindsey, when would he have had the time?"

"What about what Sheriff Dempsey said about Dad being a drug dealer?"

"I don't believe it," Erin said. "I can't prove it, but there is no way any of this is true."

She had no idea what else to say. One of the things Blake had taught her was that it was next to impossible to prove a negative.

"The sheriff seemed pretty certain about it, Mom."

"I think the sheriff is mistaken."

It nearly killed her to see the world-weary look in her daughter's eyes.

The blow from Dempsey's words was devastating. He had sounded utterly sincere in spite of his anger at her. Erin was certain Dempsey truly believed what he'd said, but it didn't square with what she knew about Blake. It wasn't just about Blake's morality. She happened to know that her husband did not like to hold hands. Not even with her and not even back when they were dating. In public, he would put his arm around her, give her hug, or maybe a kiss on the cheek, but he was uncomfortable with holding hands. He thought it looked childish. As far as the drugs, she simply could not imagine him being involved.

Nothing Dempsey said made sense, but nothing in her world made sense these days. She felt like a modern-day Alice in Wonderland who'd fallen down a rabbit hole the day she stepped off the plane from Honduras to find Marie and Josiah waiting to pick her up at the airport instead of Blake. Everything had felt strange ever since.

"Are you going to bed anytime soon, Mom?" Lindsey said. "I'm worn out."

"No. I'm too geared up to sleep. I'll visit with Josiah and Cole a bit. You go on. Try to get some rest. This has been a rough night."

Lindsey wandered up to her room, trailing the tire iron behind her.

"Are you okay?" Josiah asked after they heard Lindsey close her bedroom door.

"As okay as I can be." She sank onto the couch. "Blake would hate all this upheaval. He needed a lot of symmetry to his life."

"Symmetry?" Cole asked.

"An organized home. A specific kind of pen—he liked a black, wide-tipped felt pen. He preferred a plain coffee cup to a decorated one. Routines and schedules were important to him." She smiled sadly. "It used to bother me a little, but I think the reason for it was that his work was so messy and unsettling that it made him crave order in every other aspect of his life."

"I'm sorry, but I don't think the sheriff is correct in his suspicions about Blake," Josiah said. "Your husband and I spent too much time talking about things. I've spent too much time in my profession to be easily fooled by someone who spouts a little scripture or references a belief in God just because they happen to be around a preacher. In my opinion, Blake was the real deal. He cared too much about you, about Lindsey, about his desire to serve the people who elected him, and his commitment to Christ. Do you have any idea about the cases he was involved in before his death? What he might have been investigating?"

"The better question would be, what *wasn't* Blake involved in? There is so much corruption in this county, Josiah, so much pain. It's invisible unless you know where to look. You already know that—you just deal with it in a different way than Blake. Visitors who drive through here rave about the beauty and simplicity of these Tennessee hills. They don't see the high unemployment rate or know about the meth labs. For all I know, the intruder who was here tonight was simply another druggie, looking for something he could sell."

"Things have gotten a lot worse since I've been away," Cole said.

"It has. For what it's worth, Blake's workload tripled in the time you were gone. Government helicopters make routine flyovers each autumn now, checking the cornfields for marijuana. Several physicians have been busted for running oxycodone prescription mills. Blake was involved in all of that. So was the sheriff."

"What she says is true," Josiah said. "I know you had your own unfortunate dealings with him, Cole. It bothered me that I could never convince him of your innocence, but Blake was definitely no coward."

"He made more enemies in five years than most men make in a lifetime. Lindsey and I and this farm were his only real sanctuaries. I think that's one of the reasons he seldom talked about what he was working on. He tried to keep his home life separate except sometimes when he worked here in our home office."

"Dempsey didn't go into the office," Cole mentioned.

"Excuse me?" Erin said.

"He went through the whole house and looked into all your closets, but he didn't once glance at that alcove off the living room where I saw a desk and file cabinet. Have you checked it since the break-in?"

"It's such a small space and so visible. I glanced in, but . . . oh." Realization dawned. "Blake's files."

~~~~~

The three of them rose in unison and went to the office. Cole saw that an old-fashioned, roll-top desk took up most of the space. On one side of the desk was a four-drawer file cabinet. One drawer was opened a half-inch.

Erin gasped.

"What?" Josiah said.

"That file drawer." She pointed. "It's ajar. We always kept it locked. The lock wasn't much, but it was the only way the drawers would stay closed. Blake kept meaning to fix it, but he wasn't particularly good at fixing things like that. We kept the key in a candy dish on top. I distinctly remember locking it and putting the key back in the dish."

Cole used a pencil to pull the one file drawer that had been partially opened all the way out.

He could see that Blake had been meticulous about his filing system. Each folder was tucked into a larger, color-coordinated hanging file. A blue folder went into a corresponding blue hanging file—both labeled. A yellow folder went into a yellow hanging file and was also labeled.

"Why all this hard copy?" Josiah asked. "Even I keep most of my stuff on my computer anymore."

"Blake was careful. He always backed everything up. He said hard copy didn't catch viruses." Erin said.

"What happened to his computer?" Cole asked.

"I haven't seen it," Erin said. "The sheriff's department took it."

"You haven't asked for it back?" Josiah said.

"I did. Dempsey said they weren't finished with it yet."

Something caught Cole's attention. Toward the back, there was a red hanging file, but the corresponding folder was missing. The label read "STARK COUNTY—SHERIFF DEPT."

"If I were you," Cole used the clean, white handkerchief that Marie had put in his bureau back home, to pull out the empty file folder, open it and show it to her. "I don't think I'd put a whole lot of trust in Sheriff Dempsey right now."

⌒⌒⌒

Erin promised Josiah that she would dead-bolt the door behind them after they left, and promised to call him if anything happened or even if she just got scared. What she would not do was allow anyone to stay with her—even though Josiah offered to go get Marie and spend the night. She told him she didn't expect anything else happening tonight. He did not argue with her for long. She knew why. It was Saturday night, which meant Josiah had a sermon to preach tomorrow. She knew that Josiah and Marie seldom made any plans for Saturday night because sometimes if it had been a tough week, Josiah would be up half the night working on his sermon. Cole seemed very reluctant to leave, but both of them knew it would feel strange for him to spend the night.

She expressed her thanks but was insistent that they both go home. What she really needed was time alone to think . . . and to plan. She had no intention of being here tomorrow morning.

"Mom? Are they gone?" Lindsey came downstairs from her

bedroom. "It's scary up here by myself. I can't sleep. Can I stay down here with you?"

"Sure thing." Erin patted the couch cushion next to her.

Lindsey curled up beside her and Erin rubbed her back until she fell asleep again. Listening to the rhythmic breathing of her daughter, her mind worked through all the possibilities of what they should do.

Her faith in the local law officials' competency and skill had not been high, but she had not doubted the sheriff's honesty until tonight. Blake had worked closely with Dempsey and never given any indication that he didn't trust him as a person.

And yet . . .

Could she trust anything or anyone at all? Had she ever truly known her husband? Could Blake have been having an affair with that cheap-looking woman at the restaurant? Many women smarter than her had been fooled by unfaithful husbands.

Was there any possibility that Blake was into something so illegal he had to anesthetize himself with cocaine just to get through the day? She looked squarely at the possibilities of Blake seeing someone else. Before she had gone to Honduras, he had been coming home later and later, which most wives would consider suspicious, but she'd simply accepted his explanation that he was working on a hard case that needed his attention.

Her trust in her husband had been so absolute that she had not once considered the idea that Blake would be unfaithful to her. Of course, she had not considered the possibility that she was living with a cocaine addict either. She had never been around cocaine addiction and wasn't sure if she'd recognize the symptoms. There were times when Blake worked so hard, she wondered where he got all his energy. She'd thought it was merely his self-discipline and dedication. Now, she considered the possibility that it might have been chemically induced. And what about Dempsey's suggestion that Blake might have been dealing. *Surely* there was no possibility of that!

Was there?

She was so focused on her thoughts that the sound of the phone made her jump. Lindsey didn't stir. It was only 9:30 p.m., but it felt much later. She checked the caller ID and recoiled. It was the sheriff.

She picked up the phone and uttered a guarded, "Hello."

"Erin? This is Dempsey."

She made a face but kept her voice even. "How can I help you, Sheriff?"

"Are Cole and Josiah still there with you?"

"No." She immediately wished she had not given him that information, but lies did not come easily to her.

"Good," Dempsey said. "I want you to be very careful about Cole."

"Why?"

"I think he might have had something to do with the explosion."

"That's absurd," Erin said. "He'd been in prison up until you picked him up. When would he have been able to do anything?"

"Remember tonight how Cole mentioned that cell mate he'd had? The one he said had nearly driven him nuts talking about explosives?"

"Yes."

"I made some phone calls when I got home tonight. I found out the guy's name. Chester Simmons. He was Cole's cell mate for several months. Cell mates talk. Sometimes that's all they got to do. Chester is a little guy. The guard I talked to said that Cole kept him from being beat up a couple times."

"What are you trying to say?" Erin asked.

"Someone like that—someone who loves blowing things up

anyway—might try to do Cole a favor by getting rid of you. Chester would definitely know how."

"But he's still in prison. Right?" An ominous feeling stole over her. She didn't want to hear what came next.

"No," the sheriff said. "He was paroled two weeks before Cole."

"But Cole's been kind to me." She was suddenly so terrified she could barely find her voice. "W—we talked."

"I dunno, Erin. I've been a little suspicious about Cole ever since he came back home. He was innocent of Terri's murder, but he had good reason to hate both you and Blake. Have you ever thought that maybe he's been just a little *too* neighborly these past few days?"

Erin's heart pounded.

"Regardless of what you think, Erin, I *am* a good cop and I care about you and your daughter. Be careful of Cole—at least until I can look into this a little further."

After they hung up, she fought not to be overwhelmed with despair. She knew Cole had reason to hate her, but she didn't think he would deliberately hurt her. Had she allowed herself to be taken in by him? On the other hand, could she trust that Dempsey was telling the truth?

Her father had warned her about this sort of thing. She remembered it well because her father had drilled it into her.

Wild Bill Lesson #1: *Never trust anyone you haven't known since birth—and then be careful.*

After a childhood spent memorizing survival skills, it had been a struggle not to become as paranoid as her father, but right now, she thought paranoia might be a wise choice for her.

Glancing down, she saw Blake's Bible sitting on the coffee table where she had placed it earlier in the day after coming home from cleaning out his office. He had always preferred the King James Version. He said it was because those were the words he had memorized as a child.

She picked it up, hoping to find some courage or special wisdom that would help her cope with this confusing situation. She opened it to the flyleaf, where Blake had inscribed their wedding date. Seeing his handwriting was comforting. He had had such a strong way of writing. She remembered the pride with which he had registered Lindsey's birth directly beneath it.

A piece of yellow legal paper was folded inside. That was unusual. Unlike many people, Blake had never used his Bible as a place to file notes and bulletins. He did a great deal of underlining, but he didn't like having things falling out of it.

She unfolded the torn scrap of paper and gasped. In Blake's hurried handwriting was *"Love Is Eternal."* This was a fragment of Scripture that they had inscribed inside their wedding rings.

It was more than a promise to one another. It was also to be used as a secret code phrase in case either of them ever had to warn the other of impending danger. Wild Bill always insisted on having a danger code and she had asked Blake if they could have one too. Blake had teased her a little about it, but he had not resisted.

In their normal, day-to-day existence, she had almost forgotten about it. Now it screamed up at her from the page.

Beneath it was a date—the date he died—and scribbled beneath it was a scripture reference, Genesis 19:17.

Her hands shook as she turned the Bible to Genesis and read *"Escape for thy life; look not behind thee, neither stay thou in all the plain; escape to the mountains, lest thou be consumed."*

She covered her mouth with her hand and stared at the words. For reasons she could not fathom, on the day he died, Blake had used their code phrase for danger along with his in-depth knowledge of the Bible to tell her that she and their daughter needed to escape—and fast.

CHAPTER FOURTEEN

Erin's mind raced, trying to make sense of what she'd discovered. Blake must have been under great duress to have used such an inefficient method to warn her. Why not make a phone call? Why not a text or an e-mail?

Regardless of the method he'd used Blake's last thoughts had been of her and their daughter. Fearing for his own life, he had scribbled a warning to her that anyone else would dismiss as unimportant.

Now *that* was the man she had known!

There was no doubt in her mind that Blake was telling her to escape. And he had chosen a scripture that pointedly told her to escape to the mountains. The only mountain he could be referring to was her father's. She would stake her life that Blake was telling her to flee to her father's log fortress in Virginia. He must have been fearful indeed. He was right. There was no place she and Lindsey would be safer. If only she'd gone to clean out his desk earlier!

Although she had found his Bible in a drawer, he'd always kept it on top of his desk to be handy and as a silent statement of his faith to various people, friend or foe, who walked through the door. He would have expected it to be the first thing she would see when she walked into his office. Unfortunately, whatever deputy had cleaned off the top of his desk had evidently seen fit to stuff the Bible into the bottom drawer instead.

The mountain. Blake had hated it there. Her father and Blake had not gotten along. Wild Bill had strong prejudices and one of those was against attorneys—even good ones. Blake, having fought his way through law school on little more than intelligence, part-time jobs, and grit—took issue with her father's low opinion of his profession.

The final straw between Blake and her father had happened on their daughter's sixth birthday when Blake awoke to discover his father-in-law giving Lindsey early-morning lessons on how to handle the single-shot .22 rifle he had bought her as a birthday present.

"How dare he do such a thing!" Blake had stormed. "And without telling us!"

He had made Lindsey give the gun back to her grandfather. There had been harsh words between the two men as their relationship rapidly disintegrated. Blake had never allowed Lindsey to return to the mountain, and Wild Bill refused to visit them in Fallen Oak where Blake thought he could control the damage Lindsey's grandfather could do.

Blake said it was just as well. He did not want his daughter subjected to Wild Bill's paranoia. He wanted Lindsey to have an innocent little girl childhood of playing with dolls—not turned into some sort of mercenary by an embittered, hermit Vietnam vet.

Erin never told him that she'd learned to handle a gun at the same age.

For Blake to tell her to escape to her father's mountain was no small thing.

The explosion and the intruder now took on an even more ominous tone. Her confusion lifted and her focus narrowed to one clear objective. She needed to get out of here. Fast.

She hated to awaken Lindsey, but it was necessary. They both needed to start packing for an extended visit to her father's. She would inform no one that they were leaving. There was no one she trusted enough to tell. Cole was suspect now, and she wasn't entirely certain of Marie and Josiah simply because of their love for him.

She wasn't thrilled with the sheriff right now either. Apart from the bombshell he had dropped about Blake and the waitress, there was the missing file folder about the sheriff's department. She'd give a great deal of money right now to see what had been in it.

There was only one person in the world right now that she trusted utterly and completely and that was her father. Crazy or not, she and Lindsey would be safe with Wild Bill. He would protect them both with his life. Her father had no other agenda. He never did have. It had always annoyed her that he saw the world as a dark and dangerous place, but she had never doubted his love for her.

Once she was certain that Lindsey was safely in his care, she would return home and then, some way, somehow, find out the truth. She had no idea how to accomplish that, but she would figure it out.

The wind-up clock in the hall startled her with ten long gongs. Dawn would not break for another eight hours. If the truck held up, they would be at her father's long before daylight.

～⌈⌉～

"You know we're going to be interrogated within an inch of our lives when we get home, don't you?" Josiah said. "Marie is not going to be amused that we left her in the shower while we went to Erin's."

"Do you mind swinging past the sheriff's office?" Cole asked.

"Why?"

"I'm concerned about that missing sheriff's department file. I'd feel better about Erin and Lindsey tonight if I knew for sure where he was."

"You actually suspect Sheriff Dempsey of something illegal?"

"Frankly, Josiah, I'm not too crazy about trusting anyone in this town right now. Something's way off, and Erin and Lindsey are right in the middle of it."

"We can go past there. I'm not thrilled about facing Marie anyway. We really should have left her a note."

"We didn't think there was time."

"You help me convince her of that, okay?" Josiah's fingers gripped the wheel. "You know how she can get. I don't think I have another home perm in me."

As they drove past the sheriff's office downtown Cole saw only one car in the lot, which Josiah said belonged to the night dispatcher.

"Would you care to drive past Dempsey's house now?" Cole asked. "It isn't far from your place is it?"

"No, it isn't."

Josiah drove past his and Marie's home, past their church, past the small airport and a few other houses, and finally past Sheriff Dempsey's.

It was a squat, brick ranch with too-small windows. Nothing decorative relieved the blankness of the facade. One window blind was torn and crooked. Three newspapers still in their plastic wrappers lay in the driveway, unopened and unread. The squad car was parked beside the house.

Light flickered from a big-screen TV, illuminating the front window. Cole could see the outline of Dempsey through the shades. It appeared that the sheriff had settled into his recliner for the night.

"Doesn't he have a wife?" Cole asked.

"Yes. Her name's Michelle, but that's a whole other sad story." Josiah turned the car around in a neighbor's driveway. "A year ago, she got pregnant with twins and went almost full-term. Something went wrong toward the end and she lost them. It about killed Dempsey, but *she* never got over it. Michelle always was a fragile girl, high as a kite one minute and depressed the next. Losing those babies broke something inside of her, and she's not been right ever since. It got so he was afraid to leave her alone at home. He finally had to take her to a special-care facility over near Gatlinburg. He goes to visit her regularly and seems to think the place is doing her some good."

Cole thought about the shabby, lonely house in which Dempsey lived. There were so many different kinds of prisons, and not all of them had bars.

Just like Erin's comment about Blake requiring a certain "symmetry" to his life. It wouldn't be too much of a leap to interpret her innocent-sounding words as a description of a demanding and emotionally abusive husband. Is that what her and Blake's relationship had been? Had she actually harbored a deep resentment of her husband? And maybe she *had* known about the affair with Dinah. Betrayal made some women lose their mind with rage and do things they wouldn't do otherwise. He thought back to that moment in the restaurant when Dinah had elbowed Erin out of the way to take Cole's order. Erin had quietly left to sit with her daughter, but had that whole scenario been fraught with more emotion and implication than he had realized?

If Blake's death truly wasn't an accident, being away on a

mission trip was certainly an ironclad alibi for her. Cole had spent a lot of time listening to real murderers talking among themselves. He'd heard a couple of them mention meeting angel-faced wives paying for professional hits on unsuspecting husbands.

But that still didn't explain the car explosion. Things like that didn't just happen. Erin wouldn't have deliberately put Lindsey in danger. Her wild grief and determination to plunge herself into the burning garage could not have been feigned. Could it?

Cole drew his hand down over his face and sighed. All those years behind bars trying not to get killed by some lunatic. He had dreamed of a normal, everyday, life and it had almost been within his grasp, except for the recent happenings in this little town he called home.

Erin Ramsey, whoever she was—grieving widow, conniving murderess, innocent victim—was definitely someone he needed to avoid. He loved Marie and Josiah, but he was starting to think it might be best if he moved away and started over somewhere else. He simply could not risk being involved in this mess.

CHAPTER FIFTEEN

Erin clicked the lamp beside her off, allowing Lindsey to sleep for a few more minutes while she sat in the darkness mentally cataloguing what she would need to take to her father's.

Suddenly, she heard a noise. Then the motion sensor light they had on the back porch came on. Then off. Then on again.

She did not panic. Deer grazed so close to the porch at night that they often triggered that light. She'd wanted Blake to install one on the front porch as well, but he had said the one light was already nuisance. Their bedroom was directly over it and the light flicking on and off during the night was disconcerting.

Then—in the silence—she heard someone mounting the steps on the side porch outside the kitchen. She stiffened. Perhaps Sheriff Dempsey had asked a deputy to check on her? The downstairs interior lights were all off, so a deputy might think she was in bed and didn't want to disturb her. From within the darkness of her living room, she quietly stood up and peered into the kitchen. A shadow was standing outside the kitchen door which had a four pane, decorative window.

It would take someone zero time to break in if that was their intent. The deputy or whoever it was, quietly tried the locked door.

If that was anyone except a sheriff's deputy, Blake had been right. They needed to get out of here. *Now.*

She whirled around, put her hand over her daughter's mouth and shook her. "Lindsey," she whispered. "Wake up!"

Lindsey awoke with a start.

"Shhh," she whispered. "Don't make a sound. There's someone trying to break in through the back door. We have to get out of here. If you are ever going to obey me without question, do it now."

Lindsey nodded, her eyes frightened.

Erin blessed the fact that they were both still fully dressed. She grasped her daughter's hand and crept toward the basement as the kitchen door rattled. Lindsey stood below on the third step while Erin silently closed the door behind them.

It was then that she heard the glass shatter. He was no deputy. He had broken through the door window. There was a security chain. It might hold the man back for a few more seconds.

They felt their way down the stairs into total blackness. Even with the basement door closed, Erin was afraid that if they turned on the light, a sliver of it would show beneath the door.

For once in her life, Erin was grateful for Blake's need for order. Even in the dark, she knew exactly where everything was. It was no great trick to navigate.

The basement was full of imaginary whispers, but with Lindsey holding onto her hand, Erin felt her way to the other side of the basement where there was a door that led to the outside. The house had been built on a rise, and the basement opened out from beneath a high deck. Most people, unless they were very familiar with the house, didn't even realize it was there.

"What are you doing?" Lindsey whispered.

Erin, the reluctant daughter of a survivalist, felt along the far wall for the emergency evacuation backpacks she always kept ready and hanging on wall hooks.

Wild Bill Lesson #2: *Always keep a bag of supplies packed and ready. There will be an emergency. You can count on it.*

Her hands brushed against one, and she shoved it into Lindsey's hands. "Here. Put it on." She grabbed another for herself.

Each pack was fitted with freeze-dried food, three bottles of water, a basic first-aid kit, long johns, a Leatherman multi-tool, a sewing kit, rain gear, one change of clothes, a lightweight tarp, biodegradable soap, a space blanket thin enough to fold up and put into a pocket, iodine tablets for water purification, a rain poncho, and heavy socks. She had also secreted a couple hundred dollars in small bills in each pack.

Wild Bill Lesson #3: *Always have a stash of cash you can lay your hands on in a hurry.*

She blessed her father for teaching her to do this. In her haste to get to the basement, she had not thought to grab her purse, which was upstairs in the kitchen. She was leaving with no credit cards and no driver's license. It would certainly not be wise to go back to retrieve it.

"The truck is not an option," Erin whispered, shouldering her backpack. "We have to walk out of here to the woods. Are you ready?"

"I grabbed the tire iron from beside the couch," Lindsey whispered. "I've got your back, Mom."

Erin had never loved her daughter more than at that moment. Her strong-willed, argumentative, rebellious baby girl had courage. If things got rough—and they probably would—she had no doubt that Lindsey and she would fight side by side.

Heavy footsteps trod directly above them, and she and Lindsey froze. The footsteps hesitated, as though deciding which way to go, and then they walked toward the stairs leading to the upstairs bedrooms. Erin heard the stair treads complaining with each step as the intruder went upstairs.

"Did you leave your bedroom light on before you came down?" she whispered to her daughter.

"Yes."

"Then that's where they think we are. This is our only chance."

The outside basement door opened on silent hinges and she thanked God for having had a husband with an obsession with WD-40 oil. With Lindsey hovering behind her, Erin stepped out into the starless night and silently closed the basement door behind them.

She thanked God for a nearly moonless night too. The darkness would cover them as they made their escape.

Erin moved from bush to bush, tree to tree. Lindsey mimicked her mother perfectly as they made their way across the lawn and toward the hayfield that lay between the back of their house and the state forest that adjoined their property. She glanced back only once, saw a light go on in her and Blake's upstairs bedroom and lengthened her stride.

It wasn't yet time to cut the hay, so the crop was nearly up to their waists when they reached the hayfield and dove in.

Panting slightly, the two lay on their bellies well-hidden in the grass and looking back toward their house. They saw a flashlight sweep over the yard as someone slowly moved around the outside of the house. Erin put her finger to her lips and they both froze. Waiting. It was then that she remembered the cell phone. If that thing went off . . .

She fumbled in the pockets of her jeans but did not find the cell phone. The moving light hesitated. For a few heartbeats, Erin wondered if her search for the cell phone had given her position away, but then whoever carried the light continued on around to the other side of the house.

The cell phone was evidently still in the house. She must have dropped it in her haste to leave. She had also forgotten to grab the pepper spray that had been sitting on the coffee table. Two items that might have done them some good were still inside. There was nothing that could be done about it.

She whispered directly into Lindsey's ear. "Crawl toward the creek. I'll be behind you. Whatever you do, don't stand up, don't make any noise, try not to trample any more hay than you absolutely have to, and no matter what happens, keep going and don't stop."

Lindsey hesitated, as though debating the wisdom of Erin's plan, but then she began to crawl toward the creek that bordered their property. Erin stole one last glance toward the house. The flashlight was now circling where she'd parked her truck. Right now, their own feet and legs were their most dependable way out.

In an attempt not to create a telltale path, Erin took a more circuitous route to the creek than Lindsey. As she moved close to the ground, she realized that her subconscious had been mulling over exit plans ever since Blake had been killed.

Wild Bill Lesson #4: *No matter where you are or who you're with—always have a way of escape planned out.*

Her father's survival training was finally coming in handy. Who would have thought?

With luck, it would be several hours before anyone figured out where they'd gone. Maybe a couple of days. By then—even walking—they should be miles away. Part of her was concerned about Doc. He would be worried when Lindsey didn't show up for work on Monday.

On the other hand, part of her was also remembering another teaching her dad had drilled into her.

Wild Bill Lesson #5: *If you ever have to run, don't tell nothin' to nobody.*

Her father might be emotionally damaged, but he was no fool. The man had managed to stay alive through two tours of duty in Vietnam *and* had been one of the few POW's to escape into the jungle and survive. In a situation like this, his advice was solid.

Her greatest hope right now was that whoever was stalking her would not realize that approximately five miles from her property, at the mouth of the creek they were following, was a series of white blazes painted on rocks and trees, marking a trail that wound quietly and unobtrusively through two-thousand wilderness miles in twelve states, from Georgia to Maine.

Wild Bill Lesson #6: *If you ever have to escape, always go the direction people least expect.*

She didn't think anyone would expect a nearly middle-aged English teacher and attorney's wife to deliberately strike out on a trail so difficult that the locals referred to exhausted thru-hikers who fell by the wayside as "trail fodder."

Erin knew how to survive in the wilderness. She had simply never chosen to share that bit of information with anyone in town.

CHAPTER SIXTEEN

Cole relaxed in his pew, soaking up the feeling of being within the walls of a real church building, enjoying the sounds of having a normal, healthy congregation surrounding him. As much as he had appreciated the courageous prison-ministry volunteers who came each Sunday, it was a treat to be sitting here in Josiah and Marie's church.

Instead of the sound of metal chairs scraping a concrete floor, there were real oak pews. Instead of the sound of only men talking, there was the happy sound of women greeting friends, the smell of ladies' perfume, the chatter of children, and the cries and babbling of babies.

Normal, everyday life was sadly underrated by people until they no longer had access to it.

Marie was sitting beside him, all puffed up, proud as a peacock to have one of her "kids" with her. She and Josiah had kept close track of each child they'd helped raise and for the most part, they had turned out surprisingly well. Cole had been the only "black sheep" in their created family, but no longer. If he had anything to do with it, Marie would never have to make excuses again for him.

This building had changed in the years he had been away. An annex had been added to the back which housed new classrooms. The rooms along the side had been knocked out, enlarging the auditorium—and the auditorium was surprisingly full.

Josiah and Marie were not egotistical people but he knew they derived enormous satisfaction from the fact that the country church to which they'd devoted their lives continued to grow steadily.

Once again he thought back to the worship services he had attended in prison. Not every man who attended was a Christian, or even a wannabe Christian. Some were there simply to get a check mark on their parole papers. Others who came thought they might somehow scam the few outsiders and get something from them. Some prisoners were, quite frankly, loony tunes.

There was always danger lurking within a prison, and sometimes the volunteers who led them in song, prayer, and Bible study, were—in his opinion—far too innocent and trusting. He remembered two sweet, elderly Pentecostal ladies who'd come on Wednesday nights. One had played hymns on her accordion, while the other had taught a Bible lesson. The guards were not always paying as much attention as he would have liked. He and a couple of other prisoners had always been on the lookout, quietly watching their fellow inmates, ready to protect the innocents whenever they braved the prison walls. It had made for a stressful worship.

Now he reveled in the smell of new songbooks, the lilting sound of children talking, the warmth in the faces of the people who'd greeted him as he came through the door.

The congregation quieted as a young man in jeans and a "KISS ME, I'M IRISH" T-shirt mounted the pulpit like a victim going to the gallows. Cole settled into his seat, interested in what the young man had to say.

"Sorry, everyone. I was supposed to make the announcements today, but I forgot and Brother Josiah just now reminded me— so bear with me. We'll get through all this together."

He squinted at the paper in his hands and read woodenly. "A potluck dinner will be held next Sunday after services. Bring your own eating utensils because we ran out of forks the last time." The young man glanced up at the congregation. "That's good. Right? I mean, we're growing to the point of running out of forks?"

A smattering of laughter greeted this impromptu observation.

"Baby shower for Denise Whitfield. Bring jars of baby food." He stared at the paper. "Are you girls going to do that guess-the-baby-food-in-the-diaper game? That's so gross. I'm really glad I'm a guy."

There was applause by some of the men in the congregation.

"Alrighty, then. Moving right along. Josiah handed me a note that says Erin Ramsey's place was broken into last night. Nothing valuable was taken." He looked up at the congregation. "Whoa. That's heavy. Dude! I hope she's all right. That sister has had enough."

Several amens dotted the congregation.

Cole glanced around and saw that Erin and Lindsey were missing. He knew that Marie had tried to call them earlier, but there had been no answer. He figured they'd probably decided to sleep in after all that had happened last night. At least he hoped that was all it was.

The song leader announced the number of the hymn they were to sing, and Cole happily shared a hymnal with Marie, blending his rough voice with her country alto.

Marie, however, became more and more agitated. After another song, she leaned over toward him and whispered, "I'm going to go call Erin again. I'm getting worried. Erin hardly ever misses church."

"I'll go," he replied. "You sit still. Is there still a phone in Josiah's office?"

"Yes."

The congregation rose to their feet for the next song, so he didn't feel too conspicuous as he walked out into the foyer and into Josiah's office. The phone sat amid the clutter on Josiah's desk. *Some things never change,* he thought as he shoved some papers aside, found a phone book, and dialed Erin's number.

He let it ring until the answering machine picked up and then he dialed again and a third time. She was not at home and she was definitely not here. Where was she?

A sick feeling settled in the pit of his stomach, robbing him of the Sunday peace he had been enjoying. He *knew* someone should have stayed with her, but she was so insistent that she'd be all right.

He rejoined Marie, leaned over and said, "Erin's still not answering."

Marie's eyes grew round. "We have to go. We have to get over there. I have a feeling that something is terribly wrong."

He didn't argue. Even though he had been looking forward to hearing Josiah's sermon, Erin might be in trouble, and God help him, he still felt the need to watch over her. They left their pew just as Josiah stepped into the pulpit. He looked after them worriedly but had to begin his sermon.

As soon as they got outside, Marie asked, "Should we call the sheriff?"

"Not yet. Let's check things out first ourselves."

"Josiah told me last night before he fell asleep that the two of you are starting to have your doubts about him."

"Doubts are one thing, Marie. Knowledge is another. We don't know anything, but let's go check."

When they arrived, Cole pulled in beside Erin's truck, which was still parked where it had been the night before. From the outside, everything looked normal, except for the fact that the back door was hanging open and a window had been knocked out.

Inside, nothing was normal.

"What in the world happened?" Marie exclaimed as she started to push inside.

Cole stopped her. "Stay back, Marie. Let me go in first."

He stepped into a home that had been turned upside down. One of the things he had been impressed with as they checked out Erin's home last night was how clean and orderly everything was. This was not a family given to clutter or disorganization.

Now, it appeared that every drawer in the house had been dumped, every book or vase swept off each bookcase, every couch cushion ripped apart and left lying on the floor.

"We have to see if Erin or Lindsey are still in here," Marie whispered. "They might be hurt."

The person—or people—who did this might be also here, but somehow Cole doubted it. Still, it would be wise to have a weapon just in case. He glanced around for one. There was a fireplace in the living room and he grabbed the iron poker leaning against it. "Stay behind me, Marie."

She didn't argue. Together they began to search the house. He thought how odd it was that in the past twenty-four hours, he had become nearly as familiar with the Ramseys' home as he was with Marie's and Josiah's.

"Look." Marie pointed as they entered the kitchen. On the table was Erin's purse. The contents had been dumped. Marie grabbed a matching billfold and opened it. Driver's license, credit cards, ATM card, library card, AAA card . . . It didn't appear as though Erin had taken a thing with her. Marie and Cole stared at each other, wordless. This was bad.

"Maybe we should call the sheriff after all, Cole."

"Let's hold off a few more minutes. I want to make certain Erin and Lindsey are not still here first."

A thorough walk-through of the house did not reveal anything except more chaos. The small office alcove was a complete shambles. All the files had been pulled out and tossed.

Erin's cell phone was lying beside the couch, smashed. There was no way to tell if it had been done deliberately or if someone had simply stepped on it while searching the house.

"I can't tell you how unlike Erin it is to just take off like this," Marie chattered nervously as they headed toward the basement. "She plans, makes lists, reservations, and . . ."

"She didn't leave," Cole said. "Whoever did this either took Erin and Lindsey, or they escaped. Let's pray that they escaped."

Briefly, the dubious thoughts he had had the night before crept back in. Could Erin have possibly done this to her own home? Was this another attempt to throw suspicion away from her?

He sincerely doubted it. He couldn't see her deliberately crushing her cell phone or leaving the contents of her purse behind. In fact, with a night's sleep under his belt and in face of this huge mess, the mistrustful thoughts he'd had about Erin seemed foolish. There *was* nothing about this scene that spoke to him of a deliberate act on her part.

He turned on the light at the top of the basement stairs and went down. The room was so bare that he and the others had barely given it a glance the night before. Nothing had been tossed because there was nothing to toss.

"Did they use this room much?" he asked.

"They were in the process of turning it into a rec room," Marie said. "I remember Blake telling me that they had plans to start hosting get-togethers for the teens at church now that Lindsey is old enough to be in the youth group."

On the far side of the basement was a metal door painted the same shade of cream as the basement wall.

"Where does that lead?" Cole asked.

"To the backyard," Marie said. "It comes out under the deck they built when they moved here." She stopped in her tracks. "Now, that's odd."

"What is?"

She pointed to a lone backpack hanging on a hook beside the door. There were empty hooks on either side of it.

"That's where Erin kept all three of their emergency-evacuation backpacks. Josiah and I were over here about a month ago and they were showing us all the work they'd gotten done on this room. I asked about those packs and Blake told us that Erin always kept one supplied and ready for each of them in case of an emergency."

"Do you suppose she might have heard someone trying to break in and they escaped out this back way?" He opened the basement door and glanced around.

"It sounds possible."

Cole and Marie walked out from beneath the deck, where a brilliant morning sun illuminated the grass. It had not been mowed and was ankle-height. There appeared to be the slightest whisper of a trail in the grass, leading to the hayfield behind.

"Did they use this backyard much?"

"Not unless they were having a get-together with people on the deck. There's nothing back here except that field."

Cole got down on one knee and sighted at knee level. "I am no expert, but I think someone recently left from this doorway and went toward the field."

"I see it now. There is a slight difference."

Together, they followed the erratic line to the hayfield. Here, there was a definite, albeit narrow, path of broken hay and grass that would not have been discernible at night but was fairly clear in broad daylight. A few feet in was a larger trampled place, as though someone had lain down. Then two paths, both smaller, led away from each other, but both headed in the same direction.

"What's beyond this field, Marie?"

"There's a little creek," she said. "And a state forest past that. Do you think Erin would be brave enough to head into the woods in the middle of the night? There wasn't any moon last night."

"I think anyone would run into the woods if they were scared enough and if that was their only option," Cole said. "Does she have any family around here?"

"Erin's never talked about her family much. I know she has a father somewhere—I think she said Virginia—but I got the impression they weren't close."

"Does she have any friends she might have called to come pick them up?"

"Erin has friends," Marie said, "but if she were in trouble, I think she would call me first."

He glanced at one of the little trails through the hay. Against his better judgment, he knew he was getting ready to get involved in Erin's life again.

"I think I'm going to follow that trail for a while, Marie. See if it leads to anything. It might be nothing . . . or it might be important."

"I want to go too."

He glanced down at her church shoes. Marie was not a small woman, but she had tiny feet and took pride in wearing nice shoes to church. Today she was wearing two-inch tan heels. "Those are not exactly hiking boots, Marie."

"I know, but . . ."

"I can move faster without you."

"Don't you want me to call the sheriff?"

He pondered her question. "Not yet. Let me see if I can find out anything first."

"I don't want to be left here alone."

"Get in the car and go home or back to church. Wait for me to call you."

"Oh, all right," she said grudgingly. Marie hated being left out of anything. She fumbled in her pocket and handed him her cell phone. "Here. This gets pretty good reception in most places. I charged it overnight, so it ought to be good for a while. Call me as soon as you know anything. Call me even if you *don't* know anything. And, Cole, be careful."

He gave her a hug and was halfway across the field when she hollered at him. She was holding the other backpack, the one Erin had prepared for Blake. "Take this—just in case."

"I won't need it, Marie. I probably won't be gone that long."

"Come here and get this, Cole Samuel Brady. You have no idea *what* you're going to need."

Marie hadn't used all three of his names since he was twelve and in trouble. He decided it would be best not to argue with her. He went back, glanced inside the pack, and selected a couple of bottles of water and a small package of trail mix. "I might need these, but I'll be able to travel faster without the pack, Marie. Besides, if I find Erin, I doubt she'll be thrilled to see me toting Blake's stuff. In fact, I'm pretty certain she won't be happy to see me at all."

CHAPTER SEVENTEEN

It was a rugged, hurried hike fueled by desperation, over difficult terrain, with both Erin and Lindsey accidentally slipping frequently into the stream. Erin knew they were inadvertently leaving a trail behind, and she knew what steps to take to disguise it—but disguising footprints took time—which they didn't have and, anyway, it was nearly impossible to cover one's tracks in the dark.

She had one goal. They had to get as many miles, as quickly as possible, between them and whoever had been hunting them back at their house. With no moon and no stars to help Erin navigate, they had to stay close to the stream—or they could very well wander into the six-thousand-acre state forest adjoining their property and get hopelessly lost.

She wondered if it would be safe yet to use the small halogen flashlight she had packed . . . but she was afraid they'd be spotted. The darkness was their friend, as long as she could manage to keep from breaking her neck.

A root caught her toe just then, and she sprawled headfirst into mud and rock, bruising and cutting her knees and hands. She bit her lip to keep from crying out.

"Are you okay, Mom?" Lindsey whispered, helping her to her feet. "Do we need to take a break?"

Erin could feel warm blood trickling from her knee down her leg. The cuts she had sustained from grasping the broken window of the garage had not had time to completely heal and were now freshly torn. Dirt had gotten into the wounds and hurt like fire.

She told Lindsey none of this. "I'm fine," she said. "Let's keep going."

This was different than traipsing beside her father in the mountains. For one thing, she no longer had the elasticity of a child's body. But the familiarity of being in the woods at night did come back to her. The sound of wildlife each time they paused, the rustling of leaves as night creatures went about their nocturnal business . . . She listened for the telltale silence her father had taught her to listen to that would signal the approach of a predator—animal or human—but she heard none.

She knew that most women forced to walk in the deep woods at night would be frightened but Erin wasn't frightened; she was furious. Furious that someone had invaded her private home. Furious that because of the intruder, she had had to leave the security of her house and walk through a forest where, at any minute, she or Lindsey might step on a snake or fall and break an arm or leg. Mainly, she was furious that she had allowed herself to be comforted by the sheriff's initial lame explanation about the explosion. She should have packed a suitcase and gotten out of there the minute she discovered Lindsey alive.

No. Check that. She should have forgotten about suitcases entirely and left that very minute. Rented a car and driven far, far away from Fallen Oak, Tennessee.

One step at a time, while keeping the sound of running

water beside them, they managed to make it to where the stream crossed over the Appalachian Trail. Now, the famous white blazes painted on trees and rocks pointing the way shone out like small beacons of hope in the semidarkness that preceded sunrise.

Erin nearly fell to her knees in gratitude when she first saw that they'd made it to the well-traveled Trail—but even though they'd been stumbling along for nearly eight hours and were pretty much exhausted, she knew they could not afford to rest. Up ahead somewhere was Damascus, a small town famous for showing hospitality to hikers. On a previous trip, she had been fascinated by the way the Trail meandered directly through the middle of town. With any luck, she and Lindsey would blend in with all the other morning hikers headed north.

"I'm really hungry, Mom. We've been walking for hours. Can we stop and eat?"

"We can eat, but we can't stop. We need to make it to the town first, before people start waking up and someone notices us. If I remember right, there's a small motel on the outskirts. I want to get a room there before daybreak, if we can. There's a chance no one will see us if we get there early enough. We can rest and hide out there for a few hours until we can figure out what to do next."

"But I'm *hungry.*"

Erin dug out two packages of trail mix from her backpack and handed one to her daughter. "Here. Now that we're on a real path, we can eat and walk at the same time. I don't think it's far."

"Do I have to carry this tire iron any further? It's heavy."

Lindsey was still carrying that tire iron? Lindsey had been walking behind her, so she hadn't seen. Erin's heart ached at the thought of her lionhearted daughter carrying the heavy weapon such a long way. She had assumed Lindsey had dropped it in the darkness miles ago.

"I think it would be okay if you left it behind now."

≈

Cole walked slowly, scanning every inch of ground near the little stream. He was no tracker, but it appeared as if someone had recently been walking beside it. Near the edges, in the mud, were fairly clear indentations the size and width of what could be a woman's shoes. He saw no indications of any men's footprints, which was heartening. His fear was that someone had forced the two women to come this way.

He knew he was out here searching for them on nothing more than a hunch, but this was exactly the kind of thing he would have done if he had wanted to disappear quickly.

Erin had apparently walked off in the middle of the night into the forest instead of running to neighbors or contacting the sheriff. If so, she was braver and smarter than he had given her credit for. It was the last thing anyone would expect a woman like her to do. Erin was not an athlete or a hiker; she was a high school English teacher.

He could still see her standing in front of her classroom, years ago, wearing a lavender sweater over a white skirt with a strand of pearls at her neck. It was hard to imagine that woman finding her way through the woods in the dark—let alone choosing it as a viable option.

Of course, there was that other Erin he had glimpsed, the one who'd fought like a wildcat to get loose from his grasp so she could plunge into that burning garage. *That* Erin, he could very well imagine doing pretty much anything if it meant protecting her daughter.

It took him just under three hours to fight his way through

the brush and over fallen trees and limbs. His opinion ratcheted several notches higher for both Erin and Lindsey, thinking of them doing the same in the dark.

When he reached what he knew to be the Appalachian Trail, he hesitated, not certain whether to go north or south. For all he knew, he was on a wild goose chase anyway. After thinking it over, he turned north, toward Virginia based on nothing more than Marie's saying that she thought Erin might have a father there.

Two hundred yards up the trail, he saw something lying in front of him and smiled. Now he knew for sure he was on the right path. It was a tire iron like the one Lindsey had been brandishing last night, and there was absolutely no reason for it to be here unless she had carried it all this way and abandoned it when she hit the relative safety of the Trail.

Even though Erin could have had as much as a twelve-hour head start on him, he was fairly certain he could catch up with them now.

One of the things he had taken advantage of while in prison was the weight and exercise room. Weakness of any kind was seen as an invitation to be preyed upon within prison walls. Knowing his own strength and endurance, he fell into a steady walking rhythm, positive he'd catch up with them soon. For one thing, he needed to put Marie's mind at rest. For another, Erin and her daughter had—to his utter astonishment—begun to matter to him.

Erin awoke early Sunday afternoon, disoriented, in an unfamiliar bed. The water stain on the ceiling looked vaguely like a rabbit which was appropriate since she continued to feel like Alice in Wonderland . . . after a rough night of tumbling down the rabbit hole.

The cheap green curtains weren't quite wide enough to shut out the sliver of daylight coming through the window of the cut-rate motel.

She had been so exhausted that she only vaguely remembered showering off the mud and dirt before climbing in between the sheets.

Now as she lay on this sagging bed, Erin carefully stretched her legs and arms and flexed her toes, assessing the damage—which was significant. Every muscle and joint ached and she had bruises and scrapes all over. In spite of the pain, she gave a quick prayer of thanksgiving. She and Lindsey were alive and together. That is what her life's purpose had narrowed to in the past few hours: for her and Lindsey to be alive and together.

Her shoulders felt a little better now that she had been able to take off the heavy pack. It had dug into her back muscles as they walked last night. Toward morning it was all she could do not to cry out from the pain.

Lindsey had carried a pack nearly as heavy as Erin's and yet she had not said one word of complaint. Not one. The girl was a tougher person and a better athlete than Erin had realized. It was no small thing to discover that when the chips were down, her pouty, rebellious, back-talking daughter had plenty of grit.

Erin vowed to never, ever, let the bond between her and her daughter fray again.

This dreary motel had beckoned with a flickering, fluorescent light only a short distance from the Trail as they had struggled to put one foot in front of the other. Few places had ever looked as tempting. Now, Lindsey was tucked in beside her on the sagging mattress and Erin marveled that they had walked through the night with nothing worse than some scrapes and bruises. So far. So good.

Funny how, in the right circumstances, even a run-down motel could feel like an oasis. The coarse-looking woman sitting in the shabby office had seemed like an angel of compassion when she handed them the keys to a room.

Damascus was famous as a major hiker town. There was a festival held here every year, celebrating the long Trail as well as honoring those who had hiked the length of it. She was banking on the townspeople being so used to odd-looking hikers showing up at all hours of the day and night that no one would notice or remember her and Lindsey.

The woman who had been staffing the office last night had been so engrossed in her television show that she had shown no curiosity about them whatsoever when they came stumbling in, nor had she questioned the false name Erin had given as she handed over enough cash to cover their room. Erin was fairly certain she could have called herself Bozo the Clown and the woman would not have blinked.

Erin did not want to take a chance of waking Lindsey up by turning on the TV, but knew she would not be able to get back to sleep now. She scooted up against the headboard, wishing she had something good to read.

Without a lot of hope, she opened the drawer on the table beside her and was pleased to see that the Gideons had not let her down. God's Word was here. Even here. She pulled the Bible out of the drawer, laid it on her knees, and closed her eyes as she prayed for guidance and protection then she opened the Bible at random and found that she'd inadvertently turned to the book of Deuteronomy—definitely not her favorite. She intended to jump to the Gospels when her eyes snagged on the word "fight." She stopped to read the verse.

"Do not be afraid of them; the LORD your God himself will fight for you."

She checked the reference. Deuteronomy 3:22.

The words struck her with such force that she leaned her head back against the headboard and stared at the ceiling. Her chest heaved with emotion from the power of those words. The Lord, her God, would fight for her. Now, if only she knew who "them" were! It would help if she knew exactly why she was under attack.

There was only one thing she knew for sure—she needed to get to her father's as soon as possible.

She glanced over at her daughter. Lindsey slept on her back, her mouth open, scratches from low-lying branches marring her peaches-and-cream skin. Her tousled hair cascaded over the pillow and Erin caressed a strand. She adored Lindsey's hair—it was a vibrant strawberry blonde. Blake had always said it was never hard to pick Lindsey out of a crowd. The color of her hair was easy to spot.

Erin frowned. Maybe her daughter's hair color was a little *too* easy to spot. That would have to change. Also, they both needed breakfast and to get back on the Trail soon. The farther away from the town of Fallen Oaks they could get, the better.

She slipped out of bed and threw on her muddy khaki's and tennis shoes. She had slept in her blouse so she was already half-dressed. Quietly, she dug a few bills out of her backpack and went across the parking lot to a small grocery store.

The possible breakfast choices were slim, but Erin had not expected miracles when she came in. She just planned to get some milk and juice and maybe a package of doughnuts. She found all three and then went to study the small cosmetic section.

She found what she wanted there too. Hair dye. Black—the polar opposite of Lindsey's color. And a dark brown for her own dark blonde hair. She grabbed both and added a tube of hair gel. Lindsey was going to get her wish after all. After her stoicism last night, the girl deserved it.

She carried her selections to the counter. A stack of guidebooks about the Appalachian Trail were for sale, and she added one to her purchases. Her night flight to the Trail had been nothing more than a desperate attempt to throw off her pursuers in a way they would never suspect. Since awakening, the idea of simply blending in with the other hikers and staying on the Trail was beginning to hold an appeal. She saw a postcard rack and grabbed one with a picture of downtown Damascus, just in case she needed it. She added a postage stamp to the purchase as well.

However, as accepting as Lindsey had been last night, she doubted her daughter would be at all happy about the idea of hiking the Trail so she dismissed the idea. Her daughter had about one night like last night in her and it would be wise to figure out some other way to get to Wild Bill's.

A tattooed and multi-pierced girl who appeared not much older than Lindsey rang up her purchases, avoiding eye contact as if staying in a semi-coma would make the time go faster. Erin was pleased with her. This wasn't the kind of girl who'd remember customers. Especially not anyone past thirty.

After receiving a handful of change, she let herself back into the motel room, laid everything on the scarred nightstand, and shook her daughter awake. "I've got doughnuts."

Lindsey bolted upright. "Doughnuts?"

"A whole dozen."

"I'm so hungry, I think I can eat the entire box." Lindsey rubbed her eyes. "Where are we?"

"Virginia."

"We're not in Tennessee anymore?"

"No, sweetheart. We're just over the state line. I'm guessing we walked about twelve miles last night. Maybe more."

"I don't remember coming in here."

"You were half-asleep."

Lindsey stretched her arms above her head, yawned, and smiled at her mom. "You said doughnuts?"

"And milk and juice. I have another surprise for you too." Erin pulled the two packages of hair dye out of the grocery sack and held them up. Lindsey's eyes goggled.

"Mom, you said . . ."

"I know what I said. I was wrong. If we're going to disappear for a while, we need to disguise ourselves."

"Okay . . ." Lindsey sounded doubtful which surprised Erin, considering the passion with which her daughter had defended her desire to dye her hair a couple days earlier. "How about you go first?"

"Sure." Erin retrieved a small pair of scissors from her pack and a towel from the bathroom, and threw the towel around her shoulders. "How hard could it be?"

Fifteen minutes later, her hair was definitely shorter but lopsided. Lindsey, who'd been eating doughnuts and watching as her mother whacked at one side of her head and then the other, dusted the powdered sugar off her T-shirt and approached Erin with her head tilted to one side.

"You need help, Mom."

"You think?" Erin said, with exasperation. Arms aching from holding them up for so long, she handed the scissors to her daughter.

Lindsey snipped and cut until there was nothing left except a short mop. "I think I'd better stop now," Lindsey said. "I'm running out of hair."

Erin peered at herself in the mirror. She'd never had such a hairstyle in her life. She wasn't impressed with how it looked, but the short length felt refreshing.

"Thanks, hon," Erin said. "You want me to do yours now?"

"No offense, Mom, but no. I'd rather cut my own."

"Okay."

As Lindsey cut into her own hair, a length of red-gold fell to the motel room floor and mingled with Erin's slightly darker tresses. Their hair lay on the floor together. Just like the two of them. They were in this together, and Lord help them both.

CHAPTER EIGHTEEN

"So, Mom, what do you think?"

Lindsey's hair was now jet black, short, and spiked with gel. Erin struggled with herself before she uttered the word she thought Lindsey wanted to hear. "Cool."

"Really?" Lindsey turned her head this way and that, checking herself out in the mirror over the motel dresser. "Frankly, Mom, I kind of hate it."

"I'm not thrilled with mine, either, but you have to admit, we definitely don't look like ourselves anymore. That's a good thing. I just hope my dad doesn't think I'm a stranger and shoot me."

"Me too," Lindsey laughed then sobered. "You *are* kidding, aren't you, Mom?"

"Not entirely."

Lindsey's eyes opened wide. Erin hastened to reassure her. "It'll be fine. We just have to be careful not to sneak up on him. He's always been suspicious of strangers and he's probably gotten worse as he's gotten older."

"Oh, no, Mom . . ." Lindsey slapped her forehead. "I forgot

about Doc! He'll be depending on me showing up today! He's always shorthanded on Sunday afternoons."

"There must be others who'll be willing to help him out."

"But the horses trust *me*."

"I'm sure they do. But, Lindsey, we can't go back there. Not now. At least not yet."

"Can I at least call him? Tell him I won't be coming in?"

The normalcy of the act of hairstyling had lulled Erin into a brief, false sense of security. It sounded so innocuous—calling Doc, letting him know that Lindsey would not be in for a while.

"Sure, go ahead. I'll settle up the phone bill with the woman at the desk."

As Lindsey dialed, Wild Bill's words of warning came to mind again: *If you ever have to run, Erin-girl, don't tell nothin' to nobody.*

Erin took the phone out of Lindsey's hand and disconnected the call.

"Mom!"

"I'm sorry, baby. On second thought, I don't think it's a good idea to let *anyone* know where we are."

"I wasn't going to tell him where we are."

"Phones can be traced."

"We can trust Doc, and you know it."

"Absolutely we can trust Doc, but he's old. He might forget and say the wrong thing to the wrong person. Until we know for sure who's after us, we can't take the chance."

"You're really getting paranoid, Mom," Lindsey said. "You know that?"

Lindsey's comment took her aback. How many times had she said those very words to her own father? Unfortunately, they were true. He *was* paranoid. Still, for the first time, Erin understood how much it must have hurt him to hear her hurling those words at him when his main goal in life seemed to protect her.

"You need to trust me, Lindsey. I'm just doing this for *your own good.*"

Your own good. Now her father's exact words were coming out of her mouth!

"I do trust you, Mom. I just feel sorry for Doc, that's all."

"We'll make it up to him after this is over. The only thing I want to concentrate on right now is getting you to your grandfather's."

"I barely know him."

"But I *do* know him, and I trust him completely."

"Then why did you stay away so long? You're his daughter. You wouldn't want *me* to stay away so long."

"You're right," Erin said. "You are absolutely right. I should not have stayed away so long. But your father thought it best. I wrote Dad and sent him pictures of you through the years. He's written back. It's not like I cut off all communication with him."

"Shouldn't we call him, then? Tell him we're coming?"

"He doesn't have a phone, Lindsey."

"No phone?"

"No. And he doesn't have a computer or a car or indoor plumbing or electricity for that matter."

"What *does* he have?"

An arsenal with which to keep you safe! was on the tip of Erin's tongue, but she stopped herself from saying it just in time.

"Well, the last time we were there, he had chickens and goats and . . ."

"Horses?" A light went on in Lindsey's eyes. "Does Grandpa have horses?"

"He usually keeps a couple of mules."

"Mules! I can live with that. How are we going to get there, Mom?"

"I don't know." That was a problem Erin had been turning over in her mind since they'd fled. "I'll think of something."

If only she'd grabbed her wallet before they fled. Then she could have rented a car. Unfortunately, no rental business was going to give her a car without a valid driver's license and a credit card.

She had considered trying to hire someone to drive them to her father's, assuming there was enough money in their backpacks to pay—but that would involve conversations and explanations. Even in a hiking town, people would wonder about a mother and daughter trying to catch a nearly-two-hundred-mile ride north.

Hitchhiking? Not an option. Not with a beautiful young girl by her side. That would be an invitation for disaster.

She knew that Marie would come to get them if she called her, but that would involve Cole knowing where they were—something Erin preferred to avoid for now. There were lots of people who would come if she asked, and they probably would be willing to drive her to her father's. But aside from her reticence about getting someone else involved in her life right now, she didn't know who they might talk to. Like Doc, they'd probably mean well, but she couldn't depend on anyone keeping quiet—except herself.

Her father's eccentricities and his survivalist lair were two of her best-kept secrets and right now she intended to keep it that way. For most of her life, she'd not talked about her father because she was ashamed. Now, all she could think about was how grateful she was to have the safety and anonymity of his mountain home waiting for her.

Maybe a bus? That would be an affordable and anonymous way to get within striking distance of her father. Her spirits rose. She called the desk and asked the location of the nearest bus stop. The clerk's answer was a surprise. It was thirty miles away—which would still mean getting other people involved.

"Mom?" Lindsey was flipping through the guidebook Erin had picked up at the grocery store. "Did you look at this?"

"Not closely yet."

"Did you realize the Trail goes near where Grandpa lives?"

"Yes. He's been fussing about the Trail for the past couple of years in his letters. He's furious that they rerouted it. Now it skirts directly around his mountain. He doesn't like the idea of all those strangers walking near land he owns."

"We could walk to Grandpa's."

"It's nearly two hundred miles, honey."

"So?"

"So . . . my legs hurt, my feet hurt, and my shoulders hurt, and yours probably do too. It would take forever to walk two hundred miles. Are you sure you're up to it?"

Lindsey looked up from the guidebook with the light of enthusiasm in her eyes. "I'd like to try this, Mom. I'm enjoying being with you. I think we could do it."

Erin heard only one thing. Her daughter was enjoying being with her? Suddenly her body didn't hurt so badly after all.

"We've changed our looks," Lindsey said. "If we went on the Trail, we wouldn't have to tell anyone our names. My geography teacher, Mr. Turney, told us about the Appalachian Trail because he hiked it once. He said that people never use their real names when they're on it. It's a tradition that everyone uses made up names—like Laughing Bear or Merry Sunshine. He said one of FBI's Most Wanted criminals had escaped detection for *months* by blending in with all the other hikers."

"If the FBI's Most Wanted is on it, maybe the Trail is more dangerous than I thought."

"That was just one time, Mom. And that's not my point."
Lindsey leaned forward, pleading her case. "If someone could
escape the FBI by hiking on the Trail, then we ought to be able
to spend a few days avoiding whoever broke into our house
last night."

"It's still a long way," Erin said.

"Do the math, Mom. You say we traveled about twelve
miles last night. That was hard hiking, at night, through brush.
Nothing's going to be that bad from now on. We ought to be
able to do at least that much on a well-worn trail—probably
more. I think we could make it in ten to twelve days. Two
weeks tops."

Under different circumstances, it would have been amusing
to Erin that the more reluctant she acted, the more enthusiastic
her daughter became. "People don't just start hiking the Trail.
They purchase expensive equipment. They gear up. We don't
have the money with us to do that."

"Mr. Turney said that the first woman who walked the
entire Trail was a woman they called Grandma Gatewood. She
was sixty-seven years old and she did it in sneakers with only
a homemade duffle bag slung over her shoulder. We're already
better provisioned than her. We're both a lot younger too, and
we're only going about a tenth of the way."

"True."

"What do you think, Mom? Please?"

What Erin thought was that not only was the Trail an
excellent place to hide, but there was no way she was going
to give up this opportunity to mend fences with her daughter.
Even if it meant sleeping on the ground for the next two weeks.

"What do I think?" Erin said. "I think that, together, you
and I can accomplish just about anything we set our minds
on—including hiking two hundred miles to your grandfather's."

The look in Lindsey's eyes was gift enough for the pain and

discomfort Erin knew was ahead of them. But apart from that, with the exception of her own father, no one who knew her would ever expect her to simply take off walking to a remote mountain in Virginia.

~⚬~

He had been hiking for approximately five hours and the only sign he had seen of them besides the tire iron was a broken lime-green ponytail holder he thought he remembered Lindsey wearing last night.

There had been no good opportunities for them to get off the Trail that he could see—unless they had veered off into the woods and hidden. Somehow, he doubted that. He had been grateful for the two bottles of water and had kept hunger at bay by eating the package of trail mix. If Erin's and Lindsey's packs carried the same emergency equipment that Blake's had, there wasn't enough there to make camping in the woods all that comfortable. There was only enough to survive for a day or two.

As he neared the outskirts of Damascus, Virginia, he weighed the possibilities before him. He could quit, call Marie and Josiah, tell them he had been on a wild goose chase, and ask one of them to come get him. He could continue to hike north, hoping to find Lindsey and Erin somewhere along the way. Or he could check out the town and then make a decision. When he had taken off to try to find them, he had half expected to find one of them hurt, possibly even lying along the trail. Now that he hadn't found them, he wasn't sure what to do. He couldn't keep hiking indefinitely.

He had come at least twelve miles. If Lindsey and Erin had managed to get this far—and he was seriously impressed if they had—they would be exhausted and trying to find shelter.

Think like a girl, he told himself. *Think like a girl. What would they want to do? Get off their feet? Take a bath? Lie down in a real bed?*

At that moment, he noticed a run-down motel on the outskirts of town.

Wondering whether they might not have been tempted to stay at the first place they saw, he entered the motel's office.

A dumpy, older woman wearing too much orange lipstick sat behind the counter, engrossed in a soap opera magazine.

"Excuse me," Cole said. "I'm looking for a woman and a teenage girl. The name is Ramsey. Have you seen them?"

The woman glanced up from her magazine and scowled. "Can't say."

"What do you mean, you can't say?"

"They might be here; they might not. None of your business, cowboy."

He opened his billfold, selected a twenty-dollar bill, and laid it squarely in front of her, yet again grateful for the money Vance had given him.

"I'd appreciate any information you can give me."

The woman picked up the twenty, folded it, and stuck it into a pocket of the lavender polyester slacks she was wearing. "Nobody named Ramsey signed in here."

"Okay. Let me ask another way. In the past twenty-four hours, have you seen a thirtyish woman with shoulder-length blond hair and a teenage girl who looks almost exactly like her? They'd be carrying a couple of backpacks."

"You her husband?"

"No."

"You look like you could be her husband. Maybe you're a mean one. I had me a mean one once."

"I'm just trying to help her. Do you know anything?"

"They were here. They left. That's all I am saying."

"Did you see them go?"

"That's all I am saying."

"Were they all right? Were they headed toward the Trail?"

The woman shrugged, her attention determinedly glued to the magazine. She licked her fingers and turned a page, ignoring Cole. Evidently, on her personal pay scale, she had already given enough information to warrant the twenty dollars.

All his instincts told him that this woman was telling the truth—at least as much as she intended to share. Erin and Lindsey had stayed in that motel.

Now, if he could just find them. Damascus wasn't all that big. He would walk around and see if he could spot them—or perhaps find someone who had seen them. But first things first. He had not eaten anything except those few handfuls of trail mix. As far as his stomach was concerned, it was time to find nourishment.

He was nearly to the restaurant when a disheveled, bearded man came limping toward him and dragging a hiking pack. There was a look of weariness and pain in his eyes that caught Cole's attention.

"You okay, buddy?" Cole asked.

The man stopped. "Would you like to buy a good back pack? Fully loaded?"

"Not really. What's the problem?"

"I've been walking the Trail since Springer, Georgia. Got myself a bad case of shin splints and then pulled a groin muscle from slipping on some rocks. I'm hurt, broke, sick to death of the Trail, and headed home. I need money for bus fare."

"How much do you need?"

"A hundred maybe? My pack's worth more than that. You'd be getting a bargain."

"I don't want your pack, but I can help you out a little." Cole reached for his wallet. There wasn't a fortune in there, but he could spare this man enough for a good meal. It felt good to be able to.

The man drew himself up. "Look, buddy, I may seem like a bum after being on the Trail for weeks, but in real life I'm an accountant and I make a decent living. I lost my ATM card in a hiker's hostel in Tennessee and I don't take charity. You want a good pack or not?"

Cole thought it over. There was a chance it would take longer to find Erin and Lindsey than he thought.

"Is there any food in there?"

"I re-provisioned the day before yesterday. That was before I slipped on the rocks. There's everything a man might need for a couple of weeks in there. Lightweight tent, water purifier, camp stove, dehydrated food, eating utensils, first-aid kit—not that it did me much good . . ."

"Sounds like you've got a whole lot more than a hundred dollars invested in it."

"More like a thousand. The backpack's a Gregory-Palisade 80. It cost me three hundred used, but I'll never use it again. All I want to do is get home to Alabama." He glanced down at the dress shoes that Cole had worn to church. "You real attached to those?"

"Why?"

"Looks like we both wear around a size ten. My good pair of boots is in there, too." He gestured to his backpack. "You'll need them if you walk that Trail for very long. The rocks on the Trail will cut regular shoes to shreds."

To Cole's surprise, he had enjoyed the walk to Damascus a great deal. The Trail was more beautiful than he had ever realized. After prison, being outside in God's wilderness felt incredibly healing. Regardless of what might or might not happen with Erin and Lindsey, he had already decided to do at least a weekend camping trip on the Trail soon. He might as well get his equipment together right now and help the guy out too.

"I'll take it." Cole took out six twenties and handed them to the man. "I'm sorry for your misfortune."

"Thanks." The man took one of the twenties and handed it back. "I said a hundred and I meant it. My wife told me I wouldn't make it on the Trail and she was right. It's going to be hard facing her again, but sleeping in a real bed will be worth listening to her say 'I told you so. '"

"Did you say whether there's a bus stop here?" Cole wondered if that could be a place he should look for Erin and Lindsey.

"No. Nearest place is Marion, about thirty miles from here. A guy at the hostel said he'd give me a lift." The man nodded a good-bye and limped away.

Cole briefly wondered if he had been scammed. The pack might be stuffed with rocks for all he knew, but he didn't think that was likely. The guy had seemed honestly sick of hiking. He unzipped the top of the pack and peered in. The man had been telling the truth. It appeared that there was enough in here to sustain life for quite a while.

As he investigated, he noticed that halfway down the pack was a prize. The accountant had apparently felt the need for a weapon—a wicked-looking knife sheathed inside an ankle holder. It would probably be used for innocuous things like whittling kindling for a campfire or for spreading peanut butter, but it was long enough and sharp enough to gut a man if self-defense was necessary.

In Cole's experience, self-defense was sometimes extremely necessary. He strapped the knife onto his lower right leg where he could easily access it. He would use it only if he had no other option, but he felt better knowing it was there.

He shrugged the backpack onto his shoulders. It was heavy,

but not too bad. It was a strange and freeing thought that he could, if he wanted to, just keep walking. He wouldn't, of course. There was that job Vance was offering, and Marie and Josiah, who would worry about him—but the fact that he could, if he really wanted to, just keep walking and exploring was a heady feeling. He wondered if the awe he felt in being a free man would ever wear off.

CHAPTER NINETEEN

"There's a good hamburger joint I want to go to before we leave town," Erin said as she and Lindsey shouldered their packs and left the motel. "The woman at the desk told me about it when I checked out. She said that a local man makes a good living out of the fact that hikers crave fat and protein. We'll pick up supper there."

"I want two hamburgers and a large order of fries." Lindsey didn't hesitate to give her order. "I'm starved."

"You always are, dear." Erin said. "I think I'll get eight hamburgers, four apiece, and extra fries. That ought to hold us until breakfast."

"Are you all right, Mom? You *never* eat like that."

"People burn a lot of calories on the Trail. You, especially, don't have any weight to spare. It won't hurt either of us to fuel up before we start."

"Sounds good to me." Lindsey studied her mother. "Are you sure you're up to all this?"

"Yes. Are you?"

"Of course I am." Lindsey shrugged. "It's *you* I'm worried about."

Erin chuckled. "I am not quite in a nursing home yet, sweetheart. I should be able to hobble along."

To get her daughter to safety, she would crawl if she had to. For now, however, she would be content to hike the fifteen miles necessary to sleep beneath the roof of Lost Mountain Shelter. The guidebook she had purchased said that it had a good spring.

"Now that we're no longer inside the motel," Erin said, "I want to get out of town as fast as possible. We'll pick up that food and head straight out. We can eat while we walk."

As they passed a tiny post office, Erin dropped off the postcard she'd purchased earlier. Back at the motel, while Lindsey was in the bathroom, she had scribbled a quick note to her father. She used their old "danger" code phrase of "The catfish are biting" and had added, "Coming for a visit real soon. Hoping to find some 'sang." She'd signed it "Clyde."

Wild Bill would receive the postcard in two or three days. He didn't get a lot of mail, so she knew there was no danger of it getting lost on a desk somewhere. It would take only a couple of seconds for him to decode the message, check the postmark, and know exactly what she was telling him—that she was coming by way of the back ridge where they'd always had the best luck at finding ginseng. "Clyde" was the name of the ferociously protective dog she'd owned as a child, which would alert him to exactly how much danger she thought they might be in.

If he was the man she thought she knew, he would probably start cleaning his guns immediately, loading every clip he had and amassing supplies for a siege the moment he received the card.

Her dad might be crazy, but he wasn't stupid . . . and he loved her. The thought that she could take Lindsey to him was more reassuring than she'd ever dreamed possible.

The town was filled with hikers dressed in every possible sort of outfit. There were those who'd obviously hiked many weeks, their clothes dusty and worn, their boots scuffed, with weary expressions on their faces. Cole passed a few of them and was taken aback by their ripe smell. Hygiene was obviously a challenge on the Trail.

Then there were those he overheard talking, who were planning to use Damascus as a starting point for a flip-flop trip, starting midway, hiking to Maine with the good weather and then getting transportation to Georgia to start the northward trek back to the midway point in the fall. Those who had not yet begun their hike were full of enthusiasm. They reminded him of schoolchildren excited by the prospect of a field day.

He knew he looked odd, fitting in with neither group, wearing a worn backpack over church clothes—although his white dress shirt and black slacks weren't exactly pristine after clawing his way through creek brush.

Still, it felt good walking through a town where no one knew him. For so long, he had lived under the intense scrutiny of various guards who'd come and gone on his cell block. It hadn't been much better when he returned to Fallen Oak. He had been well aware of all the curious glances.

This was the first chance he'd had to feel anonymous, just a regular guy out enjoying a hike.

As he slowly worked his way through the length of the town, he kept a sharp eye out for a glimpse of Lindsey's red-gold hair, glancing into shop windows, scanning the people. He figured they would be easy to spot *if* they were here.

Marie would be expecting a call soon. He had put off

phoning her until he had something definitive to tell her. He kept expecting to find Erin and Lindsey around every corner.

A sudden whiff of hamburgers and onions cooking on a grill made his stomach cramp with hunger. He had been starting to feel a little light-headed, so he decided to do nothing else in the way of searching until he had downed a few of whatever someone was cooking that smelled so good. A sign that read "BEST HAMBURGERS EAST OF THE MISSISSIPPI" drew him in.

It was getting close to supper time and the place was packed; all the tables were filled. He saw a short line at the take-out counter and queued up behind a woman with raggedy brown hair. In front of her was a girl with jet-black hair gelled into short spikes.

He was reading the menu posted above the grill when he heard the woman in front of him giving her order. Strange, but her voice sounded exactly like Erin's. It was always a little disconcerting when a stranger's voice sounded like someone he knew. But still . . .

The cashier brought the woman's order to her and rang her up on the cash register. The girl grabbed the sack, turned, and saw him, and her eyes grew wide.

"Mom . . ."

The woman took one look at him and then glanced around the room as though she were planning an escape. It was Erin, and she was terrified.

"It's only me," Cole said. "Marie sent me to find you."

"How did you . . . ?" Erin stammered.

A voice coughed behind him, politely encouraging him to place an order. He was afraid that if he took his attention off Erin and Lindsey, they'd disappear. Unfortunately, he was also incredibly hungry.

"Please stay here," he said. "Let me get my food and then

we'll go somewhere and you can tell me about last night." He gave his order to the waitress, never taking his eyes off of Erin.

It hurt to see the fear and suspicion on her face. He had gone to a lot of effort to find her, thinking they might need help—and now she was ready to bolt. This was not the reception he had expected.

"Here you go." The cashier handed him the sack of food. He took his attention off Erin just long enough to pay, and when he turned around, they were gone.

⤙⤚

"What now, Mom?" Lindsey looked over her shoulder as they walked briskly down the street.

"I don't know. Just keep walking. If we run, we'll draw attention to ourselves."

"I see him," Lindsey said. "I think he's spotted us."

Now that the shock of seeing Cole had worn off, something within Erin hardened. She rebelled at the thought of taking one more step. There was a friendly looking small white church with a steeple directly in front of them, its steps leading down to the sidewalk.

"Let's sit here."

"But Cole's coming."

"Let him."

How he had found them, Erin didn't know, but if they were going to have a confrontation, she would prefer to have it here in town with plenty of people around.

"If he comes, he comes." Erin sat down on the bench. "In the meantime, I'm going to eat."

Lindsey hesitated before she sat down. "Are you sure?"

"Oh yeah. I'm sure." Erin dug into the sack, pulled out a hamburger and took a bite.

"Do you mind if I join you?" It was Cole, with a full-sized hiking backpack on his broad shoulders and hurt in his eyes.

"Oh please." Erin indicated the church steps with a wave of her hand. "By all means, join us."

Cole ignored her sarcasm, leaned his pack up against the bottom two steps, climbed to the top of the stairs, sat down, and placed his carryout bag between them.

"Looks like you came fully loaded." Erin nodded toward his backpack.

"Some guy gave me such a deal a few minutes ago that I couldn't refuse."

"What are you doing here, Cole?"

Instead of being grateful for the effort he'd gone to, her voice sounded accusatory.

"Marie sent me. I—she wanted to make certain you were all right. I agreed with her that someone needed to check on you. We didn't know if one of you might be hurt. Now I can let her know that you seem fine, with the exception of a very bad dye job."

He unwrapped his food.

Erin riffled her fingers through her short strands. "It seemed like a good idea at the time. We were trying to disguise ourselves." She allowed some bitterness to enter her voice. "Too bad it didn't work."

"Who were you trying to hide from?"

"That's just it. We don't know." She glanced at him, gauging his reaction. "We thought it might be from you."

He thought this over as he methodically demolished a hamburger. Then he took out a paper napkin and wiped his fingers and mouth.

"Erin," he said, "What happened last night after Josiah and I left? We didn't know if you and Lindsey were alive or dead."

"How did you find us?" Erin asked. "Does anyone else know we're here?"

"I saw the faint trail you left out back. I followed it. Unless Marie's said something, no one else knows. What happened?"

He didn't *look* like someone with a guilty conscience, but she couldn't trust that. There were some awfully good actors in the world, and not all of them were on the stage.

"Someone broke into our house," she said. "Lindsey and I escaped through the basement door. We walked all night to get to this town, spent this morning at the motel, saw you at the restaurant, and here we are."

"But why are you afraid of me?" His voice was raw with emotion. "I've done *nothing* to you."

"Well, for one thing, do you remember mentioning your cell mate last night?" Erin asked.

"The one who liked to talk about blowing things up?" Cole said. "Sure."

"The sheriff called me last night after everyone left. He told me the guy got out recently and owed you."

"Owed me for what?" Cole seemed genuinely puzzled.

"Keeping him from getting beat up."

"Yeah, I did that a couple times, but what does that have to do with anything?"

"Dempsey thinks he might have been acting on your behalf by trying to kill me. Probably out of gratitude."

"*What!*"

She watched him closely. As a teacher, she'd become pretty good at picking out liars. Some students, when questioned about some wrong they had committed, overreacted, brimming with feigned righteous indignation. Others were so round-eyed with pretend innocence that she could spot them in a second solely because of their ultra-innocence. Others, those who actually had a conscience, had trouble looking her in the eyes and became fixated on looking at the floor.

"No way." Cole looked at her straight on. "Grateful? Hardly. Chester was the most selfish, self-centered little snake I've ever met. He would have set *me* on fire if he could have gotten away with it. How he managed to get paroled I'll never know."

"Why did you protect him?" Lindsey asked.

"Getting beat up just made him meaner. Then I would have to deal with him later in our cell. There were a lot of nights I didn't close my eyes when Chester was in a nasty mood. I never knew what he might try to do."

"How much would it cost to hire him to blow up my car?"

"With people in it?" Cole gave a mirthless laugh. "Heck. Chester would kill you for an orange popsicle if he didn't think he'd get caught."

"Did you ever tell him about us?" Lindsey asked. "Or tell him where you lived?"

"No." Cole shook his head. "It wasn't really possible to have an actual conversation with Chester. He was in his own world most of the time."

Wild Bill Lesson #7: *Always listen to what your gut is tellin' you.*

Erin's gut told her to believe him. Her instincts told her that Cole was an honest and decent man. In *spite* of everything that had happened to him.

And yet . . .

"Here." He fished a cell phone out of his pocket and handed it to her. "Call Marie. She'll be sitting by the phone, a nervous wreck. At least let her know you're okay."

Erin dialed.

"Cole?" Marie asked the second she picked up.

"No. It's me, Erin."

"Oh, sweetheart, are you okay? You're with Cole? Thank God. How did he find you? What happened?"

Erin filled Marie in, including what the sheriff had said about Cole's cell mate. Cole calmly finished his supper and crumbled the paper sack into a ball while he waited for the two women to finish talking.

"So someone broke in last night," Marie said. "Do you have any suspicions that it might have been Cole?"

"Yes." Erin shot a glance at him sitting there acting so casual.

"Honey, I don't know what's going on around here," Marie said. "But there's one thing I do know. It wasn't Cole Brady who broke in."

"What makes you so sure?"

"I don't have insomnia often, but I couldn't get to sleep after Josiah and Cole came home last night and told me what had happened. I was so upset that I spent the whole night pacing the living-room floor, trying to pray my worry away. Ended up with some peace of mind but a bad case of indigestion."

"I'm sorry, Marie."

"Oh, that's all right. I'm fine now, but what I wanted to tell you is that Cole checked on me half a dozen times. He thought I might be having a heart attack and kept trying to make me go to the hospital. Of course that was foolish talk—I'm as strong as an ox—but I couldn't convince him. Finally he just kicked back and dozed in the La-Z-Boy. Josiah was stirring around all night too, trying to get his sermon finished. No one got more than a wink of sleep at our house last night and Cole was there the whole time. Within sight."

"Oh."

"It's a good thing to know you're all right. I was scared silly when I saw what they'd done to your house."

"What did they do to my house?"

"Didn't Cole tell you?"

"Not yet."

"Honey, somebody ransacked it. It looked like they were either really mad or really anxious to find something."

Erin's heart dropped. Her lovely home, ransacked by a stranger. Or perhaps not a stranger.

"Marie, I found something very frightening in Blake's Bible last night."

"What was it?"

"Blake had written down a passage from Genesis—the one where God tells Lot that he and his family are in great danger and to flee. Blake included a secret phrase we had chosen in case either of us ever had to tell the other that we were in danger. It was dated on the day he died."

"Oh, you poor baby." Marie sighed. "That certainly puts a different light on things, doesn't it?"

"It does."

"But why didn't Blake just tell the sheriff instead of leaving you a message?"

"You tell me. That's the question I keep asking myself."

"Uh-oh."

"What do you mean, 'Uh-oh?' "

"I meant to tell you," Marie said. "Sheriff Dempsey and his men have been out at your house all day. They're scouring the county looking for you. I don't think they've figured out yet that you got away on foot. I don't think I'd want to be found by the sheriff right now if I were you."

"I agree."

"Do you have a plan—a place to go?"

"I do."

"Well, don't tell me about it. Dempsey's already been here asking questions. I told him Cole was out looking for you, but I didn't tell him where Cole was looking. Next time he comes around, I don't want to have to lie to the man, so don't tell me where you are or where you're headed. Just let me know when you get there. I am not going to be doing anything except praying for you until you're safe."

Erin's heart swelled with gratitude for her friend. "Thank you, Marie. Where we're going, we're definitely going to need your prayers."

She disconnected the call and handed the phone to Cole.

He put it back in his pocket. "What did Marie say?"

"That you're a good guy . . . and that we should be very cautious about the sheriff."

CHAPTER TWENTY

Cole had never seen a girl Lindsey's size eat three large hamburgers before, but Lindsey finished her share and was eyeing Erin's remaining two. The teenager apparently had the metabolism of a jet engine. He remembered being that age. It had been all Marie could do to keep him filled up.

He felt a buzzing in his pants pocket, dug out the cell phone, and answered.

"Hello?"

"Cole? Is that you?" It was Dempsey.

"Hello, Sheriff."

"What are you doing with Marie's phone?"

"She loaned it to me earlier today."

"Good. I wasn't able to get hold of her at home just now. I wanted to ask if she had heard from you. Have you found out anything about Erin and Lindsey?"

Cole weighed his answer. He could lie, or he could tell the truth. There was no middle ground. He chose the truth.

"They're with me."

"You've found them?"

"Yes."

"They're safe?"

"So far."

"Do they know who broke into their home last night?"

"Not a clue."

"Okay, then, here's what we do. I want you to bring them to my office. This thing has gotten all out of control. I'm going to put them into protective custody until I can get to the bottom of this."

"I don't think I can do that."

"What do you mean?"

"I don't think I can bring them in."

Erin raised an eyebrow, looking questioningly at him, and he shook his head.

"Listen to me, Cole. Tell me where you are and I'll come get them."

"Fallen Oak doesn't seem to be a healthy place for them right now, Sheriff."

"Where *are* you, Cole?"

"I am not comfortable giving you that information."

"Listen, boy." The sheriff's voice grew ominous. "I can make your life a nightmare if you don't cooperate with me. I can have you arrested so fast it'll make your head spin. I've done it before, and I can do it again."

Cole felt Dempsey's threat like a physical blow to the stomach. The sheriff knew exactly which button to push.

All he had to do was give Dempsey a location. It was a simple thing to do. He could tell the sheriff they were in Damascus. The sheriff could be here in under an hour, and Cole could go on his way.

Handing Erin over to Dempsey would even be a bit of a payback to Erin for what she'd done to him fourteen years ago.

Erin and Lindsey watched him with fear in their eyes.

However, if Dempsey was somehow behind Blake's death, handing them over to him could mean their deaths as well.

But *not* giving them up to Dempsey could mean forfeiting his freedom. Dempsey did not make empty threats. Even though Cole had done nothing wrong, he had more reason to doubt the fairness of the judicial system than most. He didn't know for sure what Dempsey could or could not do to him. There was a real risk.

He definitely had no obligation to Erin.

One of the rules he'd learned from surviving in prison was "Every man for himself." Cole had learned it well. The second rule he'd figured out the first day was "Weakness can get you killed." Another hard-won lesson. He had the scars to prove it.

Based on his experience, the decision of whether to give over the Ramseys to Dempsey should be easy.

Ultimately, it *was* an easy decision to make. He chose not to allow prison to destroy the human being inside him. He didn't trust Dempsey. Not anymore.

Instead of giving the sheriff Erin and Lindsey's location— he disconnected the call.

"We need to start moving." He slung his backpack over his shoulders.

Erin rose from the steps. "He was trying to make you say where we are, wasn't he?"

"Yes."

"But you wouldn't tell him."

"No."

"Why not?"

"Sheriff or not," Cole said. "I don't trust him."

She stared at him a moment as though trying to figure him out. Then she grabbed her own pack. "Thank you, Cole. Now I need to go."

"Where are you going?" Cole asked.

"Mom and I were headed up the Trail," Lindsey said. "We're going to walk to my grandpa's in Virginia." She looked at her mother with pride. "It's a really long way, but we're strong, and we can make it."

"Do you mind if I tag along? I believe the sheriff intends to have a welcoming committee waiting for me if I go back to Fallen Oak."

Lindsey looked puzzled.

"The sheriff could arrest Cole for not telling him where we are," Erin explained.

"But Cole hasn't done anything wrong," Lindsey protested. "And neither have we."

"Unfortunately," Erin said as her eyes met Cole's, "that doesn't always matter."

~~~≈≈~~~

They passed a hiking supply shop on their way out of town, and Erin gazed longingly at the fluffy sleeping bags and other window displays guaranteed to make camping more comfortable. The remarkable hiking that Grandma Gatewood did aside, their own emergency backpacks had never been intended for a trek like the one they were facing. Unfortunately, the hiking shop was closed on Sunday.

Her shoes would have to do. They had never been all that comfortable, but she'd liked the way they looked with her dress-up jeans when she had gone out to dinner with Lindsey last night. Now she was paying for her small vanity.

It definitely wasn't going to be easy. As they crossed the weathered, wooden footbridge leading away from Damascus, she sent a prayer heavenward for a safe and uneventful journey.

There were fifteen miles to hike before they could rest again. She estimated approximately four hours of light left. If they walked nonstop at a fast pace, they would be doing well to make four miles an hour. She calculated that they would make closer to three an hour, barring mishaps, putting them into the shelter well after dark. That might not be a bad thing. They would be less visible and less memorable to other hikers in the dark.

"Marie said that Dempsey and his deputies are combing the county for you," Cole said. "You realize, don't you, that he can't officially cross state lines? He'll have to contact Virginia state authorities for that. Since he doesn't know where we are, he'll probably hold off until he knows for certain that we aren't still in Tennessee. That should give us time for a head start."

"Do you think he'll figure out we're on the Trail?" Lindsey asked.

"Eventually."

"So what do we do?"

"We keep walking. Does anyone in Fallen Oak know where your father lives, Erin?"

"I never talk about him."

"Why not?"

"It's a long story."

"We have a long walk."

"It's very hard to explain my father . . . so usually I don't try."

"That will work to your advantage. Even if Dempsey suspects that you took to the Trail, he won't know whether to go north or south. If he searches the Trail at all, it will probably be south—the section in Tennessee."

A mile up the Trail, Erin had to stop and change the position of her pack's shoulder straps. Two miles into the hike, she had to take off her right shoe and shake a pebble out of it. Three miles into the walk, after having worked up a sweat, gnats came out to play their suicide game of trying to dive into her eyes, throat, and mouth. She envisioned a tiny gnat scoreboard—with points for each hit.

Lindsey and Cole were batting at the air in front of their faces too. The gnats were getting to all of them, but they kept moving forward in spite of the cloud of pests. Speed was essential.

The insects grew even more persistent as the three hiked farther and farther into the forest. She desperately tried to think whether she had ever seen Wild Bill fight these tiny winged demons that were driving her nearly wild. Suddenly, a long-forgotten memory sprang up—her father walking out of the woods with small, leafy sassafras limbs tied around his head, secured with his ever-present bandana. He had looked so strange with all those branches swishing around in front of his face. She had asked him what he thought he was doing, and he'd informed her that sassafras helped keep gnats away.

At the time, she could have cared less. Now, desperate, she grasped onto the memory. They rounded a bend in the Trail and there, as though heaven sent, were an abundance of new-growth sassafras.

"Let's take a short break, gang," Erin said. "I've got a plan."

$$\sim\!\!\infty\!\!\sim$$

Cole looked forward to arriving at Lost Mountain Shelter. It should be coming up any minute now, not a minute too soon. Hiking in the dark was difficult.

They would be able to rest when they got there and he was ready. He had gotten little sleep the night before with Marie pacing the floor. He still wasn't convinced that she had not been having heart trouble; one of his earlier cell mates, an older man, had the same symptoms. They found out later that it had been a heart attack.

He had hiked nearly twenty-seven miles today, counting the trek from Erin's house to Damascus. He couldn't have done it had it not been for the good hiking boots of his accountant Trail friend. His church shoes would have been in pieces by now.

The backpack had the guy's name and address written on it. Once things got back to normal, Cole intended to write to the man, letting him know how much he had needed the pack after all.

Erin's guidebook said there was a good spring near the shelter. He looked forward to it. They were nearly out of water. He was grateful they'd taken the time to fill their water bottles at a municipal tap in Damascus before leaving town.

As they'd crossed over the first stream, Erin had explained to Lindsey that the biggest Trail danger they faced was getting sick from drinking impure water. She said her father had taught her that some people, unacquainted with the woods, became so thirsty that they threw caution to the wind and drank from what looked like pure streams. Wild Bill had taught her about some nasty parasites a person could get—bugs that would hospitalize you.

During one short rest stop, Cole dug into his pack and discovered a supply of iodine tablets and a filter. Erin said she and Lindsey both had iodine tablets, too, so he figured they would be fine. Two tablets for regular water, the instructions said, and three if it were especially bad.

Cole shifted his shoulders beneath the backpack—about fifty-five pounds, he estimated. He could bench-press two hundred easily, so the extra weight wasn't that much of a hardship. Still, he would have pared it down along the way if he only had himself to think of . . . but Erin and Lindsey were traveling light and they might need something he carried.

If he had only himself to think of. Funny. He had had only himself to think of for so long. It felt . . . nice, having these girls depending on him and chattering back and forth around him.

He knew that, from the beginning of time, God had placed men in a protective role. He suddenly wondered whether there wasn't something innate inside men, some vital piece of their identity missing, if they had nothing precious to protect.

He and Erin had pored over the guidebook while Lindsey filled the water bottles back in Damascus. They had roughed out a hiking plan. Leaving Damascus, they'd had a choice of sticking strictly to the Appalachian Trail or of taking a parallel side path called the Virginia Creeper until it hooked back up with the AT.

In the end, they'd flipped a coin. Such a simple act, but one of self-determination he cherished. It continued to feel so amazing—the simple fact of not having all his decisions made for him, of not having his days regimented, of being able to plan his next step, his next stop, his next meal. He never, ever wanted to go back.

The light from a campfire appeared in the distance, interrupting his thoughts. Several people were clustered around it. A few colorful tents had popped up.

"I think we might want to drop these sassafras branches now," Cole said, pitching his into the woods. "There are people up ahead."

Lindsey and Erin dumped theirs on the side of the path as well.

"Hi there, hikers." A young man in cutoffs was hunched over a small camp stove, stirring something that looked like gray gruel, as Cole, Lindsey and Erin walked into camp. "What's your trail names? Have we met up with you before?"

"Trail names?" Cole asked.

"Yeah. Trail names. You haven't been hiking long, have you, fellow?"

Lindsey stepped in front of Cole and took over. "Hi, I'm Sunshine. This here is my mom. Tell him your trail name, Mom."

Cole heard Erin hesitate a moment. "Sonnet."

Sonnet? Ah, the English teacher in her was coming out. It

fit her and "Sunshine" fit Lindsey perfectly, or at least it would when the black, spiky hair grew out.

"Sonnet. Now that's real pretty. I haven't heard that one before. Good to meet you, Sunshine and Sonnet. I'm Coyote."

Cole stared at the young man. He looked more like Daffy Duck, with his big feet and the baseball cap pulled down over his eyes. But if he wanted to be Coyote, that was fine with Cole.

"And you are?" Coyote prompted him.

Cole recalled a nickname Marie had given him when he was a teenager. Sometimes when he would dawdle about getting out of bed and dressed for school, she would put her hands on her hips and say, "You're about as fast as greased lightning this morning, aren't you, boy?"

"Lightning." Cole shook hands with the man.

"Good to meet you, Lightning," Coyote said as he stirred his pot. He took a spoonful and blew on it, then ate the steaming goo while breathing in noisily through his mouth. "Hot, hot, hot," he said. Then he went through the same ritual again.

"What are you eating?" Cole asked. It was dusk, but the stuff still looked disgusting.

"Oatmeal. We practically live on it out here. It sticks to your ribs. That and macaroni and cheese. Plus, it's cheap. What kind of food are you carrying?"

"I have no idea," Cole said truthfully. He started toward the shelter, ignoring the puzzled look on Coyote's face.

The shelter was three-sided and made entirely of logs. It rested upon a few of the large rocks that naturally jutted out of the earth all around the campsite. He looked inside and saw a variety of people lying stretched out, fully clothed, on top of sleeping bags laid out on wooden benches built into the wall. There was a long bare spot on the left side of the shelter, just the right size for his sleeping bag. However, he was looking forward to setting up the one-man tent that was strapped to his backpack. It would not only keep the elements outside, but it would protect him from the cacophony of snores that were inevitable inside the shelter with this motley crew.

But what about Erin and Lindsey? Where were *they* going to sleep? This wasn't something that had occurred to him until this very moment. He wasn't used to looking out for other people.

Cole turned and scanned the campground. At the far edge of the camp, Erin was kneeling, stretching out a small tarp on the bare ground. She gestured to Lindsey, who obediently lay down on the tarp. Then Erin put something that looked like a space blanket over her daughter, tucking it in around her. Was that all the women had? It would grow cold long before sunrise up here in the mountains. They would be miserable with nothing but a thin tarp between them and the ground.

Once again he felt the tug of self-preservation. He had a nice tent. He had a warm sleeping bag. He also would not get a wink of sleep while knowing they were out here, cold and miserable.

He went over to where Erin had spread out her own tarp.

"Is that all you have?"

"Afraid so. I wasn't really expecting a trek like this when I prepared the packs, but we'll be okay. These space blankets are amazing."

He looked at the thin, shiny material. "No doubt, but they can't be all *that* warm. What about the shelter? It would at least block some of the wind."

"I feel really uncomfortable about Lindsey sleeping in there with all those strangers. We'll be okay. It's a clear night. There shouldn't be any rain."

Cole dropped his pack and undid some straps, shook out the tent, and, after a few moments of figuring out how everything went, set it up.

"What are you doing?" Erin asked.

"Fixing you a place to sleep."

"I told you, we're okay. That's your stuff. You're the one who lugged it all the way here, you're the one who should use it."

"Lindsey," he asked, "Are you cold there on the ground?"

A small voice came from beneath the blanket. "Y—yes."

He gave Erin a look, and then he unfolded and unzipped his sleeping bag and spread it out inside the tent. It covered the entire space, making a snug mattress for the girls. Even though it was a one-man tent, there would be room enough if they snuggled together. "Here. This will be a lot more comfortable for the two of you."

"But what will you do?"

"Me? I just spent the past fourteen years sleeping on hard steel bunks with mattresses thinner than your space blanket. Those benches inside the shelter will feel like a feather bed to me."

"You'll need something."

"I won't say no to one of those 'amazing' space blankets you're so impressed with."

A few minutes later, he tried to get comfortable by wadding up an extra pair of pants for a pillow, ones he had found in the pack, while someone on the other side of the shelter nearly took off the roof with the intensity and volume of his snores.

The air was cold, coming in through the open side of the shelter, the plank bench as hard as stone. But as he drew the thin blanket over his shoulders, he warmed himself with the memory of the gratitude he saw in Erin's eyes before she crawled inside the tent, and by her parting words: "Cole Brady, you are a good man."

CHAPTER TWENTY-ONE

Erin awoke well before sunrise with Lindsey's knees jabbing her in the back.

"Wake up, sweetheart," she whispered. "We need to get out of here before the others get up."

Lindsey groaned and flopped over.

"I mean it. Get up."

Her daughter dragged herself upright and rubbed her eyes. "I'm hungry."

"Eat some trail mix. Right now we need to pack as quietly as possible and get out of here."

"It's still dark."

"Exactly."

As Lindsey pulled on her socks and shoes, Erin crawled out of the tent. So many of her muscles hurt, she didn't even take the time to catalog them. Pain was part of hiking. She had known that before she started.

Cole was already awake, sitting alone on a large log near the campfire. He stirred the embers with a stick, which made sparks fly up into the dark sky.

Memories of his generosity last night humbled her. She

wondered if he had gotten any sleep at all. Despite his claims to the contrary, she knew that lying on those bare boards couldn't have been comfortable.

A twig cracked beneath her foot. He glanced up and smiled when he saw her. Not wanting to wake the others, she went over and sat close beside him on the log, where they could plan the day in whispers. He had the blanket wrapped around his shoulders against the cold morning air, and he pulled it around both of them, sharing his warmth with her.

For a few moments, they watched the glowing coals of the fire in silence. The early morning breeze carried the sweet perfume of nearby honeysuckle. It was a heady scent. She wished she could bottle it up and keep it with her.

She was reluctant to leave the camp but knew they must. As lovely as the morning promised to be, the reality was that someone, somewhere, was after them and they had to keep moving. "We need to go," she whispered.

"I know." He nodded. "I filled our water bottles earlier at the spring. How far is it to the next shelter?"

"Twelve miles away—Thomas Knob."

Neither of them moved. It was definitely chilly and she knew that Cole's arm around her was only to hold the blanket in place, but this moment of physical contact was too comforting to break off.

Reluctantly, she stood just as Lindsey left the tent and headed to the privy. In less than ten minutes they were packed and hiking again as the first red streaks of dawn peeked over the horizon.

Lindsey, now fully awake, was exuberant. "I am going to start calling this 'Sunshine, Sonnet, and Lightning's Excellent Adventure.' "

"You can call it anything you want," Erin said, "as long as you keep walking."

As Lindsey hiked in front of them, Erin said to Cole, "If she thinks *this* is an adventure, just wait until she meets her grandpa."

"Hasn't she ever seen him?"

"Yes, but it's been a long time. Blake refused to let me bring her back after he caught Wild Bill trying to teach her how to shoot a rifle."

"Wild Bill?"

"That's his nickname, and it fits in more ways than one."

"Well, teaching your daughter how to shoot doesn't sound so bad. A lot of people teach their children and grandchildren how to conscientiously use a gun."

"She'd just turned six."

"Oh. That's a little young."

"The target was the outline of a man. Dad was instructing her to aim at the head just in case the person was wearing body armor—and when Blake saw what was going on, he was furious. Blake said that my father was a danger to himself and to the community, and he refused to allow me to take her to Emory Mountain again. Of course, my dad refused to visit us in Fallen Oak, so we've been in a stalemate for the past eight years."

"Was Blake right? Is your father a danger to himself and to the community?"

"I don't know. Maybe. It's so hard to see your own flesh and blood for what they really are. All I know is that he would never be a danger to Lindsey. She's his granddaughter. He would die for her."

"Or kill for her?"

"Without hesitation," Erin said grimly.

"How old is he?"

"Sixty-seven this month—a healthy sixty-seven from working his land and eating the pure foods that he grows himself. He doesn't own a car. He used to take me several miles to school every day, but now he walks into town maybe twice a year at most. A couple of relatives bring him the mail and a few supplies in return for the honey he collects from his beehives. From what I can tell he's pretty much turned into a hermit."

"Have you stayed in contact at all?"

"Oh, yes. It was just that Blake didn't want Lindsey around him. He didn't say I couldn't stay in touch. But Dad doesn't have a phone, and of course a computer is out of the question. We've written each other once a month for the past eight years."

"He knows about Blake's death then?"

"He does."

"But he didn't come to the funeral?"

"Dad doesn't leave his mountain."

"Oh."

"In some people's eyes, he's probably nothing more than a cantankerous, damaged old man." As usual, she felt the need to defend him, which was another reason she seldom talked about her father. "But he knows where all the wild medicinal herbs grow that have been used for centuries in these hills. He always found the rare lady's slipper wildflowers for me to admire each spring. And he can deliver a baby lamb with the gentleness of a midwife."

"Actually, he sounds like someone I'd enjoy getting to know."

"Yes, but he can also take offense at the drop of a hat and be barricaded behind his foot-thick log walls with a shotgun poking through a window before an outsider has time to say 'Anybody home?' "

Cole laughed. "But being barricaded behind that thick oak door of his sounds pretty good to me right now."

"He also terrifies census ladies, door-to-door salesmen, and Jehovah's Witnesses," Erin said.

"You miss him, don't you?"

"Yes, I do," Erin said. "And I have for a very long time."

"Do you think he'll be okay about me being with you?"

"I have no idea." Erin pondered the question. "Dad has his own yardstick for judging people, and I've never been able to discern exactly what it is. I thought he would like Blake, but he barely tolerated him. It didn't take Blake long to return the dislike.

"Do you think he'll like me?" Lindsey asked. "I'm half Dad's."

"He'll love you. You're blood kin and his only granddaughter. You could be a serial killer and he would still love you."

"Any advice for those of us who are not blood kin?" Cole asked.

"Yes," Erin answered. "Don't say much. Let him do the talking. Whatever you do, don't disagree with him or try to reason with him. Just accept anything he says at face value and leave it alone."

"Like what?"

"Well, for one thing, it would help a lot if you believed that man hasn't yet walked on the moon. It was a hoax. Something made up by Hollywood."

"Really?" I don't think . . ."

"Just agree with him."

"Okay. What else?"

"The assassination of President Kennedy was a Communist plot and they still haven't found the real killer."

"Got it. Any UFOs in the picture?"

"Of course not. Dad's not crazy."

"Has he seen Elvis lately?"

Erin stopped and gave him a look.

"Sorry," Cole said. "That was out of bounds. He's your father."

"Yes. And he can shoot the eye out of a squirrel at a hundred paces, but he prefers to make pets of them."

"What hurt your dad, Erin?" Cole asked. "What made him this way?"

"There's a lot I don't know about him, but what I do know is that he was one of the best sharpshooters the military had during the Vietnam War. A helicopter he was being transported on was forced down, and he was captured. My father was a POW for eleven months. He was tortured and starved."

"He told you all this?"

"No. He never told me any of it. I only found out a few years ago when one of the other American POWs called me in Fallen Oak, trying to track down my dad."

"Oh." He digested this information. "I'm sorry I teased you about him. It will be an honor to meet him."

"Thanks, Cole, but you do need to be careful about what you say. He's a hard man to read."

"Do you love him?"

"Yes, I do, and I've saved every letter he's ever written to me."

"What's it like to get a letter from Wild Bill?"

"Dad's letters sound like they come from a different time. He'll write something like, 'Shod the mule today. Mulched the garden and harvested the beehives. Got two full tubs of honey. It's been a good year for clover. Bees are doing good.' " Erin smiled. "Things like that."

"Still sounds like someone I would enjoy knowing."

"Being with him can be confusing," Erin said. "For instance, when I was a kid, I found a box of his medals. When I asked him about them, he called them 'fool's gold' and took them out and threw them into our pond. I was ten."

"He just threw them away?"

"He did. But later, when he thought I was asleep, I watched

from behind a window curtain while he dived repeatedly where he had thrown them until he had retrieved the medals, dripping, from the water. Nothing in my childhood ever made sense. The only thing I ever knew for certain was that my father loved me and wanted to protect me. He wanted to protect me a whole lot more than I wanted to be protected."

"But not now?"

"No. Not now. Now I'll take any protection he wants to give—if I can manage to get there."

Two hours later her backpack straps were biting into her shoulders again, but they had outdistanced the hikers they'd left behind back at the shelter and had seen no others so far.

"How are you doing?" she asked Lindsey. "Are you okay?"

"I'm fine, Mom. This is *so* cool."

"Easy for *you* to say, Little Miss Soccer Player!" Erin laughed. "This is evidently nothing but a walk in the park for you."

Lindsey hiked as though her leg muscles were made of well-tempered steel, but Erin's felt like hers were made of gelatin. With a little sleep and a shower at the hotel, Lindsey had bounced back like a rubber ball. One day of rest for Erin made her feel like she could sleep for a month. The adrenaline that had sustained her during the long night flight and then their trek from Damascus had drained away, and there was nothing left except sore muscles, aching shoulders, and bruised feet.

Cole, quiet and uncomplaining, brought up the rear, frequently scanning the trail behind them. Never in her life would she have dreamed that having Cole Brady walking behind her would make her feel more secure, but things had changed. Now it did.

As they crested a mountain, Erin wearily dropped her backpack and sat down on a fallen log. "Let's take a break."

"We'll never get there at this rate, Mom. You're taking a break every half mile."

"I've got a blister." Erin pulled off her shoes. It might have been her imagination, but she would have sworn that steam rose from the inside of her shoes. She rummaged in a pocket of her backpack for a Band-Aid.

Her feet were hurting worse than she wanted to let on. These shoes had never fit her exactly right, but she'd kept them because they looked good with her jeans. A vanity that was costing her now. She'd never intended to walk long distances in them. A couple places had been rubbed raw, in spite of a pair of socks and trying to keep Band-Aids on the bad places.

Lindsey, her hands on her hips, unconsciously adopted a wide-legged stance and gazed at the panorama before them.

Erin had been so busy enduring, leaning over to balance the backpack, and staring at the forest floor that she had not raised her head to see the beauty around her. Fresh Band-Aids re-applied, she staggered to her feet with her shoe in her hand, leaned against the rough bark of a pine tree, and gasped at the sight before her. "Wow."

"You see, Mom? We've been going uphill all morning. That's why it's been so hard."

Erin nodded, drinking in the horizon. There was forest as far as her eyes could see. Pastel colors streaked the sky. Strangely enough, it made her homesick—not for the farmhouse she and Blake had shared, but for the view from her father's.

It was a scene she could have gazed at for hours. But she didn't have hours. They had miles to go before they could rest.

"Let's roll," she said.

Several hours and many rest stops later they heard voices and singing.

Lindsey came to a halt in the middle of the path. "It sounds like there are a lot of people up ahead. Should we keep going?"

Erin looked at Cole. "What do you think?"

"The only choices we have are to walk on, go back, or camp here until whoever is ahead of us leaves. It's nearly supper time, so that might not be until tomorrow. I vote we keep going."

Loud laughter drifted toward them.

"Sounds like they're having a really good time." Lindsey sniffed the air. "Do you smell what I smell?"

The unmistakable scent of meat roasting on a grill wafted over them. Lindsey's stomach growled in response. "Mom . . ." Her voice was strained. "I vote we go check this out."

Erin didn't need much persuading. As they approached a flat space several yards from the shelter, there were a half dozen people all happily holding hot dogs in one hand and soft drinks in the other. A man in an apron and a homemade chef's hat had managed to drag a grill there via a four-wheeler parked off to the side, and he was forking hot dogs off a hot grill as fast as the hikers could gobble them up.

Lindsey groaned in anticipation. "Oh, man."

"Hey, hikers!" the man doing the cooking shouted at them. "Come on and eat. There's plenty."

They were so sick of trail mix, they didn't wait to be invited a second time. Erin's hands shook as she accepted the first hot dog. It was the most delicious food she ever remembered eating in her entire life. Who would have thought that plain hot dogs could taste like a gourmet meal?

She downed three before she stopped long enough to take a breath. Then cold Cokes, dredged from a Styrofoam ice bucket and still dripping, were placed in each of their hands. One of the hikers, a ruddy young woman in Heidi-type braids asked, "Have you three been hiking long?"

"A couple of days," Erin said.

"Then you might not have heard of Trail Magic," the girl said. "Good things happen that you'd never expect—like the

Preacher here getting a windfall from a local food pantry and deciding to share with us."

"The Preacher?"

The cook tipped his white chef's hat. "That was my Trail name back when I through-hiked in '81."

Erin liked the kindness she saw in the gray-haired man and the way his blue eyes crinkled when he smiled.

"I'm Sonnet, and the one still stuffing her face is my daughter, Sunshine."

Cole shook the man's hand. "My name is Lightning, and we appreciate this meal more than you'll ever know."

"Oh yes, I know exactly how much you appreciate it." Preacher laughed. "I was pretty much down to gnawing bark off trees before I finished my trek. You folks going the whole distance?"

Erin hesitated. How much should she tell the people they met along the way?

Cole came to her rescue. "We don't know for sure how long we'll be on the Trail. We're just enjoying ourselves and seeing how far we make it."

The Preacher gave them an appraising look and then handed his grill fork to one of the hikers standing nearby. He stepped from behind the grill and ushered the three of them off to one side. Reaching into his hip pocket, he drew out a card with his name, address, and phone number on it and handed it to Cole.

"I'm called the Preacher because that's what I am. Retired these past four years. Now that I'm no longer chairing deacon's meetings, scrubbing out the baptistery, and keeping the members of the ladies' auxiliary from tearing each other's hair out, I've got some spare time to actually *help* people. The three of you have a look of trouble about you. I am not asking what's wrong, but here's my number in case you need me."

Erin felt tears hot behind her eyes. It was as though God

had given them a direct message that they weren't alone. "Thank you." She swallowed hard.

"You're welcome." The Preacher turned to go, but Cole placed a hand on the man's shoulder. "Why are you doing this? You've gone to all this trouble and expense to feed people you'll probably never even see again."

The Preacher hesitated. "Do you want the easy answer or the hard one?"

"The hard one," Cole said.

"When I was a young man, I thought I was smart enough and strong enough to convert the world." The Preacher's face was serious, his infectious smile gone. "I did a great deal of damage with my arrogance. Because people weren't responding like I thought they should, I came to the mistaken conclusion that the world didn't want to be saved . . . but I was wrong. The world wants very much to believe in a risen Savior. Unfortunately, too many of us who are believers think that we have to come up with the right words, the right arguments, the right scripture."

He ruffled Lindsey's black hair, which had lost its gelled spikes and now lay in soft feathers around her pixie face. She looked up at him, entranced with this man who'd magically appeared and fed her.

"What happened to change all that?" Cole asked.

"I read something St. Francis of Assisi wrote that changed my life." The Preacher cleared his throat and quoted, "Preach the gospel by every means available. If necessary, use words."

"What does that mean?" Lindsey asked.

"It means he's preaching the gospel by feeding hungry hikers," Erin said.

The Preacher winked. "You got it." He bent toward Lindsey and whispered loudly enough so that Cole and Erin could hear. "Besides, grilling hot dogs is a heck of a lot easier than trying

to write a thirty-minute sermon that won't put people to sleep."
He straightened and continued. "Now you three see if you can
stuff a little more food in you. It's another eleven miles to Old
Orchard Shelter. Are you going to make a try for it now or stay
here for the night?"

Cole glanced at Erin. "What do you think?"

She looked around at the people still crowding around the
grill. "I'd like to keep going, but I am not sure my feet and legs
can make it. Do you and Lindsey mind if we rest here tonight?"

"Of course not," Cole said.

"What about you, Lindsey?"

"I'm tired too, Mom."

"I've got something you'll need to take with you on your
way to Old Orchard Shelter tomorrow, young lady," the
Preacher said.

Curious, they all followed him to the four-wheeler where he
brought out a small plastic sack of apples and handed them to
her. "You don't know why I'm giving them to you, and I am
not going to tell you. You'll have to find that out for yourself.
Just make sure you keep them until tomorrow."

"What's going to happen tomorrow?"

"When you get to the Grayson Highlands, you'll see
something rare and special and you'll know exactly what to do
with the apples."

"Thank you." Mystified but happy, Lindsey gave the
Preacher a hug.

Some of the hikers were already drifting toward the shelter,
getting ready to set up for the night. Others were heading back
to the Trail to get a few more miles in before daylight faded
completely. Cole, Erin, and Lindsey helped the Preacher load
up his grill and empty containers.

Before he left, the Preacher asked permission to say a prayer
for their safety.

"Of course." Cole surprised Erin with his lack of hesitation. "We welcome it."

The Preacher put his arms around the three of them in a loose huddle, and then he prayed for their safety and success. After he finished, he looked at them. "It's going to be okay," he reassured them. "I promise."

As the man drove away, he called out something to them. Erin caught his words in the wind and knew that his parting thought would forever echo in her mind. "Remember, children, preach the gospel by any means available. If necessary, use words."

CHAPTER TWENTY-TWO

Marie wished she had not eaten that extra piece of pie. At least not that late at night. She'd made the crust with pure lard which made for a delicious and flaky pie crust, but she should have known better. That much grease always played havoc with her digestion. Right now it felt like she'd swallowed a handful of thumbtacks. The pie had been so good it had *almost* been worth the discomfort, but not quite.

She knew better than to eat pie this late at night, but she couldn't help it. When she was worried about something, she ate, and she was worried sick about Cole, Lindsey, and Erin. She didn't know where they were. She didn't know if they were safe. She didn't know when she'd hear from them again. Her heart was deeply troubled which didn't help her heart-burn one iota.

All her life she'd admired people who had the spiritual discipline to give their problems up to God in prayer and then sleep soundly. That's the way Josiah was. He had more faith than anyone she'd ever known. Unfortunately, she wasn't built that way. She prayed often and heartily, but she didn't feel quite right unless she also spent a fair amount of time *worrying* about things! It seemed wrong, somehow, not to worry about people you cared about.

The problem was, when she worried, she ate. And recently, when she ate, she got indigestion. It was a vicious cycle but she couldn't help it. Tonight she was worried about whether they'd get to wherever they were going safely. She worried about Cole not being here to start that new job. She worried that maybe Cole was right and she actually *did* have heart trouble instead of just simple indigestion. She worried about Josiah if she died from a heart attack. Then she worried about who he'd marry if she died.

The more she lay in bed and worried, the more nervous she got. Finally, she threw back the bed covers, climbed out, and put on her robe. Tonight was going to be one of those nights when she took a lot of antacids and dozed while sitting up in her recliner.

"Is everything all right?" Josiah mumbled sleepily. His head was practically buried beneath covers.

"I can't sleep. I'm going to read for a while." She tied the belt of her robe and slipped on her house shoes. "By the way, if I die of a heart-attack tonight, don't you *dare* get re-married in a month like Pastor Frankie did after Verla passed. That kind of thing is just *rude!*"

Just thinking about all the casseroles that would start showing up on Josiah's doorstep by the women of her church if she died of a heart attack made Marie practically spoiling for a fight—but Josiah was already snoring.

She grabbed the antacids out of the medicine cabinet, poured herself a glass of milk, and picked up the book she'd been reading earlier. Her interest in genealogy had begun to pall almost before it started. She'd given up on her search for a new hobby and indulged in the one thing besides cooking and eating that she'd always thoroughly enjoyed—reading. Maybe a good story would calm her down.

She had tried to read books that would help her become a better manager, how-to books on improving her personality or spiritual life, even books on finding one's passion in life. None had kept her attention. She'd tried reading non-fiction books about other countries or historical events and those had been slow-going as well.

What she *really* enjoyed was a good mystery novel! A story where all the clues were there but buried within the story and the reader could figure out the mystery if they really tried.

She had discovered over the years that she could almost always figure out the mystery before the author's revelation at the end. This had led her to think maybe she could have become a detective if she'd started at it younger. Of course, she wouldn't want to actually deal with dead bodies or have to carry a gun or anything—but she did like working out mysteries in her head. Especially if the author had been thoughtful enough to sprinkle clues throughout the book.

Soon, the antacid and milk began to cool down her heartburn and she became so involved in the novel she was reading that she didn't realize that several hours had passed.

When she heard the small jet land in the airport behind the parsonage, she glanced up at the clock and was surprised to discover that it was already three o'clock in the morning. It seemed awfully late for a flight school to be training pilots. If all that was happening was young pilots being taught to land after dark, like Sheriff Dempsey had said, it seemed to her like that could easily be accomplished long before midnight.

She marked her place in the book with a homemade bookmark that sweet little Kaylie Jo at church had made her when she was in the five-year-old class Marie taught, then walked over to the kitchen window. This was the window that looked out over the church cemetery and gave her a view of the airport. Sure enough, the landing strip lights were on, and she could see a small jet taxiing down the runway.

It didn't stop in front of the main airport building but continued to the very end of the field where it parked for about fifteen minutes before flying off again. All she could see were the blinking lights on the plane, but she thought maybe she could see more if she used a good set of binoculars—which she didn't have.

It occurred to her that if someone wanted to do something illegal, this small country airport, surrounded by woods and cornfields would be an ideal place. Especially since she and Josiah were the only people who lived close and the small airport restaurant closed down around eight o'clock every night. There was simply no one around to see anything.

She wrote down the time on the calendar, chewed one more antacid, and crawled back into bed, planning on purchasing a good pair of binoculars the next day. She had an inkling that she and Josiah had been wrong in trusting Sheriff Dempsey's explanation about the night-flight school. Well, she might be too trusting sometimes, but she wasn't stupid. Tomorrow she'd do a little sleuthing. She'd solved every last one of Agatha Christie's novels long before the end, and it would be interesting to try her hand at solving a real life mystery. Perhaps she'd finally found something she was good at!

~⧓~

After the Preacher had packed up and left they approached the crackling fire in front of Thomas Knob Shelter. It appeared that, besides them, there would be four others staying the night. The same young man in grimy cutoffs and duck-billed baseball cap—who Cole thought they'd left behind at Lost Mountain Shelter—greeted them from beside the fire.

"Hi. I'm Coyote, and these are my new friends, Snoring Bear and She-Who-Talks-in-Her-Sleep. Mellow Yellow is inside, sweeping out the shelter."

A silent young woman, who appeared to have Native American ancestry, nodded hello. A large bear of a man smiled at them, his white teeth splitting his bearded face.

The fire lit up the ground around the two-story structure that was surrounded by packed earth filled with boulders and large stones. A picnic table sat at a slant between the rocks. Cole saw that it would be near suicide to try to pick one's way through the jagged rocks to the shelter in the dark.

Erin suppressed a groan as she lowered herself onto a large rock. He wished he could get her away from these people, but he didn't think she could take another step tonight—and besides, there didn't seem to be more than a foot of clear ground anywhere near the shelter to pitch his tent for her. He had never seen such rocky ground.

The fire was welcome of course; the company—under the circumstances—was not. One of the reasons they'd gotten up early and walked so far was to try to outdistance this very pack.

Coyote looked at Cole more closely. "Haven't we seen you before?"

"I'm Lightning. This is Sunshine and Sonnet."

"Oh, yeah. I remember you." Coyote pushed the brim of his hat back from his forehead and stared at them. "Did you walk all the way here from Lost Mountain Shelter?"

"Yes."

"That's a long way, and it's some steep climbing."

"Yes, it is." Cole tried to keep the irritation out his voice. They had left this morning long before daylight, and pushed themselves mercilessly to get here, hoping to outdistance this crew. "How did you get here before us? Is there a shortcut we didn't know about?"

"We yellow-packed."

He saw Erin staring at the ground, seemingly too tired to enter into the conversation. Twelve miles wasn't a long way for someone who was used to hiking or was wearing hiking boots, but Erin was neither. He was beginning to wonder whether she had the stamina to make it the whole way. What would he do if she couldn't make it to her fathers' place?

Lindsey still had enough energy to be curious. "What's 'yellow-packed'?"

Coyote chuckled. "We hitchhiked, of course." He gestured toward the shelter. "There are a whole bunch of bunks still open. This shelter has room for sixteen if you count the loft. Just remember to hang your packs up high where the bears and mice can't get to them."

A man who looked to be in his mid-twenties appeared in the large, open doorway, sweeping the floor with vigor.

"I can't *believe* what a state these shelters are in!" he complained, shoving dirt and leaves outside with the ragged broom. "You'd think people were raised in barns."

Erin rose without a word, limped past the man into the shelter and Cole heard her whimper as she collapsed onto a sleeping platform. Lindsey looked at Cole in alarm. "Are we going to sleep with all these people?"

"It's part of the Trail, Lindsey," Erin answered from inside the shelter. Her voice betrayed her exhaustion. "It's safer than being in a tent if a thunderstorm hits."

"That's not what I heard," the sweeper intoned. "A man was struck by lightning last year. Dead as a doornail. He'd flipped a coin with his buddy to see who got the bottom bunk . . . and he lost. In more ways than one."

Lindsey looked at Cole, wide-eyed.

"What did you say your name was?" Cole tried to distract the man from any other revelations that might spook Lindsey.

"Mellow Yellow." The man dug at a corner with the tattered broom, dragging out a chewing gum wrapper. "You see what I mean?" He shook the offending piece of paper at them. "People are just awful."

"It's a shelter, Mellow," Coyote said, "Not the Hilton. We're in the middle of the wilderness. Lay off with the housekeeping and don't scare these people."

Mellow Yellow ignored Coyote and raised his voice. "And then there was this couple they found two years ago at the shelter down in Georgia. She was stabbed to death, and he had been shot. And the two women who were killed and . . ."

Mellow headed back inside the shelter, presumably to find more dirt.

"You think he's been on the Trail too long?" Cole asked Coyote.

"Mellow? Don't worry about him. He just needs to get to the next post office drop and get his meds. He'll be fine."

Cole wasn't so sure. He entered the shelter and found Erin lying in a fetal position on the bare wood.

He dropped his pack, pulled out his sleeping bag, and he and Lindsey tried to make her more comfortable. Erin was sound asleep before they had even finished getting the sleeping bag spread out with her situated on it. In spite of the narrowness of the bunk, Lindsey crawled in beside her mother and protectively put one arm over her.

"I've got this, Cole," Lindsey said. "You get some rest, too."

Cole placed one of the space blankets over the girls, climbed up to the loft where the other men were sleeping, and stretched out beneath the second space blanket. As he closed his eyes, he gave a brief thanks for having met the Preacher and the blessing of his stomach-filling hot dogs. The hardness of the wooden planks barely registered as he fell asleep.

⚬⚬⚬

Erin was jarred awake by a loud noise and discovered that she was lying on a sleeping bag she didn't remember crawling onto, with Lindsey sound asleep and pressed tightly up against her. The noise that awakened her was Snoring Bear, asleep in the loft with the other men. He had been aptly named. His snores were so loud that the whole shelter seemed to vibrate with them.

An interesting counterpoint to Snoring Bear was She-Who-Talks-in-Her-Sleep muttering to herself on a bench a few feet away from Lindsey and Erin. Though virtually silent when awake, the woman had long, rambling conversations while sound asleep.

While the other hikers slept, Erin watched the mice, illuminated by the dying campfire, come out to play. She had heard stories about the intrepid field mice that inhabited these shelters, but the stories had not begun to do them justice. They were acrobats, fearless, swinging upside down to crawl all over the food bags in spite of the tin cans threaded over the wire suspending them that was supposed to keep the mice out.

Earlier, she had been awakened for a few moments by the sound of Coyote emptying his backpack and turning out all the pockets before he went to bed.

"It lets the mice indulge their curiosity without having to gnaw through my pack to see what's in there," he explained when he saw her watching him.

She-Who-Talks-in-Her-Sleep started another long, agitated monologue.

"I don't know what that woman's saying"—Lindsey stirred

beside her and whispered—"but she certainly feels strongly about it."

In spite of her aches and pains, Erin giggled. As bizarre as this whole situation seemed to be—total strangers rolled up in cocoon-like bags as the fog rolled in and enveloped the shelter—and as much as she hurt—it still felt good to be sharing something this unique with her daughter. They would talk about it for years.

If they survived. Erin sobered. None of this was funny. This Trail might be a vacation or a lark to others hiking it, but it was life or death to them, and she had better pay attention.

Determined to get an earlier start tomorrow morning, she forced herself to ignore the snores and mutterings of the other campers. She fell asleep again to the sound of mice feet pitter-pattering on the tin roof of the shelter, but not until she'd given thanks to God for the unexpected blessing of Cole Brady's help and forgiveness.

Cole awoke with a start, and realized that the knife he'd been wearing in the ankle sheath was in his hand. His subconscious instincts had detected danger before he was completely awake.

It wasn't the snoring that had awakened him. He was used to the sound of men snoring. Nor was it She-Who-Talks-In-Her-Sleep's impassioned conversation with someone in her dreams. He was used to hearing people talking in their sleep, and sometimes crying in their sleep.

What had awakened him wasn't noise—his subconscious filtered out regular noises—it was stealthy quiet. A shadowy presence was trying not to make any noise while rifling through the pack Cole had hung from the low ceiling.

Without thinking, Cole slipped out from beneath the space

blanket, grabbed the person from behind and held a knife to his throat. "You need something, buddy?" Cole said.

The person investigating his pack turned his head, and Cole saw the duck-like profile of Coyote's hat.

"Yeah," Coyote said, his voice slightly strangled. "I didn't want to wake you, but I was hoping you might have some Vitamin I. Mellow Yellow used up the last of mine two nights ago."

Cole was confused. "Vitamin I?"

"It's what thru-hikers call Ibuprofen. The pain killer? Some of us practically live on it while we're hiking. I pulled a muscle this morning and I'm hurting so bad I can't get to sleep. Most of us keep it handy in an outside pocket—I thought you might carry yours there, too."

Cole let loose of Coyote, slipped his knife back into its sheath, grabbed a flashlight and rummaged in his pack until he found the bottle of pain killer and handed it over. Coyote shook a couple tablets into his hand, tossed them into his mouth and swallowed them with a healthy swig from his water bottle.

"Thanks," Coyote said, as he crawled back into his sleeping bag. "But you really need to chill out, man. People share stuff on the Trail. They don't threaten to slit a man's throat over a couple of Vitamin I tablets."

Cole lay back down, pulled the space blanket over himself and realized that he was shaking. It wasn't from cold. It was from adrenaline overload. He had fought in prison, not only to survive, but to hang onto his few possessions. None of the prisoners had much and it was important to protect what little he owned.

His pulse was pounding as he tried to bring his breathing under control. And then he heard it. A soft giggle, a little spluttering sound, and then another giggle from the sleeping area below. The only ones sleeping down there were Erin, Lindsey, and She-Who-Talks-in-Her-Sleep, who, judging by the muttering going on, was living up to her Trail name. The giggling was coming from Erin and Lindsey.

He felt himself smile, and then his body began to relax, and then the pounding of his heart lessened just from the sound of those two sharing a private joke.

Whatever else was happening on this trek, he felt the dregs of anger he'd carried so long against Erin draining away. She wasn't the only one who had been at fault when it came to his years in prison. It wasn't entirely Blake's fault, either. It was also the fault of the unprepared, too-young, court-appointed attorney. It was a town willing to convict a kid they thought would never amount to anything. It was the girl's grieving father and mother who wanted to punish someone, anyone, for their daughter's death.

He had known when he walked out of prison that he had two choices in front of him—living the rest of his life in bitterness over the lost years, or building a life. It was his intention to get on with his life. Spending time on this hike with Erin and Lindsey was helping strengthen this resolve. Erin was flawed, but by far not the monster he'd thought her to be. He thanked God for having put him in a situation where he could get to know her as the human being she really was.

CHAPTER TWENTY-THREE

They left Thomas Knob Shelter silently, while it still lay in darkness. When dawn finally broke, they were on top of a mountain and could see the sun creeping over the horizon.

"We have a red sky," Erin said.

"Not a good sign." Cole switched off the flashlight with which he had led the way. "We'll probably have a storm before we reach the next shelter."

"Red sky in morning, sailors take warning," Lindsey chanted. "I've heard that. Is it actually true?"

"I guess we'll find out," Cole said.

Several miles later the sky darkened and rain began to pelt them from all directions as they fought their way up a steep incline. Pine trees swayed in front of them. Rain slashed at their faces.

"We have to stop," Erin shouted. "We need our rain gear."

They huddled in a grove of pine trees while hurriedly jerking on the ponchos they carried in their packs.

"We have to get out of here." Cole pulled his hood over his head. "It isn't safe to be under these trees if the storm worsens."

Mud splattered the backs of their legs as they slogged out of the pine grove and back onto the Trail.

Cole knew they had been extraordinarily lucky, so far. Clear skies. Near-perfect hiking conditions. Not to mention the Preacher and his hot dogs yesterday evening. This was the first really bad weather they'd hit. As long as it didn't start lightning, they'd be okay.

As though the sky had read his thoughts, a bolt of lightning struck in the distance. Lindsey and Erin jumped in unison. Cole calculated that the strike was about a mile away. It had been clearly visible as it split the sky.

"This could get interesting," Erin shouted as she increased her speed.

"Still wanting to walk to your dad's?" he yelled.

"Not much choice now!"

There was nothing they could do except keep going and hope the lightning moved in a different direction.

Instead, it crept closer.

Another lightning strike. This time there wasn't even a full second between the flash and the thunder. The thunder volleyed so loudly it shook the ground.

"We need to find cover!" Erin shouted against the wind and the rain.

Without shelter, Cole knew that the only thing left was to lie flat on the ground and hope the lightning passed over them. He thought of all the metal they had on them—the frame of his pack . . . the snaps, hooks, and zippers of their clothing. They were in danger no matter what they did.

Lindsey pointed. "I see something!"

Up ahead, there was a grouping of large boulders that looked as though they'd been scattered by some primeval giant. They ran toward the boulders, their backpacks flopping, all three of them clumsily slipping on the rocky path.

Lindsey reached the giant rocks first and climbed in between two boulders the size of freight cars that were wedged together, creating a ragged, peaked roof. Cole noticed that Erin was limping badly as she ran. He put an arm around her waist to help her and they made it to the boulders together just as a lightning bolt struck near the spot where they'd been standing less than thirty seconds before. He could feel the hair on his neck rising from the static electricity.

Erin leaned against one of the boulders, panting, Rain coursed down her face in rivulets. "What *is* this place, anyway?"

Lindsey had already pulled out the guidebook. "It's called 'Fat Man's Squeeze.' It says hikers have to crawl through part of it."

They were not completely protected from the rain here— plenty still blew in—but it was a small concern compared to the very real threat of the lightning that now crackled all around them. He had always loved thunderstorms when he was a kid, and now he experienced the same feeling of wild excitement brought on by the pyrotechnic display they were watching from this rocky cavern.

Erin had taken a seat on a wide boulder, and Lindsey sat next to her mom, with the guidebook safely stashed beneath her poncho. Cole leaned against a rock just inside the opening, looking back at the trail they'd just hiked, grateful the storm had held off until they were close enough to access the protection of these rocks. As the rain-laden wind blew in on them, Lindsey made a strangled sound. Cole went over and peered beneath Lindsey's rain visor. "Are you okay?"

Lindsey threw back her head, allowing the rain to pelt her on the face. She laughed out loud, a full belly laugh of sheer delight, as water streamed down her poncho and her short black hair plastered itself to her cheeks. "Oh yeah, I'm good! This is the most fun I've had in *ages!*"

The rain quit nearly as quickly as it had started. The clouds scuttled away as though late for an appointment elsewhere. The sun came out, the sky turned a brilliant blue, and Cole was filled with energy. He didn't know whether it was the ozone-charged air or the adrenaline rush of being narrowly missed by lightning, but it was intoxicating.

They clambered the rest of the way through the tight, rocky cairn in which they'd sheltered, dragging their packs behind them.

"That was close." Erin shook out her wet poncho.

"Sure was." Lindsey still had the light of adventure in her eyes.

"It was dangerous," Erin said.

"But it was fun." Lindsey grinned.

"Okay. It was a little bit of fun," Erin conceded.

Lindsey pointed. "You can see forever up here."

"Only a few more miles to the next shelter," Cole said. "Are you women up for it?"

"What are you talking about? I'm turning into a hiking machine," Erin said. "Of course, my feet and back don't seem to know that, but my head does."

"Are you having trouble with your feet and back?" Cole had noticed her limping, but this was the first time he had heard a complaint.

"A couple of blisters that have been giving me trouble. I can stand it, though."

"What about your back?"

"It hurts some, but I can deal with it."

"Take off your shoes."

"Why?"

"Blisters are not something to take lightly."

"We'll be at my dad's in a few more days. I can stand it 'til then. I don't want to slow us up."

"Don't be stubborn, Erin. If your feet are hurting you need to stop and take care of them."

"You've been limping for miles, Mom," Lindsey pointed out.

There was certainly no lack of small boulders to sit on. Both sides of the path were covered in them. Erin reluctantly sat down and slipped off her wet shoes. The heels of both socks were bloody.

"What the . . . ?" Cole saw the blood. "Why didn't you tell me?"

"There was nothing anyone could do. The little first-aid kit I put in our packs was pretty basic. Antibiotic ointment, some aspirin, a few Band-Aids. I tried to use the Band-Aids, but they kept rubbing off. I didn't want to stop, so I figured I could stand it for a few more miles."

"Another hundred-plus miles is a lot of pain."

"I want to get Lindsey to her grandfather's."

"Don't move."

Cole had already discovered a well-equipped Trail first-aid kit in Greg's pack and drew it out now. Unlike Erin's kit, Greg's had been put together with the Trail in mind. Carefully, he cleaned the backs of Erin's feet with antibiotic towelettes while Lindsey looked on with concern.

"I'd have given you my shoes, Mom. You know I would have if I'd known how bad it was."

"Thanks, sweetie, but I think my feet have swollen too much to fit anything but these."

"I can't do a lot," Cole said. "But I think I can make you feel a little better."

Erin didn't make a sound, but he noticed that she did bite her lip while he cleaned her wounds. Then he spread a packet of soothing, healing cream on the raw skin.

"Oh, that feels wonderful," Erin said. "Can I just sit here all day?"

"Not a good idea," Cole said. "It's pretty up here, but I don't want to risk another lightning storm."

"I'm kidding anyway." Erin reached for her socks. "I'm ready to walk."

"Not like that." Cole gently put sterile pads on the back of both heels, bandaged them in gauze, and taped them with surgical tape. "Now put your socks on."

Erin did, and then pulled on her shoes. She stood, testing her weight.

"How does it feel?" Lindsey asked.

"Better." She took a few steps. "Much better. Now, let's get some miles behind us."

⤜⤛⤜

"Where did you say this airport was?" the flight instructor on the other end of the phone asked.

"Fallen Oak, Tennessee," Marie said. "It's pretty small, and practically in my backyard. No one is ever at the airport at night. I was told some flight schools in Virginia had recently begun using it to teach students how to do night landings."

"None of the trainees from my school are. Even if we were using it, we don't train pilots at three in the morning."

"Thank you so much!" Marie said. "You've been a great help."

She hung up and crossed out the last name on the list she had printed out from her internet search of flight schools even remotely within reach of Fallen Oak.

All this time she had tried to give Sheriff Dempsey the benefit of the doubt—she really had—but one thing was obvious now. The sheriff was lying and Marie wanted to know why.

Cole and Erin had not called back. She had told them she didn't want to know where they were, and she didn't. Not really. But she did wish they'd let her know they were safe.

She'd left a couple messages on the cell phone they had, telling them that she was worried sick, but they hadn't contacted her. Either the phone's battery had died, they were someplace where there were no cell towers, or . . . something bad had happened. Her mind was the kind that immediately imagined the worst. How she wished they would call!

A few minutes later, she revised that thought and was grateful they had not called after all. A car pulled into the driveway, and when she looked outside, she saw Sheriff Dempsey. This did not make her happy. Josiah was on a hospital visit and she was alone. She didn't *think* she was in danger from the sheriff, but the man *had* deliberately lied to her. Just like in the mystery novels she loved solving, a lie was almost always a clue, and she was at the point where she was starting to suspect *everyone*.

She said a quick prayer for wisdom and safety, filled the electric tea pot with fresh water and started it heating, smoothed down her still-frizzy hair, and went to answer the door. She'd been a preacher's wife for a lot of years and had carefully honed the skill of pretending to know a whole lot less about people than she actually did. Today, that skill might come in real handy.

—✕—

"Mom!" Lindsey gasped. "Do you see what I see?"

Erin plodded along, staring at the ground. Enduring. Cole's ministrations to her feet had helped, but the trail was rocky and she was miserable. She just wanted to get to the next shelter. The last thing she wanted was to admire more scenery.

"You need to stop and check this out, Erin," Cole said. "I've never seen anything like it in my life."

Erin lifted her head. Laid out before them was a sweeping natural pasture dotted with rocks . . . and ponies.

Ponies? Up here? The scene was so breathtaking that Erin forgot her misery for a moment.

"Snoring Bear and Coyote were talking about this last night before they fell asleep," Cole said. "They're called the feral ponies of the Grayson Highlands."

"Feral?" Erin said. "You mean wild?"

"That's what Coyote said."

Lindsey was already walking toward the ponies with her hand extended, one of the apples the Preacher had given her in the palm of her hand.

"Lindsey, stop," Erin called. "Be careful. If those ponies are wild, they might . . ."

She should have saved her breath. The pony her animal-loving daughter had approached was already contentedly munching on the apple.

Lindsey looked back at her mother with a smile of such pure joy that Erin's heart ached. The brown-and-white pony finished crunching his apple and nuzzled Lindsey's shoulder, wanting more.

There were pregnant ponies and newborn colts beside their mothers. The scene looked like something out of a fairy tale. She longed to pet one also, but each time she or Cole got close, the ponies would start backing away.

With Lindsey, it was different. Erin finally sat down on a boulder and simply watched her daughter. Lindsey's apples were soon all gone, but still there was a circle of ponies clustered around her.

Lindsey was utterly oblivious to anything except these wild ponies, and she was laughing aloud at the sheer joy of it all.

"She's beautiful, isn't she?" Cole said.

"Yes, she is," Erin said. "In so many ways I never saw or understood before."

The panic with which she had begun this trek felt far, far away up here on this high place. She memorized the scene, knowing that the vision of her daughter communing with the wild ponies of Grayson Highlands would be embedded in her mind forever.

CHAPTER TWENTY-FOUR

It was hard to watch Erin walk the final three miles to Old Orchard Shelter. The woman was in agony. The bandaging had helped for a while, but after seeing the state her feet were in back at Fat Man's Squeeze, he knew that nothing except plenty of rest with her feet up could help her recuperate . . . and possibly some antibiotics.

The shelter, when they arrived, was completely open on one side and had no sleeping benches.

"Is this it?" Erin said. "It isn't much."

"It's going to be like sleeping on a small, open, stage," Lindsey said. "But at least it has a privy. See you later."

Erin dropped her pack on the ground and sat down on the open floor of the shelter with her feet dangling off as Lindsey left.

Cole squatted in front of Erin.

"How can I help you?" he said.

"Is there any of that cream left?"

"There is."

"Please. Whatever you can do."

"Scoot back." He unrolled his sleeping bag and made a

place for her to lie down. Then he pulled the first-aid kit out of his pack, sat down with his back to the log wall, and pulled Erin's feet onto his lap.

He gently pulled off her shoes, still sodden from the rain, and then peeled off her socks. When he tried to disengage the blood-soaked, gauze bandage, she cried out—the first he had heard her do so.

"I don't want to hurt you," he said. "But I've got to see what's going on."

"I know, Cole. I'm sorry."

He carefully unwound the bandages and was shocked at what he saw. The bottom of Erin's feet were so bad, they resembled raw meat.

"Oh, Erin," he breathed, "why didn't you tell me?"

"I can stand the pain long enough to get Lindsey to her grandfather's."

"What's wrong with Mom?" Lindsey asked as she entered the shelter. Then she saw her mother's feet. "Oh." She bent over to take a better look. "That's really bad, isn't it?"

"I don't know how she's endured it this far."

"My dad always said that my Mom is a lot tougher than people think," Lindsey's eyes grew moist. "She was hurting so bad and all I could do was talk about those ponies."

"It probably helped keep her mind off the pain, seeing you so happy," Cole said. "It was the best thing you could have done."

"Maybe." Lindsey sounded doubtful. "What are we going to do? Mom can't go on like this."

"I know. For now, hand me my pack and help me get fresh bandages on her. I want to get some food in all of us. Then we need to rest until morning. I don't want you getting sick on me too."

No one came to the small shelter that evening—something Cole thanked God for.

"Where do you suppose Coyote, Mellow Yellow, and the others are?" Lindsey asked.

"Maybe the rain made them decide to stay and rest up at the shelter for the day." Cole stirred the re-constituted beef stew Lindsey had chosen from the selections in his back.

Lindsey giggled.

"What?"

"Oh, nothing." She giggled again. "I was just thinking that it's going to be one very clean shelter if Mellow stays there for another day."

Erin ate a little, but she had a restless night, tossing and turning in pain. None of them got much sleep and none of them needed other hikers to deal with.

The morning was a welcome sight, but it was chilly out. He managed a small campfire for warmth and cheerfulness, and then he set up the camp stove from his pack, ready to cook for the three of them. The equipment was unfamiliar to him but simple enough to figure out in a few minutes. He thanked God for the umpteenth time for the weary hiker who had sold him this outfit.

When Erin opened her eyes that morning, she saw that Cole was up first and yet again taking care of them as he bent over his small camp stove.

"What are you making?" she asked.

He added a spoonful of something to the steaming water.

"Coffee," he said. "Ready for a cup?"

"Not yet."

Had the man gotten any sleep? She swung her legs over the edge of the shelter and lightly put her feet on the ground. "Ouch!"

Cole's head came up. "Are you okay?"

She nodded, but she felt tears prickle from the pain.

Cole came over to check on her.

She looked down and saw that her feet were badly swollen and she was wearing a thick pair of men's socks. Cole was evidently now sacrificing his own footwear for her. She glanced up and saw her shoes on the rafters of the shelter.

"I thought they might dry out a little better up there," Cole explained. "Can you walk?"

"I have to." As difficult as it was, Erin put her full weight down on her feet. Her knees buckled and she fell to her knees, dizzy from the pain.

"You won't be going anywhere today," Cole said.

"You don't understand." She couldn't believe she had to say this to him. "I have to go to the bathroom."

"Of course you do." Cole's voice was kind. "No problem."

With little effort, he scooped her up in his arms and headed toward the outdoor privy. "Lindsey, please come help your mother."

Feet dangling, encased in Cole's thick hiking socks, she held tightly onto his neck while he carried her to the privy. She knew he was strong, but it was a bit of a shock that he could carry her so easily. He deposited her inside and returned to the campfire, telling Lindsey to call for him when they were finished.

For the first time in her life as a mother, their roles were reversed with Lindsey taking care of *her* instead of the other way around. Her daughter was solicitous and patient—so much more than Erin would have expected. How had she and Blake managed to raise such a wonderful daughter?

Eventually Lindsey opened the door and called for him, and he carried Erin to the picnic bench. He sat her on the tabletop, so that her stocking feet could rest on the wooden seat instead of the ground.

"I am going to fix us something hot to eat," he said. "What do you want?"

"It doesn't matter." It really didn't. She had no appetite. Instead, she felt achy and half-sick to her stomach.

Lindsey sorted through the freeze-dried packets that had come with his pack and chose precooked eggs and bacon, ready to reconstitute with boiling water. As Cole worked with the stove and camping kettle, Erin watched the dried stuff fluff up into something that almost resembled real food—just like the beef stew last night.

There was a buzzing sound, and Cole looked confused. Then he grabbed at his pocket and pulled out Marie's cell phone.

"Hello?" He listened for a moment. "Yes, we're okay, Marie. I tried to call yesterday but there wasn't any reception." He hesitated and then handed the phone to Erin. "She wants to talk to you."

Erin grabbed the phone like a lifeline. "Hi Marie." It felt so good to be connected to the outside world again—at least it felt good until she heard what Marie had to say.

"Erin, I'm going to talk fast. Don't tell me where you are. I still don't want to have that knowledge. Just listen."

"Okay."

"Your pictures were all over the local news last night." The older woman's voice sounded strained and worried. "Dempsey put out an APB for Cole's arrest. He stopped by to tell me to tell him if I heard anything from him."

"But Cole hasn't done anything," Erin protested. "Neither have we."

"I know that, but it's not stopping Dempsey."

"What's he charging Cole with?"

"Kidnapping of a minor for starters."

Erin glanced at Lindsey. There had been no kidnapping, but Lindsey was a beautiful young girl and Cole had been in prison. Guilty or not, the media would have a field day with the story and Dempsey knew it.

"You said 'for starters.' What else is there?"

"Dempsey is also accusing Cole of kidnapping you, and of breaking and entering and attempted murder."

"Attempted murder?"

"The car bomb, and it gets worse, Erin. The national media has gotten hold of it, and this morning it was on all three main news networks. Your pictures, Cole's time in prison, Blake's death, the whole thing. If you look at it from their perspective, this is a juicy story with lots of human interest, and it's all being fed to them by a respected law official. There's a major manhunt going on now that the pictures are out. And Erin, there's even more."

Marie hesitated as though she had not yet told her the worst part. How could there be any more after all that?

"What is it, Marie. Tell me."

"He's accusing Cole of Blake's murder."

"That's ridiculous! Cole was in prison."

"Exactly. Dempsey is telling the press that he believes Cole had an accomplice in prison who got out first and acted for him. He says that Cole intended all along to get back at you and Blake for being a witness and putting him in prison. He says Cole had been plotting revenge ever since he was put in."

Erin glanced at Cole who was in the process of carefully spooning food onto a plastic plate for her. "That's not possible."

"I know it isn't possible. That's why I am calling. If Dempsey gets his hands on Cole, I don't know what will happen. I don't know if he can manage to send him back to prison or not, but I wouldn't bet against it."

"I'd tell the press and the courts the truth."

"And they might not believe you."

"Why not?"

"In case you haven't noticed, Erin, Cole is a good-looking

man. You've been on the run with him for several days. A good attorney could dismiss anything you might have to say."

"What do we do, Marie?"

"Stay hidden for now. I've got an idea I'm working on. I'll call you back when I know more. Where you are, can you keep this phone charged?"

"No."

"I was afraid of that. Hang up and turn the phone off to keep the battery charged. I'll leave a message as soon as I hear something. You can check it again tonight."

"Thanks, Marie." She clicked the phone off and told Lindsey and Cole what Marie had said. Cole silently absorbed the news—and the implications.

"Like I said before," Lindsey said, "Now what?"

"Cole?" Erin asked. "What do you want to do? You have even more at stake here than we do."

"The only thing I can think of is to get you to your father's where we can regroup and you can heal. How much farther is it?"

Erin did a quick calculation in her head. "About a hundred and forty miles if we keep hiking. Maybe a hundred by the road."

"The road?" Lindsey said. "Are you thinking of yellow-packing?"

"I'm thinking we need to get there any way we can and as fast as we can," Erin said.

"But Marie said that our pictures are on TV. Don't we need to stay out of sight?" Lindsey asked.

"Yes, we do. Cole, why don't you and Lindsey hike on ahead? You're both stronger than me and in better shape. You'll be able to travel twice as fast without me. Leave me here with some water and food. I'll spend the day letting my feet heal, and if I can, I'll start out alone tomorrow. Dad will come after me as soon as you tell him what's happened."

"Would your father leave you here alone, Erin?" Cole asked.

"Probably not, but . . ."

"I won't either."

"But . . ."

"We started this trek together, and we'll end it together. We won't separate. Not when you can't even get to the toilet alone."

"I won't put you in any more danger of being arrested," Erin said. "I've already done that. I won't be responsible for doing it again. I can endure some physical pain, but I cannot endure that. Bring me my shoes."

"Erin . . ."

"Hand me my shoes."

"I won't allow you to . . ."

"Hand me my *shoes*."

〰〰〰

After making slits in her shoes with his knife so she could get them on her swollen feet, Cole watched Erin knock back two ibuprofen tablets, swig some water from her water bottle, and then stand up. Slowly. He could see the pain in her face as she took her first step. He wasn't happy with her decision, but then, he wasn't happy with any of the other options before them, either. One thing he knew: she couldn't go another one hundred and forty miles like this. He would be surprised if they made it a mile before she collapsed.

"We have phone service here, Erin. Let me call for help. You need medical attention."

"Everyone's looking for you, Cole." She took another step and another, sweating with the effort. "The Trail is our best shot."

"I've seen your feet, Erin. If you continue to abuse them they'll become infected. They may already be."

"That doesn't matter. That . . ." She took another step, wincing in pain. "Doesn't . . ." Another step. "Matter."

She fell.

Lindsey rushed to her and touched her face. "Mom?" She looked at Cole over her shoulder. "She's burning up, Cole."

He dropped his pack and knelt beside her, gathering her in his arms. Even with the ibuprofen, she felt as though there were a furnace burning inside her. He should have gotten her to a hospital last night.

He grabbed a bottle of water, pulled a small hand towel out of his pack, soaked it, and began to bathe Erin's face. The towel turned hot in his hand. He poured more water on it, thanking the Lord for the cool spring and the bottles he had filled early this morning.

"Maybe I should call Doc," Lindsey said. "Doc could tell us what to do."

"He could tell us what to do, but we don't have the equipment to do it," Cole said. "We don't have any other medical supplies. I think we need to call 911 and get some real help."

"No." Erin, revived by the cool water, came to long enough to argue. "Don't call 911. They'll know who you are."

"I don't care. You're sick. We have to get you some help."

"What about the Preacher?" Lindsey said. "He said he would help us."

A small light went on in Cole's world. It was a long shot— not everyone meant what they said when they offered to help— but maybe the Preacher was one of those people who did.

And maybe, just maybe, the Preacher had not seen the news today. Maybe, just maybe, even if he had, he would not turn them in to the cops until they could get Erin some help.

He reached into his back pocket and dragged out the card the Preacher had given him.

Cole left his backpack in the shelter with a note saying that anyone who needed it could have it. He instructed Lindsey to leave Erin's pack there as well. Lindsey carried nothing in her own except the cash they had left, a bottle of ibuprofen, and three bottles of water. Lord willing, it would be enough.

It was a long way to carry someone—but he thought he could do it. At least it was downhill. The Preacher was an expert on the Trail and knew the area well. He had instructed Cole to take Erin north two miles, where the Trail and a state road intersected. He had said he would meet them in the parking lot there.

After a mile and a half, Cole was panting so hard that Erin begged him to let her try to walk. He put her down, but she screamed from the pain. Lindsey shoved her shoulder beneath her mother's left arm and with both of them supporting her, Erin was able to bear a little of her weight and walk long enough to give him some respite. In a few minutes he was able to carry her again. She didn't complain.

The gratitude he felt when he saw the Preacher waiting for them at the parking lot was overwhelming.

Then he saw the Preacher bring up a rifle and point it straight at his head.

CHAPTER TWENTY-FIVE

"Sunshine," the Preacher said, "come over here and stand behind me."

"No!" Lindsey said.

"Come here, child. I'm just trying to make certain that he can't hurt you anymore."

Lindsey put her body between Cole and the gun and shook her head emphatically. "No!"

"You don't have to be afraid. I know this man kidnapped you and your mother. I saw it on TV this morning. I've come to take you back home."

"It's a lie." Lindsey, tired and hungry, had a meltdown right there in the middle of the parking lot. She threw her pack on the ground and stomped her foot. "Everything you saw on the TV is a lie. And Sheriff Dempsey is a big, fat liar too. Mom and I had to run because someone is after us, but Cole helped us even though my mom and dad helped put him in jail, even though he was innocent, and my mom didn't have good shoes and she hurt her feet and can't walk and now she's got a fever, and . . . and our preacher and his wife will tell you that Cole's a good man, and I thought we could trust you and now you're here pointing a gun at us and . . . and . . ." Lindsey finished her tantrum by sitting cross-legged on the ground at Cole's feet and folding her arms across her chest. "And I quit."

At that, the girl burst into tears.

Cole, his arms filled with a woman who was burning up with fever, felt ready to quit too. The Preacher had been their only hope, and now he had turned on them.

"That's good enough for me." Preacher lowered his rifle. "Put the girl's mother in the car, Cole, and the two of you get in too."

Lindsey stopped crying and wiped her nose with the tail of her shirt. "Where are you taking us?"

"Where do you want to go?"

Lindsey sniffed and stood up. "Grandpa Emory's."

"Do you know where he lives?"

"Kind of."

The Preacher smiled. "Do you know the general direction?"

"Erin said he lives not far from Pearisburg, Virginia." Cole shifted Erin's weight. "Up in the mountains."

"You were trying to walk there?"

"Yes, sir."

At that moment, hearing the older man's voice, Erin roused and lifted her head. "Dad?"

"No, darlin', I'm not your father. Can you tell me where your daddy lives?"

"I'll . . . show . . . you."

"I brought some pillows and a blanket to make her more comfortable." The Preacher jerked his head toward his old Ford Taurus. "Any man who'd carry a sick woman that far, risk his own neck when he could abandon her, and then have the girl he was supposed to have kidnapped throw herself between him and a gun to defend him—you can't be the person they're saying you are on the news. What in the world did you do to get that Dempsey fellow so mad at you?"

"I wish I knew."

The Preacher opened one of the back doors. "You can sit in here with her. The child can sit up front with me."

Cole gratefully placed Erin on the backseat and cushioned her head with pillows as Lindsey scrambled into the passenger seat.

The Preacher stowed his rifle in the trunk then got behind the wheel. "Sorry about scaring you back there, Cole. It was hard for me to take you for a kidnapper when I recognized your face on the TV. That's not how I read the situation at Thomas Knob Shelter at all. But I had to make sure that little girl was okay."

"I thought there might be a chance you'd turn us in, but I didn't expect you to come toting a gun. Is it normal for preachers in this neck of the woods to be armed?"

"Only those who do a little hunting."

"Ah."

"Thanks for coming to get us." Lindsey clicked her seat belt into place. "I'm not mad at you anymore. Can we get something to eat? I'm starved."

"Of course you are." The Preacher chuckled. "How would you feel about my pulling through the first McDonald's drive-through we see?"

"I want two Big Mac's and double fries and an extra-large Coke and two cherry pies," Lindsey said, happily. "And something for my mom when she wakes up."

The Preacher glanced into the rearview mirror as he backed out of the parking lot and winked at Cole. "You've had an interesting few days, haven't you?"

"You have no idea, Preacher."

Now that Lindsey's menu order had been placed and food

was imminent, she had something else on her mind. "Guess what! I got to feed those apples you gave me to the wild ponies yesterday. It was *so cool*."

⤙⤛⤜

Erin felt a gentle rocking motion and a roughness against her face. There was a smell of horse. A large bear of a man walked beside her, steadying her, as the horse beneath her climbed higher and higher.

Strong, gentle hands lifted her down. More hands carried her into a cool room. A feather bed. Her face against sheets that smelled of sun. Her hair smoothed back with calloused hands. Her daughter's voice. Someone washing her face and neck with soap and water. Something bitter going down her throat. Cooling ointment on her burning feet.

Sleep.

⤙⤛⤜

Lindsey had been the first to spot her grandfather—waiting at the end of the wagon road that led down Emory Mountain toward the Trail. Cole had no idea how Wild Bill knew they were coming, but the older man had been prepared. He had even thanked the Preacher with the gift of a mason jar of honey. The rays of the late-afternoon sun made the jar and its contents glow like gold.

The Preacher accepted it with a grace that gave dignity to the homey gift . . . and to the large, gruff man who offered it.

Wild Bill had come for his daughter by leading a snow-white mule off the mountain and his tenderness toward her won Cole over from the moment Bill lifted Erin onto the mule, murmuring to her as though she were a babe, "It's all right, daughter. It's all right."

The mule, with Erin on its back, seemed to know it was carrying something precious by the way it carefully picked its way over the rocks and roots of the path.

Cole didn't know how much Erin would remember, but he would never forget that journey up Emory Mountain. The long stretches of silence. The occasional words of encouragement to the mule. The entire time, Wild Bill steadying his feverish daughter with one hand, his other resting lightly on the reins.

"Careful, girlie," he would say. "Watch out for that rock."

Cole didn't know if he was talking to Lindsey or the mule. There were no words at all for Cole, but that was all right. He was being allowed to come with them, which was something he had not been entirely certain would happen.

Wild Bill's fortress looked as though it had been built directly into the mountain—designed to accept the contours of the land—in such a way that it would be nearly impossible to sneak up on anyone inside the massive log structure.

No wonder Erin had been so certain that Lindsey would be safe once she got there.

When they entered the cabin, Wild Bill immediately mixed up a potion for Erin. Cole half expected some ancient mixture of roots and berries but found out later that Wild Bill had real antibiotics on hand. Drugs he'd gotten from the vet for his animals—which he judged to be effective for Erin's infection, as well.

After Bill got her and Lindsey settled, he showed Cole into a room filled with massive primitive bedroom furniture. There was a tin basin and a pitcher filled with water beside a rough, clean towel. A side table held a loaf of dark bread and a hunk of goat cheese on a clean linen dishcloth.

"Thank you," Cole said.

"Rest," Wild Bill said. "Eat."

After Wild Bill left, Cole moved to the window and looked out. It felt as though the earth had fallen away; all he saw was empty space with mountains in the distance. It was beautiful, but he was too worn out to enjoy the vista.

After washing off some of the grime of the Trail, Cole collapsed onto a bed that consisted of a feather mattress strung over a web of ropes. He had never lain on anything like it before. It definitely beat the hard floor and benches of the shelters.

He slept like a rock for two hours. Then he went to check on Erin. Her father was keeping vigil by her side, a shotgun within easy reach. Lindsey was asleep on a trundle bed next to her mother. Cole nodded to Erin's father, then went back to his room and fell into another deep sleep, grateful to temporarily hand over the responsibility of Erin and Lindsey into Wild Bill's hands.

CHAPTER TWENTY-SIX

ole slept for eight straight hours. In a half daze he found his way outside, relieved himself and slept another four. When he awoke, it was nearly noon. Famished, he fell upon the bread and cheese that he had been too exhausted to bother with the night before. A tin cup of tea, still hot to the touch, was waiting for him on the bedside table. Wild Bill must have brought it and, in coming into the bedroom, had awakened him.

He sat on the edge of the bed and sipped the strong brew. Sunlight streamed through the bare window. A clean, threadbare pair of pants and a mended shirt were folded and draped over the wooden chair.

The dirty water in the basin from the night before had been removed and the pitcher filled with fresh water. He washed himself, put on the loosely fitting borrowed clothes, and emerged from the bedroom.

Erin was still sleeping when he looked in on her, as was Lindsey. An adult potty chair sat beside the bed, and he wondered at its presence here in this mountain home. He knew Erin had been raised by her widowed father, but he had never thought to ask how her mother had died. Now he suspected a long illness.

The only thing he knew about the layout of the huge log house was the two bedrooms in which he and Erin and Lindsey had spent the night and the way they'd entered last night. Half-worried that his presence might be an unwelcome intrusion upon Erin's father, he padded, barefoot, down a long corridor with glistening wood floors. Now that he was rested and fully awake, he marveled at the craftsmanship of the giant timbers.

He didn't know a lot about logs, but the size of these made him think that the place must have been built out of virgin timber—something that, to his knowledge, no longer existed.

His nose led him to a huge room that appeared to serve as both kitchen and living room, and he found Wild Bill standing over a wood cook stove, feeding pieces of kindling into the flames. Bacon sizzled in a cast-iron skillet. In spite of his hasty breakfast of cheese and bread, Cole's stomach growled, responding to the scent.

"Good morning," he said. "I thank you for all you've done for us."

Wild Bill kept his eyes on the stove and acknowledged Cole's words of thanks with a curt nod. Somehow it was hard to reconcile this neatly dressed, freshly shaven host who was bending over a frying pan, with the picture of the wild man Erin had drawn in his mind.

The man had cared for his daughter with the tenderness of a mother, and he had provided for Cole's needs with thoughtfulness and kindness. He had probably even plied the needle that had neatly patched the hole in the elbow of the shirt Cole was wearing. But Cole cautioned himself to be careful. He knew, from Erin's description of her father, that this seemingly gentle man cooking breakfast was no tame lion.

Wild Bill forked the bacon onto a plate and then broke two

eggs into the bacon grease. A minute later he slid the eggs, perfectly fried, onto the plate. He sat it on a rough-hewn table, along with a fork.

"Eat," he said.

Obediently, Cole sat at the table as Wild Bill turned back to the stove. Grateful beyond words for this respite and food, he bowed his head and gave silent thanks. When he finished and raised his head, he saw that Erin's father had been watching him.

Wild Bill put his own filled plate on the table directly across from Cole and began shoveling food into his mouth. They ate in silence, broken only by Wild Bill's retrieving a flame-darkened coffeepot from the stove and pouring two cups of black coffee. Cole thanked him, but Wild Bill didn't so much as nod in reply.

When both had cleaned their plates and finished their coffee in silence, Wild Bill laced his hands behind his head and trained his eyes on Cole.

"Blake talked too much," he said.

Cole thought he had been given a compliment, but he wasn't sure. He nodded in honest agreement. Blake *had* talked too much. *Way* too much. Especially in front of the jury that had convicted him.

"How's Erin?" Cole asked.

"Better," Wild Bill said.

"Good."

Wild Bill abruptly rose and motioned for Cole to follow him. They entered another large room with windows looking out over the valley. It was directly beneath the room Cole had slept in, so again the earth dropped away from the window. Looking out, Cole thought he now knew what it might feel like to be sitting in an eagle's nest.

The opposite wall was solid bookshelves. It was before this that Wild Bill stood. "You can read. If you want."

Cole ran his fingers along the spines with appreciation. There didn't seem to be any fiction, but there was an impressive array of books on history and nature. He saw a fat tome on birds, another on plants, several on natural medicine.

"This is a wonderful library," he said. "And an amazing house."

Wild Bill didn't smile, but his features softened slightly. He stuck out his hand. "William Harrison Emory."

"Colton Samuel Brady," Cole said, matching the man's words as he shook Wild Bill's hand. "You can call me Cole."

"I'm Bill," Wild Bill said.

Cole tried to wipe the "Wild" from his memory for fear he might slip and accidentally offend the man.

Bill pulled a well-thumbed history book off a shelf and riffled through the pages. He showed a chapter heading to Cole. It was about Captain Samuel Brady.

"Any kin?" he asked.

"My mom thought so."

Bill's eyes grew wide. "Really?"

"When I was a kid she said my father's people always gave the middle name of Samuel to every boy. It was a tradition. We were supposed to be related to the Captain, but I've never formally traced it back."

"He was a great frontiersman."

"And a great athlete," Cole said.

"Brady's Leap," Bill said. "That Sam Brady jumped twenty-two feet across the Cuyahoga River running from the Indians."

"Yes."

"You must have something of him in you. You brought my daughter home to me—alive. My granddaughter said they could not have made it without your help."

"It was an honor."

Bill nodded. "You can stay."

~~~

Erin awoke to the sound of water. Then she slept. Then she awoke yet again to the sound of water. She opened her eyes and watched her father bringing bucket after bucket of water into the room, pouring them into an elongated tin tub on the floor in front of the fireplace in her bedroom.

He carried in two wooden chairs and placed them in front of the tub, draping a quilt over the back of them to provide a sort of screen to hold in the heat from the fireplace. It was a makeshift bathroom, one she was familiar with from her childhood. She propped herself up against the pillows and the ropes beneath her mattress squeaked.

He glanced up from his work of creating a bath for her, sat on the edge of the bed, and laid a work-roughened palm against her face. "Daughter."

There was such a world of love in his voice that a lump came to her throat and a tear escaped down her cheek.

"You're safe." He wiped the tear away with his thumb. "It's all right. The fever's gone."

"Fever?"

Lindsey poked her head in the room. "Are you finally awake? You've really been out of it, Mom."

"Tell me what happened?"

"Your feet got infected," Lindsey answered for him. "Grandpa was up all night working with you, giving you medicine, taking care of you. He even sat you on the pot, Mom."

Her grandfather shot a warning look at her, and Lindsey stopped talking.

"After such a fever, you'll want to bathe," her father said.

He went over and sprinkled a handful of what appeared to be herbs and some sort of crystalline substance over the top of the water. "Soak in this until the water cools." He nodded at Lindsey. "Help your mother."

Lindsey went to inspect the makeshift bathing arrangements her grandfather had prepared. "Cool! Can I take a bath too?"

Erin saw a glint of mischief in his eyes and knew what was coming next.

"First your mother bathes," he said. "Then you. After you finish, come outside. With so many here, we'll need more kindling. I'll show you how to split it. Tomorrow, instead of me, you will draw the buckets of water from the well, heat them on the stove, and prepare a bath for you and your mother."

Lindsey loved her long, hot showers and to Erin's knowledge, had never questioned the fact that all she had to do was turn a knob to have unlimited water. Erin expected Lindsey to rebel right then and there. Instead, Lindsey, mesmerized by her grandfather and the novelty of the situation, simply said, "Yes, sir!"

He closed the door.

"If you'll help me to the tub," Erin said, "I'll do the rest."

It was only five feet from the bed to the tub, but it felt like five miles. Erin hobbled over and collapsed onto one of the wooden chairs her father had set in front of the tub. Lindsey helped remove the bandages on her feet and then steadied her as Erin wrestled out of her clothes.

Putting her feet into the warm water was torture, but once she had sat down in the aromatic water, whatever her father had sprinkled in it began to do its work, and being there felt heavenly. She could almost feel her aches and pains draining away.

Lindsey fell into Erin's bed and plumped up the pillows behind her back. "This all belongs to Grandpa?"

"Yes."

"The entire mountain?"

"The entire mountain."

"It's huge."

"That's why it's called a mountain." A bar of homemade soap lay on a flannel rag on the floor beside the tub. As she worked up a lather the homey scent took her back to her childhood.

"How could one guy end up owning an entire mountain?"

"By inheriting it from an ancestor who was awarded it for valor in the Revolutionary War."

"Wow. You're kidding."

"Nope. I've seen the deed. It's on parchment and has Washington's signature on the bottom."

"I'm impressed."

"The Native Americans weren't."

"What do you mean?"

The warmth of the crackling fire caressed Erin's bare neck and shoulders. Even though it was summer the logs held in the cool of night and the fire felt good this morning.

"They thought it was a joke. They spent the first fifty years trying to dislodge our Revolutionary War grandfather from the mountain."

"How did he hold out?"

"Did you get a good look at your grandpa's fortress when we came home last night?"

"It was dark."

"You'll understand when you go outside."

"Oh, yeah. I'm supposed to go chop wood after I get finished with my own bath."

"Are you okay with that?"

"I think it sounds pretty cool, Mom."

Erin smiled herself. She would see how Lindsey felt about it in a couple of hours.

"Hand me that towel, please."

Lindsey helped her dry off, laid another towel on the floor so Erin would have a clean surface upon which to walk, and then helped her back to the bed. Her father had left an old-fashioned throat-to-toes nightgown on the end of her bed. Probably her mother's. He never threw anything away, and thank goodness. She hated the idea of putting on dirty clothes after that lovely bath.

She watched with amusement as Lindsey sank into tepid bath water instead of the hot shower she'd always seemed to think was necessary to her survival.

Marie sat in front of the television with the sound turned down low so Josiah could get his sleep. She seemed to have lost the need for sleep. Ever since the news about Cole, Erin, and Lindsey had hit the national news, she'd not been able to tear her eyes away from the reporters who had gotten everything so very wrong.

She was so nervous, the habit of chewing her fingernails that she thought she'd broken herself of years ago, came back with a vengeance. Seeing Cole being accused of kidnapping after all he'd been through was so infuriating it was . . . well, it was almost enough to make a preacher's wife cuss!

At that moment she heard a small jet engine approaching their little country airport. There had been none the night before. She checked the clock on the wall. 3:30 a.m. Then she went to the calendar hanging on the wall Josiah got each year from the local funeral home, and jotted down the time. She didn't know why these jets were landing, but she had a strong suspicion this information might be important.

⚊⚊⚊

Erin sat on her father's porch, wrapped in a shabby quilt with her freshly bandaged feet resting on a chair. A plate of fried potatoes and sausage was at her elbow.

Cole accepted more coffee. He had helped by grinding the beans a few moments ago in an old iron coffee grinder that looked like it was at least a hundred years old. It was, hands down, the best cup of coffee he had ever tasted.

Bill had also shown him where the well, a tub, and a washboard were and handed him a sliver of soap to wash out his clothes. They might not be exactly clean after he finished, but they were cleaner and now hung on a taut wire clothesline out back. It was early afternoon, and they had a clear view down the mountain path.

Any rift between Erin and her father seemed to have already healed. At the moment she was filling him in on the details of their flight. Cole noticed that Bill's hands were gripping the table edge. It was apparently not easy for him to hear details about the danger his daughter had been in.

"Do you mind if I ask a question?" Cole said when Erin had finished.

"Go ahead."

"How did you know we were there, Bill? I mean, how did you know to be waiting for us?

"The stars sang to me." Bill looked straight at him with eyes so light blue they looked as though they had been leached of pigment. They were strange eyes . . . eerie eyes. "They told me that my daughter and granddaughter were on the Trail."

Cole was almost ready to believe anything this man said.

For some reason the idea of stars singing to someone like Bill sounded almost plausible.

Erin laughed softly. "Before you caught up with us, Cole, I sent Dad a post card with a code telling him we were coming and we were in danger."

Bill smiled. "Now, Erin, I almost had Cole believing me there for a minute. Yes, I got the post card and have pretty much been camped at the base of the mountain ever since. But I also heard from Jeff. He saw you on the Trail while he was hunting 'sang."

"A relative of yours?" Cole asked.

"A cousin. Jeff pretty much lives on the Trail between here and Georgia," Bill said.

"It's too early to harvest ginseng," Erin said.

"He's just looking. He'll harvest it in the fall if the hikers don't take it."

"I doubt most Appalachian Trail hikers even know what wild ginseng looks like, Daddy." Erin took a bite of potatoes.

"True. But it's nice to have someone to blame for it becoming so rare."

"Well, it isn't the hikers. It's mountain folk who have hunted it to death. You told me yourself that Daniel Boone gathered twelve *tons* of dried ginseng in one season, trying to get rich quick, and then lost it all when the boat he'd stacked it on overturned."

"That was a real shame," Bill said. "Daniel and his boy worked awful hard to gather that crop."

Cole noted that Bill talked about people like Daniel Boone and Samuel Brady as though they were personal friends. He wondered if the fact that Bill apparently spent more time reading his books than with actual people made these historical figures more real to him than to most.

Lindsey came out onto the porch, her hair still wet from her bath. She was wearing Bill's oversized long johns.

"And here's my grandbaby." Bill held out his arms.

Lindsey was all skinny, gangly arms and legs, but she curled up on her grandfather's lap like a five-year-old and snuggled. Bill laid his cheek on the top of her head and closed his eyes.

Erin watched her father and daughter with sadness in her eyes. "I'm sorry, Dad."

"It wasn't your fault." Bill rocked his granddaughter. "I knew seeing Lindsey target practicing on a man's silhouette would set Blake off. I did it deliberately just to watch him fuss. I never figured on it costing me the right to see her again. I had her pictures these past few years, though," Bill said. "Thank you for those."

Cole had also seen those pictures. Bill had nearly papered an entire wall with them in the living room. As Bill and Erin continued to talk, Cole wandered over to the window again. He simply couldn't imagine what it would be like to wake up to this view every day.

Of course, Bill Emory probably couldn't imagine waking up to any other. Erin said he seldom left the mountain anymore. For the most part, her father depended on relatives to take the honey he harvested, the goat's milk he sold, the woodcrafts he carved, down the mountain to sell and bring back the few supplies he needed.

Cole supposed that if a man were to have to stay someplace for a lifetime, this would be the place to do it.

CHAPTER TWENTY-SEVEN

Three days later, Erin, wearing a pair of her father's slippers and her mother's old bathrobe, shuffled outside to where he kept his four goats. She scratched the head of the one nearest her.

"Looks like you've made a new friend," Cole said, as the goat bumped her hand, wanting a treat.

"My dad treats his goats better than some people treat their children." She gave the goat one final pat and turned away from the split rail fence. "Where've you been? You were gone when I got up."

"I walked down to the village. It was time to find out what was going on back home and I knew Marie would go into a meltdown if she didn't hear from us soon."

"Weren't you afraid of being recognized?"

"I wore sunglasses and an old hat of your dad's as a disguise."

"What did you do down there?"

"I bought a phone charger. Went to the library where I read the newspapers while it charged. By the way, your picture doesn't do you justice. Fortunately, my picture's old. I've changed a lot since that mug shot was taken. And your new hair color does help disguise you. I like you better as a blonde, by the way."

"I can hardly wait to change it back. Did you get hold of Marie?"

"I did, and she was just chock-full of information."

"That's Marie." Erin's voice was resigned. "What's happened now?"

"Marie has been doing some sleuthing."

"Sleuthing?"

"That's what she called it. Says it's her new hobby. She'd contacted Sharyn Pierce, who was another one of their foster kids. Sharyn recently got hired as a clerical worker with the FBI."

The goat Erin had patted poked its head through the fence and began to nibble her bathrobe. "Does Sharyn know something about this mess?"

"Not a lot. She's new there and her clearance isn't high, but she told Marie she had heard Fallen Oak mentioned recently."

Erin pulled a mouthful of bathrobe out of the goat's mouth and moved a few feet away from the fence. "What had she heard?"

"That Stark County is rumored to be a major drop-off point for cocaine from Mexico."

"Cocaine? That's how Blake . . ."

"Exactly."

"What else did Marie say?"

"She thinks she knows where the cocaine is brought in. She's making plans to gather enough proof to give to the FBI."

"*Marie's* going to get the proof?"

"That's what she said."

"Marie needs to stay out of this," Erin said. "She's going to get herself killed."

"I know." Cole said. "I have to get back there."

"Did she say what she was intending to do?"

"It involves taking photos at the Fallen Oak airport. When I was at Marie and Josiah's this past week, I heard a small jet landing behind their house late at night. She said she'd mentioned it to Dempsey and he'd told her that a pilot-training school had started using the airport as a safe place to practice night landings."

"That sounds plausible."

"Except that Marie's been busy. She made some phone calls and found out that none of the schools within flight range of Stark County are teaching their students to do a night landing there."

"Dempsey lied to her."

"He did. There's such big money in drugs, I think it would take a stronger man than Dempsey to say no if the price was right. He doesn't make all that much of a salary. Josiah had already started to wonder how Dempsey has been able to afford the private hospital his wife's been staying in. Now I think we know."

"Do you suppose Blake found out?"

"I don't know, but you're here with your dad now and safe. You don't need me anymore but Josiah and Marie do. I need to get back there before they stumble into something they can't handle."

"You might not be able to handle it either, Cole."

"Maybe not, but I'm better able to read a dangerous situation than they are. Marie's the kind of person who thinks all the ills of the world can be fixed with a smile and a nice bowl of soup. Josiah thinks it just takes a good, in-depth Bible study to show someone the error of their ways."

Erin smiled. "And you don't?"

"There is true evil in this world, Erin." He did not smile in return. "I've seen it. I've experienced it. I know it exists. I'm not sure Marie and Josiah would recognize it until it was too late. I'm worried about leaving them alone for too long right now."

"Then it's time for us to go back," Erin said.

"Us?" He shook his head. "No."

"Yes." Erin ignored him. "You really can't stop me. I only wanted to get Lindsey to my father. I always intended to go back."

"Your dad won't be happy about that." Cole said.

"No, but he'll take care of Lindsey. Are there any planes coming in tonight?"

"Marie says it is usually between one and three o'clock in the morning when the planes arrive."

"Do they come on any particular night?"

"She says she hasn't been able to figure out any kind of pattern yet, so for the past few nights she's been staying up all night logging any landings, and napping during the day."

"I need to go get ready."

"But it isn't safe."

"Sorry, Cole, but I'm going to Marie's and Josiah's tonight."

As Erin went back to the house, she stopped to watch Lindsey feed the chickens, all of which her daughter had given pet names. The white mule that had carried Erin here grazed inside a split-rail fence. Three hogs rooted in the mud beneath a beechnut tree. Her father was milking the cow inside the barn and she could hear the milk hitting the pail.

Lindsey, surrounded by multicolored chickens pecking at the corn she was scattering around her feet, saw her and waved.

"Looks like you're having fun," Erin called.

"I love it here, Mom."

"Then you won't mind staying for a while?"

"I wouldn't mind staying here forever," Lindsey said.

"Good," Erin replied. "Because I'm going back home for a few days."

"To Fallen Oak? Why?"

"Now that we've gotten you safely to your grandfather, I have some things I need to do."

Lindsey dropped the chicken feed and the biddies scrambled to get as much as possible. "I'll go back with you."

"No. Seriously, Lindsey. I can't concentrate if you're with me. I'll be trying to protect you. I'll be worrying about you."

"And you think I won't be worrying about you? Wanting to protect you?"

She loved Lindsey so much her heart hurt just looking at her. There was no way on earth she would put her daughter at risk again.

This must have been something of how her father had felt—why a man who'd been exposed to the horrors of war had become such a recluse, hiding his wife and child away from the world. Like Cole, her father had known firsthand that there was true evil in the world. He had seen it. Heard it. Felt it. Still had scars, both physical and emotional, from it. Instead of talking about it, he had surrounded his family with farm animals and beauty and vegetables from their garden.

According to one of her relatives who'd told her the whole story long after she'd grown up and moved away, her father had been only seventeen when he joined the military—a Virginia mountain boy flush with patriotism and thirsty for adventure—only a few years older than Lindsey was now. He had been eighteen when he shipped off to Vietnam, twenty-two when he came home broken in spirit and in body. He had eventually married a girl he had known in high school and brought her home to his family's mountain, and then pulled it around them like a warm quilt.

The mountain had not been enough to protect his bride

from the cancer that had stolen her life. Another tragedy he had swallowed quietly, without words, while becoming more and more reclusive.

How it must have hurt him to see Erin so determined to go off into the world, barely glancing over her shoulder as she left.

But he had loved her enough to let her go. What he could not bring himself to do was love the man who had kept her away. Erin thought of the wall he had made of the pictures she had sent him through the years. The pictures she had taken while going about her everyday life . . . while here, she and Lindsey were still his world.

What would it cost him now—to see her leave again?

"Dad?" Her father was still milking as she entered the barn.

"I'm almost finished, Erin."

There were few cozier sounds than a stream of fresh milk ringing against the side of a tin bucket. She took a seat on a square bale of hay and waited.

Her father stood and gave the Guernsey cow a pat. "All done."

He carefully laid a clean linen towel across the top of the bucket, sat it on a low wooden bench, and then untied the cow and let her wander through the barn door to the pasture.

"She's giving well," Erin observed.

"Nearly four gallons a day and plenty of cream. It's nice to have someone here to help drink it."

"Now that Lindsey's safe with you and I can walk again, I have to go back. You know that, don't you?"

"To find out who murdered Blake?"

"Yes."

"Can't Cole do it?"

"It's not his fight. He's done too much already. More than most men would have under the circumstances."

"How long will you be gone?"

"I don't know. Will you keep Lindsey for me?"

He adjusted the towel over the pail of milk, centering it so that both sides hung exactly the same distance. "Of course."

Her father's easy capitulation surprised her. She had expected a longer argument.

"I came close to coming to see you a couple times, but in the end I decided to wait for you to come to me. I prayed that Blake would let you bring Lindsey back to me and trust me with her again."

"You prayed?" Erin was shocked. One of the issues between them when she was growing up was that she had wanted to go to the friendly little church down in the village, and her father had forbade it. He had even railed against organized religion.

"I've changed since you left. I even help keep the church building in good repair these days."

If her father had told her he had flown the space shuttle to the moon and back, she couldn't have been more surprised.

"How did this happen?"

"Long story. I'll tell you about it when you get back." He glanced at her, worried. "You are coming back?"

"If you'll have me, Dad," Erin said. "After this is over, I don't think I'm going to want to stay in Fallen Oak anymore. I was wondering whether you'd mind if Lindsey and I came and lived with you."

"The two of you underfoot all the time?" He grunted. "Making noise? Messing up my kitchen?"

"Yes."

"I suppose if she stays here Lindsey will be wanting a dog that will chew up things and dig up my garden and chase the chickens."

"Most likely."

"I don't suppose I'd mind that so much. I've had a bellyful of silence since you left—but what about Cole?"

"What about him?"

"Will he be coming to stay too?"

"I can't imagine why. He has his own life to live, Dad."

"I may be just an old hermit, but even I can see that he cares about you."

"No, Dad. He's just being kind to us."

"Too bad that's all it is," he said. "I like him."

She could hardly believe her ears. "You what?"

"I said I like him." His voice was irritated. "Anything wrong with that?"

"There's nothing wrong with it, but it surprises me. You hated Blake."

"I didn't hate him. Didn't like him much, either. I thought you could do better."

"Blake was a good man, Dad, no matter what you thought. He was just different than you."

"I didn't say he wasn't a good man, but he reminded me of a friend in Vietnam. Always had his mind somewhere else. Reading when he should have been cleaning his gun. Looking at flowers when he should have been looking for the enemy."

"What happened to him?"

"Got his fool head blown off. Almost got mine blown off too. Blake looked like him, acted like him, talked like him. Gave me the creeps the first time you brought him around here."

"Oh, Dad. You would have liked him if you could have gotten to know him better."

"Too late now."

"Can you get in touch with Cousin Ronnie and see if I can borrow something to drive. He still sells used cars, doesn't he?"

"I'll do that on one condition."

"What's that?"

"You go armed."

"Dad, you know Blake didn't believe in owning guns."

Her father hawked and spit. Then he looked her straight in the eyes. "My point exactly."

~~~

She drove well within the speed limit, carefully using her turn signal, with eyes on the road, watching every sign. Even though she had no driver's license with her, at least she owned one and Cole didn't. Still, she was extra careful. She didn't want to take any chances at being picked up—at least not until she had reached her destination.

Her feet, nearly healed, were encased in old hiking boots her father had rummaged that had once belonged to her mother. They were terribly out of style, but they fit her well. Strapped to her left ankle was a derringer. A holster and loaded Glock nestled beneath her left arm. Beneath an oversized shirt of her fathers, she wore a Kevlar vest. In one pocket of her jeans, she had a walkie-talkie—the twin of the one Cole carried. Cole carried a camera specially made to take pictures at night. Both of them carried night-vision goggles. She had no idea what sort of war her father thought he might have to wage some day with all the gear he'd collected, but right now she was grateful for it. Hopefully, all they'd have to do was take a few pictures of the mysterious jet's license numbers and give it to the FBI as proof that there was something strange going on in Stark County, Tennessee. Sneak up, click, and leave.

On the other hand, strange things seemed to keep happening in Fallen Oak and it didn't hurt to be well prepared.

She knew she was probably breaking a few laws armed like this, but she hadn't really had a choice. Her father had refused to let her leave unless she suited up to his satisfaction. Lindsey had been wide-eyed when she had seen her grandfather's underground arsenal and even wider as he prepared her mother for battle.

He had also insisted on setting up targets, checking her reflexes, making certain she was familiar with each weapon. Cole had been put through the same steps, given the same instruction, suited up in the same way. She almost hated to admit it, but she had discovered that she had more of Wild Bill in her than she'd realized. The bad guys—whoever they were—had made her mad, and now that Lindsey was safe, she was spoiling for a fight.

There was a phrase she'd used too many times back when she and Lindsey were always fussing with each other. She would say that she was "sick and tired" of whatever Lindsey's behavior was. She had resolved to never say that to Lindsey again, but the phrase definitely suited her mood tonight.

She was sick and tired of not knowing what had happened to Blake, sick and tired of wondering what the heck was going on, sick and tired—most of all—of being afraid. Being with her father again had given her the backbone she needed to go face whatever was waiting in Fallen Oak.

Having Cole with her didn't hurt either. She had an idea that a man didn't survive years of prison without knowing how to protect himself.

〜〜〜

"WELCOME TO FALLEN OAK." Cole read the sign out loud as they neared the outskirts of town. "FRIENDLIEST TOWN IN TENNESSEE."

"Right." Erin said, grimly. "As long as you keep your head down and don't ask any questions."

"It's a better town than that," Cole said. "There are still plenty of good people here."

"I know," she grumbled. "I've had several of them as students, but right now I'm in no mood to feel warm and fuzzy about this place."

Marie and Josiah lived on the far side of Fallen Oak. When Erin and Cole arrived, Erin took the precaution of parking her cousin's borrowed car well behind the parsonage—which put it almost in the small church cemetery.

They'd deliberately timed their trip to put them at the Newmans' door at eleven o'clock which was a time when they could depend on most of the people in Fallen Oak being home watching TV or getting ready for bed. They had not told Marie they were coming for fear that she would share the information—in strict confidence of course—with half the congregation.

It took only one knock for the door to fly open and for Marie to launch herself at them, hugging both so hard that Erin was torn between gratitude for the older woman's enthusiasm and worry that she might strangle them both.

When Erin finally got a good look at Marie, she was doubly grateful she had come. Marie was dressed in camouflage pants that she'd had to roll up quite a ways, a camouflage shirt that hung nearly to her knees, her hair had been tucked up under a camouflage hat, and she had smeared black paint under each eye like a football player. An old camera hung around her neck.

Cole looked her up and down. "Were you planning on going somewhere tonight?"

"Yes." Marie seemed somewhat abashed. "I was going to take some pictures of the plane if it came in."

"I asked you not to do that."

"Well, *somebody* needed to!"

"You're right," Erin said. "Somebody did need to. That's why we're here."

"By the way," Cole said. "That blacking is supposed to help

keep the sun from reflecting into the player's eyes. It's pretty dark outside."

"Huh! So *that's* why they wear it!" Marie said. "I wasn't sure."

"What did you use?" Cole asked.

"Josiah's dress shoe polish."

Marie wiped at it with the tail of her shirt but it still left a black smear on her skin.

Cole gave Erin a look. *See why we needed to come tonight?*

"Have you eaten?" Marie asked. "I have stew. It won't take but a minute to warm it up."

"We ate right before we came, Marie," Cole said. "Have you heard any planes landing tonight?"

"Not yet."

A door opened and she whirled around. "Josiah! I'm so glad you're awake! Erin and Cole are here!"

"I heard." Josiah stumbled out of their bedroom, his thinning hair disheveled. It seemed strange to see him in his pajama outfit of gray sweat pants and a white T-shirt. Erin had never seen him without a dress shirt and tie.

He automatically went straight into the kitchen and came back in a few minutes carrying a coffeepot and four mugs hanging off the fingers of his left hand.

"Couldn't find the tray, Marie," he said. "So don't scold me."

"That's okay, dear," Marie said. "I was so nervous last night, I reorganized the kitchen."

Josiah had awakened enough for the camouflage outfit she was wearing to register.

"Really? My hunting clothes, Marie?"

"Well, you weren't using them."

He sighed. "I will be so glad when this is over."

Marie relieved him of the mugs, poured the coffee, and they

spent the next few hours getting caught up. Marie was alert and inquisitive. Josiah kept dozing off.

"He's had a rough week," she explained when he started to snore sitting upright on the couch. "Mrs. Haney had her gallbladder taken out. Her family called him from California and asked him to go sit with her. They said they figured he didn't have anything better to do. We're getting ready for Vacation Bible School next week—you know how much work that is. Then last night the Smith family called him in the middle of the night to come sort out a fight they were having."

"Did he get them calmed down?" Erin asked.

"He kept them from coming to blows." Marie said. "He also did a session of pre-marital counseling with a couple who are getting married in a month and are so crazy in love they don't think they need it, of course. Engaged couples are so cute. And he prepared a sermon and taught a class on the book of Hebrews."

"Did he get a raise this year?" Cole asked.

"No," Marie shrugged. "It's been . . . awhile."

"I'll start helping out once I start my new job. It's the least I can do after all you two have . . ."

A low-flying jet roared over the little house, rattling the dishes in Marie's cabinets. Cole froze, Josiah woke up, and all four looked up at the ceiling

"There it is," Josiah said, glancing at his watch. "One o'clock. It's a little early tonight."

"Are you ready?" Cole asked Erin.

"You have no idea how ready I am."

"Just take the pictures." Josiah admonished. "No heroics. If these people are as bad as we think they are . . . don't let them see you. I don't need any more funerals to preach and I *really* don't want to preach either of yours anytime soon!"

"Oh, goodness," Marie said. "Funerals . . ."

They all looked at her. "What?"

"The idea of funerals. I just remembered something." Marie seemed stunned. "I did mention the jets to someone other than the sheriff."

"Who?" Erin asked as she and Cole headed for the door.

"It was a couple days before I said anything to Sheriff Dempsey. I told Blake one morning at church that there was some unusual plane traffic behind our house."

"When was this?" Cole prompted.

"It was the day of old Mrs. Johnson's funeral. I was in the church kitchen getting things ready for the funeral dinner— Mrs. Johnson had a big family and we were trying to cook for about fifty people—and Blake came by early to drop off those two cakes you'd baked, Erin. I was worried over whether I'd ordered enough fried chicken and Blake came through the door and asked how I was doing, and I said I'd be doing a whole lot better if some jet hadn't landed behind the parsonage in the middle of the night and woke me up and he acted real interested and said he would look into it, but then he . . ."

"Died," Erin said. "Why didn't you mention this to us earlier, Marie?"

"The conversation was over so fast. My memory just isn't as good as it used to be. I'm so sorry."

"It probably doesn't need to be said, but if anything happens tonight, *don't* call the sheriff's department," Cole said. "Try to get hold of the state patrol instead. There's a fighting chance they're not involved in this."

CHAPTER TWENTY-EIGHT

The small, dark, air terminal sat approximately a quarter mile behind the country parsonage. It had been built in the middle of Tennessee farming country and except for the cemetery directly behind the church and parsonage, it was surrounded by woods and cornfields.

Cole could see the airport runway clearly because the lights had been activated, but he didn't see a jet standing where the planes usually parked or refueled.

As they stepped quietly through the cemetery and into the strip of woods behind the parsonage they walked through another, older pioneer cemetery buried in the dark woods. It was a creepy place, with tall trees pushing against old tombstones. He'd stayed away from it when he'd lived there as a kid.

Through the trees he saw the lights of a plane parked at the far end of the runway.

He and Erin picked their way around the tilted and overgrown tombstones. The few sounds they made were masked by the subdued roar of the jet's engine as it idled. Men's voices were faintly audible.

The hidden location of the jet, the sound of the voices—Cole knew without a doubt that something illegal was happening just through the copse of trees.

They crept closer until they could almost read the numbers on the tail of a black jet sitting on the runway. Two men were in the process of unloading something heavy. There was a forklift in play. Two other men were standing guard, each one with machine guns held ready.

Whatever was in that shipment was apparently extremely valuable.

"Don't go any closer or they'll see us," Cole whispered.

Erin nodded, lifted the camera, sighted through the telescopic viewer, and began to softly click pictures of the operation while Cole kept watch with his night vision goggles as he scanned the area for any possible lookouts that might be positioned in the woods around them.

The men who had been helping with the unloading, their job done, got into the plane first. Then the guards with their guns still at the ready, backed into the doorway. The jet's passenger door closed.

Cole heard the jet engines speed up, a high-pitched whine that signaled an imminent departure.

He began to relax slightly. The evening had been a success. They'd gotten what they came for; no one had gotten hurt and it was time to leave.

But then as the plane taxied down the runway, he heard Erin make a sound in the back of her throat as though she were in pain. He saw her drop her dad's good camera to the ground. Then his heart nearly stopped. Erin had apparently lost her mind. She was sprinting across the airstrip straight at the man on the forklift and her gun was drawn.

This was not part of their plan. They had agreed that they would remain safely hidden, doing nothing but taking pictures as proof that something illegal was going on.

He had only a split second to react and chase after her. She was going to get herself killed if he didn't stop her. At the very least he needed to protect her. He only prayed that the jet would take off without the armed men seeing Erin.

As the jet pulled away, it revealed what had been parked just outside his vision. There was a truck attached to a horse trailer and the forklift operator was in the process of loading the bulky, shrink-wrapped pallet into the trailer. He prayed that whoever was operating the forklift was too preoccupied to notice the figure bent on overtaking it.

"Stop!" he heard her scream.

The forklift paused.

"Get down from there!" Erin was standing a few feet away from the forklift, her Glock pointed directly at the man's chest. "Now!"

Cole drew his own weapon but at that moment, he felt something thump into his chest so hard it threw him to the ground.

As the jet roared off into the sky, he lay struggling to get his breath, fighting back against the darkness that threatened to consume him as Sheriff Dempsey emerged from behind the horse trailer.

"Put the gun down, Erin," Dempsey said, his voice calm and reasonable, his weapon now trained on Erin. "I don't want to hurt you. I *never* wanted to hurt you. You should have left this whole thing alone."

"I *knew* you were involved," Erin said. "How could you do it? Blake was your friend!"

"Put the gun down," Dempsey said. "I'm warning you."

Finally, Cole was able to suck in great gulps of oxygen. He was shakily attempting to get to his feet and find where his own weapon had landed when a shot came out of nowhere and he heard a curse as the Sheriff's weapon flew out of his hand.

At that point, he saw that the forklift operator had wasted no time in getting into the truck and starting to drive away—the small horse trailer bouncing along behind.

Four more shots rang out in rapid succession and the two tires on the left side of the trailer collapsed, then it began to dig into the ground. The driver of the truck had a dilemma. To continue driving away at any speed would involve stopping, getting out of the truck, and unhitching the trailer—leaving the contents behind. Or he could continue to drag the horse trailer behind him.

The driver did neither. The man in the truck climbed out and tried to run into the weeds on the other side of the airstrip, but he didn't seem to be able to run very fast. A figure dressed all in black caught him, and in seconds the man was face down on the runway with a knee in the middle of his back and both wrists twisted behind him.

"Don't move," Erin said, training a gun on a suddenly unarmed Dempsey. "You have no idea how badly I want to hurt you right now, so just don't move."

"Are you alive, Cole?" she shouted over her shoulder.

"The vest," he said. "Your dad's bulletproof vest saved my life."

"Are you sure you're not hurt?"

"Nothing except my pride." He walked over to stand beside Erin.

"I didn't mean to hit you, Cole." the sheriff suddenly attempted to be conciliatory. "I thought I was shooting over your head. I always liked you. Even when you were a kid."

Cole ignored him.

"Who's the other shooter out there?" he asked Erin.

"I have no idea. Whoever he is, I think he's on our side."

The person dressed in black now had the man from the truck on his feet and was walking him toward them. The man from the truck was wearing a floppy hat pulled low over his eyes. As the pair drew nearer, Cole could clearly see the face of the figure in black. It was the waitress with whom Dempsey had accused Blake of having an affair.

"You have the right to remain silent," the waitress was saying. "Anything you say can and will be used against you in a court of law. You have the right to speak to an attorney, and to have an attorney present during any questioning. If you cannot afford a lawyer, one will be provided for you at government expense."

Dinah looked nothing like she had at the restaurant. Her face was devoid of makeup and her hair was pulled straight back in a ponytail. She was dressed in black jeans and a long-sleeved black sweatshirt. "DEA," she said as she prodded the masked figure toward them. "Are either of you hurt?"

"We're fine," Erin replied, mystified. "You're from the Drug Enforcement Administration?"

"Yes. Glad you're both okay," Dinah said. Gone was the wad of chewing gum, the flirty attitude and the Southern accent. Instead, she was all business.

The man who'd been driving the van had his head bowed, as though weary or resigned or both.

"Who *is* he?" Cole asked.

Dinah pulled his hat off.

At first, Cole thought his eyes were mistaken. What he was seeing made no sense. The person standing before him in handcuffs was Doc Wilson. His normally genial, kind face was filled with anger.

"You have no idea what you've done," Doc said. "You've destroyed the Little Acorn's last chance. Why couldn't you have just stayed out of it, Erin? You and Blake both. If you'd just stayed out of it, nothing bad would have happened to you. We weren't hurting anyone—but neither of you could leave it alone."

Erin was so shocked at seeing Doc Wilson there, her attention was drawn away from the sheriff who began to reach down for his gun.

"Watch out, Erin," Cole said. "He's . . ."

A tall figure materialized, seemingly out of nowhere, and grabbed the sheriff. In less than a second, Dempsey was handcuffed and the tall figure quickly informed the sheriff of his Miranda rights.

Once again, Cole wondered if his eyes were playing tricks on him. The person who had cuffed the sheriff looked and sounded awfully familiar.

"Coyote?" Erin asked, stunned.

"Good to see ya'll again," Coyote drawled. "Been yellow-packin' lately, Sonnet?"

"You are DEA, too?" Erin said.

"Thought it best to keep an eye on you and Lightning here for a while. We didn't know if either of you were involved in this."

"That's why you were going through my pack that night." Cole said.

"You wouldn't be the first to use the Trail to transport drugs, but I was mainly concerned about the little girl."

"But I don't understand why." Erin still couldn't seem to take it all in. "Why did you do it, Doc?"

"I want a lawyer." The old man wouldn't meet her eyes.

"It was the farm." Dempsey said. "His wife's dream. He's been funding the Little Acorn out of his own pocket for years. The drug money was digging him out of debt and putting the farm on solid footing."

"Is that true, Doc?" Erin said.

"You think I made enough money to run that place?" The doctor's voice was bitter. "By the time I shelled out for office expenses and malpractice insurance and my own health insurance—not to mention floating the people who don't pay their bills . . ."

"But . . . did you kill Blake?"

"Do you see any expensive cars at my place? Do you see me taking any fancy trips?" The doctor ignored her question. "What you see are a bunch of hurt kids riding horses. Your husband was going to ruin it all. I couldn't talk him out of it."

"But . . . Lindsey loved those kids too. She was there at the farm constantly trying to help. How did my husband die, Doc?"

The doctor seemed to have gone somewhere else in his head. It was as though he were talking to himself, rehearsing the same justifications he'd used in order to do what he'd done.

"I didn't create the market for drugs in this country," he said in a sing-song voice that sounded so rehearsed that Cole could imagine the doctor having said it over and over to himself to justify his actions. "I didn't push anything on anybody. I just stored the stuff in my shed until their people pick it up. I used the money to do good! If I didn't take it, someone else would. It fed my horses and paid therapists to work with the children."

"Was it that wooden shed with the big padlock on it?" Marie asked. "I always wondered what you kept in there."

Cole whirled and saw Marie and Josiah standing behind them. Josiah held a ball bat in his hand, and Marie—still dressed in camouflage—had a badminton racket in hers.

"We heard shots," Josiah said, in explanation.

"And you came to save us with a baseball bat and a badminton racket?" Cole said.

"Well . . . I did pray a good deal as we came through the woods," Josiah said.

"What happens now?" Marie said.

"We'll call the state patrol," Dinah said. "I don't want to use any of Sheriff Dempsey's people. We suspect there's a couple of his deputies in on this. My own people will be here soon, but the state patrol can get here the quickest."

Marie tucked the racket beneath her arm, pulled her cell phone out of her pocket and punched in a number. While she explained what they needed, Josiah cleared his throat.

"Did you help with Blake's death?" Josiah asked Dempsey. "Were you part of that?"

"No," the sheriff shook his head. "Two members of the cartel killed Blake. They figured that if Blake died of an 'accidental' overdose, the DEA would discount anything he might have reported. Doc filled the hypodermic they used on him to make sure plenty of the stuff got in his bloodstream, but he refused to administer it. The only thing I did was take payoffs to keep my mouth shut. That's why I was here tonight. All I did was take a bribe. I didn't kill anyone. The facility where my wife is staying is not cheap. I had nothing to do with the murder."

"There was an autopsy," Cole said. "Wouldn't it have shown that Blake didn't die accidentally? Blake would have fought back. There would have been bruising."

"You've been gone too long," the sheriff said. "Want to take a wild guess who has been functioning as a coroner for the past few years?"

All eyes turned toward Doc Wilson.

"How very convenient," Dinah said.

"I'm confused." Erin turned to Dinah. "You've been a DEA agent all along? Dempsey told me you were having an affair with my husband."

"There was no affair, Erin." Dinah said. "And for the record, I've seldom met a man more in love with or as protective of his wife. I've been working undercover, gathering information, trying to figure out a pattern. We've been coordinating a major bust. This is just one of many destinations this particular cartel targeted. We suspected Doc and Dempsey, but they're small potatoes and have been in way over their heads from the beginning."

"The sheriff said he saw you together."

"Yeah." Dinah shifted her weight. "He probably said he saw me and Blake holding hands at some restaurant outside of town. Right?"

"I *did* see you together," Dempsey said.

"The drug cartels have gotten very advanced. They knew about every phone call you made to the other law officials around the country, trying to talk them into coming here to investigate Blake's death. That's probably why you were targeted—they figured you were never going to back off. We knew that some of the cartels target the families of those who get cross-ways of them as a warning. With Blake gone, I thought they'd leave you alone, but they didn't."

"But about you and Blake . . ."

"Small rural towns are hard to infiltrate and doing so is my specialty. I worked my way through college waiting tables. People tend to overlook waitresses and waiters. It's possible to learn a lot about a small town if you keep your ears open. Blake was suspicious that something major was going on. He also suspected at least some of your local law officials were involved. He and I met a few times miles from here to safely exchange information. Unfortunately, Dempsey ran into us once. I was in my Dinah makeup and clothing, so I grabbed Blake's hand and tried to make it look like a romantic liaison. It wasn't, but it fooled the sheriff."

As the stars shined down from the heavens on the ragtag little group, the sound of an ambulance and a state patrol siren split the air.

"Here come the cavalry," Marie said. "And it's about time."

Coyote glanced into the woods. "Ya'll can tell your shooter to come in now."

"Our shooter?" Erin said. "I thought it was someone *you* brought."

"Then who . . . ?" Coyote waved his arm in the air. "Hey! Whoever is out there. We got 'em now. Come on in."

Two figures came walking out of the woods across the airstrip. One was carrying a rifle.

"Daddy?" Erin recognized them as they grew closer. "Lindsey?"

Lindsey's face was a tear-streaked mask of grief as she walked toward them.

"I saw the whole thing." Lindsey walked up to the doctor. "I thought you were the best person I'd ever met!"

Doc Wilson looked away.

"How did you get here?" Erin asked. "When?"

"We were behind you the whole way." Lindsey turned her back on Doc. "Grandpa was afraid you and Cole might need him, so he borrowed Cousin Ed's truck. While you parked in the cemetery, Grandpa parked out behind the airport. I showed him where to go to wait."

Erin didn't know whether to hug her father or shake him for putting himself and Lindsey in danger. Her fear for her daughter overcame her gratitude for his presence.

"You lied to me, Dad. You said you'd stay there and keep my daughter safe."

"Nope. Never said I'd stay there. I only said I'd keep Lindsey safe and I did. And you. I'm sorry I didn't see Dempsey behind the truck until after he'd fired on you, Cole. "

She should have known that Wild Bill would never stay safely on his mountain when his daughter was in danger. She didn't yell at him. She didn't hug him. She said the one thing she knew her father would appreciate the most. "Good shooting, Dad."

CHAPTER TWENTY-NINE

Doc Wilson looked as though he had aged ten years. She steeled her heart against the pitiful sight of him in prison garb, sitting at a table in a room usually reserved for low-risk prisoners meeting with their family or lawyers. Doc had a lawyer, John Phipps, whom Blake had helped train years earlier, but Doc had no close family. She, Lindsey, and Blake had probably been the closest he'd had to that—and yet he had still filled the syringe that had ended Blake's life.

She'd given a lot of thought to what she wanted to do and say. It was unusual for a jail to allow the wife of a victim to spend time alone with a criminal, but the circumstances were different here. With Sheriff Dempsey no longer in charge, the sheriff's department was in disarray. Richard Conrad, the deputy with the most seniority, was trying to gain control of the situation, but he was harried, overworked, and distracted.

Erin was a respected member of the community and Doc Wilson had been nearly idolized. The trial had not taken place to this point, so many of the details were not yet public. Richard had not hesitated when she'd asked him if she could spend a little time with poor old Doc.

Now she was sitting across the table from one of the men who had helped murder her husband. A man she had entrusted with her daughter, a man who she had once, along with the rest of the town, dearly loved.

"Hi," she said.

"How nice it is of you to come see me, Erin," Doc said, cautiously. "Most people have stayed away."

"I'm sorry for that, Doc. You have done a lot of good in this community."

He visibly relaxed at her kind words.

"I've wanted to talk to you, Erin. I've wanted to explain. I wasn't exactly at my best that night at the airstrip."

She noticed that his hands, which he had clasped together on the table in front of him, were trembling.

Richard Conrad stuck his head in. "Everything all right in here, Mrs. Ramsey?"

"We're fine, Richard. Thanks for asking. Doc and I are going to visit awhile, if you don't mind."

"Take all the time you want, ma'am."

"You were saying?" she prompted.

"You can't possibly understand what it is like to get old, Erin. You can't know how helpless it feels to be facing an infirm old age with few resources. The horse farm for handicapped children was the only thing I had to leave to this town. It was my legacy, my dream."

"And a great one," she agreed.

"Exactly." He brightened and sat up a little straighter. "When the man from the cartel approached me, I had two options: to blow the whistle on them—which would only make them go someplace else—as well as put my life in danger. Or I could take their money and put it into something worthwhile, something lasting."

"In other words, the end justified the means."

"Yes. I was able to get better horses, better equipment, and better trainers. A few more months and the farm would have been back on solid footing financially."

"That would have been wonderful."

"Blake was going to ruin everything."

"Blake tended to see things in black and white . . . but how did he find out?"

"He started to get suspicious. One day when I was gone, he found a package of cocaine we'd dropped in the tall grass at the far end of the airport. I'd searched for it—the stuff is like gold—but I hadn't been able to find it yet. He put two and two together and came to me in my office."

"Why?"

"He said he hated for me to get hit with the fallout when the DEA got hold of what I was doing. He said if I stopped and would tell him exactly who I was working with and testify against them, he would personally represent me and make certain I got off as easily as possible. He said he understood the position I'd been placed in."

"What did you do?"

"I pretended to go along with it. I said I'd think about it and meet him in his office later—but he should have known better. There was no way I could allow my name to be connected to something like this."

"Of course."

"Do you think parents would allow their children to come to the farm if they knew? Do you think I'd still have my volunteers? Think about it, Erin. Would you have allowed Lindsey to come help at the farm if you'd have known what was going on out there?"

"No."

"Everything I did, I did to protect the good work we were

doing there. It was my wife's dream and became mine. There was no way I could let that dream die."

"What about Dempsey?"

"When the cartel approached me," the doctor said. "I knew Dempsey was in serious financial trouble. I'm a family doctor. People confide in me. He'd already mortgaged his house to pay for his wife's treatment and he was facing bankruptcy. Getting Dempsey to turn a blind eye for a kick-back wasn't hard."

Richard stuck his head in again. "Are you ready to go yet, Mrs. Ramsey?"

"Not yet, please. Doc and I haven't quite finished our visit. Would you mind coming back in about ten minutes? I think we'll be done by then."

"Sure thing, Mrs. Ramsey."

There was silence between them after Richard closed the door.

Then she asked the question that had been keeping her awake nights ever since she'd heard that Blake had been murdered.

"Did my husband struggle?" she asked. "Did he suffer?"

"No, not . . . not after the injection. I—I liked Blake. I made certain it was enough to knock him out."

"Were you there? Did he know you were helping with his death?"

"I told him I was sorry," Doc began to look wary. "I told him it was out of my hands . . . and by that time it was."

She pulled out her father's Glock and laid it on the table.

Doc's eyes were wide. "How did you get that in here?"

"Did you really think Richard would search me, Doc?" Erin smiled. "When I walked in, he was trying to figure out where Dempsey kept the key for the storage cabinet that holds the toilet paper. I used to be his teacher. I'm the one who gave him C's on the tests he took and he was grateful to get them.

I know Richard. I knew he wouldn't have the nerve to search me."

"You wouldn't dare . . ."

She took the safety off and pointed the gun directly at him, her back toward the door, her body blocking the sight of the gun if anyone glanced in—and the single security camera. Theirs was not a financially flush county.

Don't ever point a gun at something or someone you don't intend to kill, daughter.

Deliberately, she turned off her inner Wild Bill dictum.

"Do you have any idea what you put me or my daughter through, Doc? Did you think about the fact that her father would never see her graduate, never walk her down the aisle, never hold his grandchildren in his arms?"

"Erin, I . . ."

"Shhh. Don't say another word." She put a finger up to her mouth and shushed him. "It's my turn to talk, and I've been rehearsing what I would say to you ever since I recognized you at the airport."

"I didn't mean to . . ."

"Because of you, both Lindsey and I were nearly killed by a car bomb. Because of you, a cartel thug nearly killed us later at home. Because of you, I nearly died from an infection while trying to escape to my father's mountain. All of this grief and pain and suffering because of that horse farm."

She noticed that Doc watched the barrel of the gun with the same sick fascination he might have watched a poisonous snake about to strike, and she felt happy about it.

"Put the gun away, Erin." He stared at the gun. The color had drained from his face. "Have you lost your mind? I know a good psychologist . . ."

The irony of Doc Wilson offering to set her up with a psychologist was just too rich. She chuckled softly. It really was laugh-out-loud funny, but she didn't want to draw Richard to the door again. Not before she was finished.

"On the contrary, Doc. I know exactly what I'm doing. I've planned it out, second by second. I've imagined you lying on the floor, dead, from a bullet from this gun in my hand. I've fantasized about how satisfying it would be to kill you after what you did to Blake and to us."

Doc's eyes darted around wildly. He started to get up.

"Sit down, Doc." She cocked the gun. "*Now.*"

He sat.

"You can imagine how tempting it was for me to think about killing you, can't you?"

"Y—yes."

"Good." She propped both elbows on the table and with two hands, pointed the Glock directly at his forehead. "Because I want you to remember this moment for the rest of your life. I want you to know that if it weren't for the teachings of Christ—if all I had were the laws of men to hold me back today—I would already have blown your brains out and claimed temporary insanity. I would have done my time and it would have been worth every second to see the surprise on your face when I pulled the trigger."

"I don't understand . . ." A droplet of sweat trickled down his forehead.

"Let me put it in simpler terms. The only reason you aren't lying dead on the floor right now, is because Jesus told me not to commit murder and I have chosen to be obedient to his teachings. That's the only reason. You owe Him your life."

A dead silence filled the room as she let Doc absorb what she'd said.

Slowly, she un-cocked the gun, reengaged the safety, carefully placed the Glock in her purse, and stood up. "You might be tempted to tell someone what happened here today.

Don't bother, because no one would believe you. There's not a person in this town that would expect me to be capable of this."

She knocked on the door, calling out, "Richard, I'm finished here."

Before Richard came to usher her out, she remembered one last thing.

"There have been times in the past where my respect for you was so great I found myself wishing that I could have had someone nice and normal like you for a father. But my war-damaged father would never, ever have done what you did, no matter what the cost. My dad would have fought the cartel all by himself single-handed before he would have helped them kill a friend."

Richard was at the door. "Are you ready, Mrs. Ramsey?"

"I sure am, Richard." She smiled at Doc. "I feel so much better after our talk, Dr. Wilson. I hope you do too. Please let me know if there's anything I can do for you."

The last image she had of Doc was of him sitting at the table, staring into space.

She had considered and rejected the idea of ultimately telling him that she had unloaded the gun before her arrival. It wasn't that she was afraid it would accidentally go off—she was afraid she would be tempted to use it.

CHAPTER THIRTY

Weeds had grown up to the bumper of the old farm truck. It sat rejected and weary-looking beside the barn. The whole place looked derelict except for Erin's new black Jeep sitting out front.

Cole waded through the tall grass to Erin's porch. The front door was open, and he heard voices within.

He stood in the open doorway for a moment, enjoying the sight of Erin and Lindsey. He had missed those two. Erin was on her knees, picking up glass from a shattered lamp. Lindsey was dumping things from the kitchen into a large trash can sitting between the two rooms.

"Hello," Cole said.

"Cole." Erin glanced up and smiled. "It's so good to see you."

Lindsey squealed and ran toward him. "We've missed you!"

"I've missed you, too."

"Can you *believe* what those people did to our house?" Lindsey said, giving him a hug.

"I'm sorry this happened, sweetie," Cole wrapped his arms

around the girl. Her hair was back to its natural color he was glad to see. "But it's over, now."

After giving him a hard hug, Lindsey went back to her job and he was left to talk to Erin.

"Marie said you were back from your dad's."

"Only temporarily. Just long enough to clean this place and put it on the market."

"You're moving permanently, then?"

"It's the best thing to do. Lindsey hates it here now. I need to get her away from everything that's happened. A new start in a new place would be the healthiest thing all around. Plus, Dad's getting older and I need to be close to him if he needs me." She rose and carried a dustpan of broken glass to the trash can. Then she pointed to the overturned couch. "Can you help me with this?"

"Sure." He grabbed hold of one end and she took the opposite side. They hefted the couch and put the cushions back into place.

"Now the armchair."

He lifted it back in place as she stood back, hands on her hips, and surveyed the room. "That's a little better."

"Ew! Ew! Ew!" Lindsey came in, picked up a bowl from the floor beside the overturned couch and dropped it into the trash can. "A moldy cereal bowl. Mom, he ate stuff while he was here! Probably waiting for us to come back." She ran to the kitchen to wash her hands. She came back into the living room using a paper towel to wipe each finger individually.

"I'm definitely looking forward to getting out of here," she announced.

"Because a stranger used a cereal bowl?" Erin said.

"Because things have been way too weird around here."

"Why don't you just concentrate on your own room for

now?" Erin said. "It's not as bad up there. I'll keep working down here."

"If you're sure you don't mind."

"I don't mind."

"Fantastic." Lindsey ran up the stairs.

"I'm ready for a break," Erin said. "Have a seat Cole, and I'll get us a couple of soft drinks—I stashed some in the fridge this morning."

She went into the kitchen, came back, and handed him a bottle. "Is orange soda okay? It's Lindsey's favorite."

"It's fine."

She collapsed into the armchair next to him, put her feet on an ottoman, and raised her soda bottle in the air. "Here's a toast to surviving."

He clanked his bottle against hers. "Here's a toast to two very brave women."

She took a sip then raised her bottle again. "How about a toast to a man willing to forgive?"

"To a woman worth forgiving." Cole said. "How about a toast to William Emory, one of the most interesting men I've ever met—not to mention an excellent sharpshooter."

"Amen," Erin said. "Here's to Marie and Josiah."

"Absolutely." Cole thought for a moment. "To Coyote and Dinah."

Erin raised her bottle again. "To Old Orchard Shelter and all the other shelters and the volunteers who built them."

"To the Preacher, his hot dogs, and his willingness to rescue three filthy hikers."

"To the DEA catching the men who killed Blake. May the cartel guys spend the rest of their lives in prison regretting what they did."

"To Sheriff Dempsey and Doc Wilson also being behind bars."

Erin hesitated. "It seems so strange to be grateful that Doc is in jail. How could he have done what he did, Cole? It boggles my mind that someone we loved so much would do such a thing."

"Like so many people, Doc Wilson believed that the end justified the means. He was wrong."

"The Little Acorn has done a lot of good . . . but it wasn't worth murdering for. I wonder what will happen to it now."

"Marie told me that volunteers are already out there feeding the horses and keeping it open. One of the newer ones is a local grant writer and thinks the state might kick in some funds if Doc will sign it over to make it into a nonprofit."

"I wouldn't count on it," Erin said. "He's a doctor, a respected man. This is his first offense. He's old. They'll give him a slap on the wrist and he'll be living there again soon."

"Maybe, but there's something you might not know about him," Cole said.

"What's that?"

"He has Parkinson's disease. I noticed the tremors in his hands when he bandaged my arm. I mentioned it to Marie and she confirmed it. That's one of the reasons he was willing to risk what he did—he knew he wouldn't be able to work much longer and didn't know what would become of him or his ranch when he couldn't practice medicine. He has no savings. Everything went into the farm."

"It's hard for me to feel sorry for him, Cole. There had to be some other way. How could someone as kind and as giving as Doc—someone who put all their money and energy into creating a place as wonderful as the Little Acorn—help kill a friend?"

"He was desperate. He felt backed into a corner. Desperation makes people do a lot of things they shouldn't."

"Blake used to talk about that. As a prosecutor, he ran

into a lot of people who believed they had no choice in what they'd done. If they had any kind of belief in God, he would sometimes quote 1 Corinthians 10:13 to them."

"I don't know that reference," Cole said. "I'm not the Bible scholar Blake was."

"Me either, but he quoted it so often I have it memorized. *No temptation has overtaken you that is not common to man. God is faithful, and he will not let you be tempted beyond your strength, but with the temptation will also provide the way of escape, that you may be able to endure it.*"

"From what Marie told me," Cole said. "Doc has never followed the same code as we do. That's why it's hard for us to understand his actions. I can see how someone who has no belief in anything outside of creating a legacy of good works might think that killing one person to protect what he considers the greater good could make perfect sense. I'm guessing it still makes perfect sense to him, except that he got caught."

Erin sighed. "The world is an ugly place."

"It isn't always," he said. "I saw many small acts of kindness even in prison. I didn't care for Blake for obvious reasons, but I know he was a man of integrity. He did what he thought was right. In your classroom, you'll use literature to help show hundreds of children how to discern between right and wrong. Josiah will prepare and preach his sermons until the day he dies, and Marie will welcome sojourners into her home and love on people until she can't anymore—and she'll probably try to continue even then. It's best to remember all the decent people we meet and all the acts of kindness we observe."

"I appreciate you reminding me of that right now, especially in the middle of the chaos of my home. Hey, here's a toast to the best thing of all." Erin touched her bottle to his. "To true friendship."

"Yes. To true friendship." Their eyes met and locked. "I'll miss you, Erin Ramsey."

"I'll miss you too, Cole." To his surprise, her voice cracked with emotion. She cleared her throat. "My dad says that a relative of Samuel Brady is welcome in his house anytime. You'll visit, won't you?"

"I'll try." He rolled his soda bottle back and forth between the palms of his hands. "I'm working full-time for Vance these days. We're building a vacation home over on the lake near Deer Run Ridge. I'm going to be pretty busy until it's finished."

"Do you like your job?"

"It's satisfying work and I'm getting better at it. Vance treats me well. I like the crew I work with. Frankly, after all those years in prison, construction work feels like play."

"I hope you have a good life. No one deserves it more than you."

"I hope the same for you. Will you be living with your dad or just getting a place near him?"

"Both, I think. There's a cottage in the village that caught my eye. It's only a short walk to the school. During the school year, especially if I can manage to get a teaching job and in the winter when it snows, it would make more sense for us to live close to the school and visit Dad on weekends instead of trying to make the trek down from the mountain every day. I had to do that as a kid and it was rough. We'll also stay with him a lot during the summer. I know my dad will love having us around, but he's been a loner for a long time. I think he might welcome some days to himself."

"Probably." Cole sat his soda bottle on the floor and stood up. "I need to be getting back. We're putting trusses on that house this afternoon and Vance needs all the muscle he can get. Otherwise I'd stay and help you with this." He gestured at the jumbled room.

"We can handle it. Besides, Marie and Josiah are coming over this afternoon and some other friends from church who said they'd help." She rose with him. "I'll see you out."

They walked as far as the front door until he turned suddenly and faced her. He could hear Lindsey moving around in the room directly above them.

"There's something I've been debating whether or not to say to you." Cole's heart was pounding. This was going to be hard, and there was a chance it could be humiliating.

"What's that, Cole?"

"Back when you were a first-year teacher and I was a janitor, I thought you were the most perfect woman I'd ever known."

Erin shook her head. "You certainly learned better than that in a hurry."

"I just wanted you to know before you left . . . that I still do."

Tears welled up in her eyes, and he wondered whether it would be okay to kiss her. Reluctantly he decided against it. Too soon. Way too soon. The woman needed time to heal. Time to grieve. And he needed time to figure out exactly how to live this new life he'd been given.

As he pulled out of the driveway in the new truck he'd bought, he saw her standing in the doorway, one hand lifted in farewell.

CHAPTER THIRTY-ONE

LATE SPRING - ONE YEAR LATER

E rin sat on her father's handmade porch swing, pushing herself back and forth with her bare foot, the prayer journal she had started by her side. She had worked hard today, helping her father build a new chicken coop for the fancy breed of chickens Lindsey had taken a shine to after viewing a 4-H exhibit at the county fair last fall.

She ruffled her hands through her short hair. It had grown out enough that Lindsey had been able to clip most of the dye off, and her natural color was back—albeit only about three inches of it. It was still wet from the makeshift outdoor shower her dad had set up for her and Lindsey. The shower involved a large, black bladder of water that was heated by the sun, providing just enough for each of them to lather up and have a few seconds to rinse off each night. It was a lot easier than lugging buckets of water.

Wild Bill, however, still preferred to bathe in the bone-achingly-cold mountain stream a quarter mile from their house. Her dad was as tough as old leather, except for where she and Lindsey were concerned, and Erin loved him beyond words.

At the moment, Lindsey and her grandfather were checking

out a patch of wild mulberry trees on the other side of the mountain. They'd invited her to go with them, but she had wanted this moment of solitude—to think, to pray, to thank God for His continued care. She had promised to make a cobbler for them tonight if they brought back enough ripe berries.

She glanced down at her journal and added yet another thank-you, this time for the teaching job she had been offered yesterday. After a winter of sporadic substitute teaching, there had been a sudden full-time opening in the local high school. Her own much-loved former English teacher had decided to retire, recommending Erin as her choice to fill her position. Erin was flattered to be considered and thrilled to accept.

Her grief over Blake had subsided into a dull ache. Moving away from Fallen Oak had helped a little because, there, everything reminded her of him. She and Lindsey had ended up selling or giving away nearly everything they owned. Their house and everything in it had felt sullied after all they'd been through.

She had given Blake's law library for free to a law student who'd answered her ad and couldn't believe his luck. She was certain Lindsey would not be needing her father's books. Her daughter had a very different talent, one that would probably always have to do with the outdoors and animals, and she was getting the best education of all just by hanging out with her grandfather.

It was strange how little emotion Erin felt about getting rid of all the things she had accumulated over the years as she tried to create her idea of a normal life. Each item she gave away or sold left her feeling lighter.

Lindsey was the only truly important thing she had—and her dad, who had been relieved to get back immediately to his mountain once he had made certain that his daughter and granddaughter were safe.

Wild Bill was opening up to people a little more these days. After he met Marie and Josiah that night at the airport, Marie had insisted he and Lindsey spend the night as well before driving back to Virginia. In return, to Erin's astonishment, he invited them to visit him. They'd been gracious about it and had come for a short stay in the fall. Her dad had wanted to show them all his animals and favorite places on the mountain. She had never been more grateful for their kindness and Marie's ebullience than when she had seen her father enthusiastically explaining the intricacies of a survival farm.

Marie's latest enthusiasm had therefore immediately become backyard chicken farming. The people at church were being gifted with organic eggs when the hens were laying well, and hearing more about chickens than they ever wanted to know every Sunday as Marie and Josiah stood around visiting with everyone after church.

From the proceeds of the sale of their house, she and Lindsey bought a small cottage in the village. It was sparse in decor, but Erin liked it that way these days. She didn't want to waste her time dusting and cleaning. She wanted to spend her time doing important things—like teaching at the high school and enjoying the companionship of her daughter.

There was one cloud on her horizon, one hurt that would not go away. She had not heard a word from Cole since that day he had come to say good-bye at the house. It was to be expected, of course. He owed her nothing and had a life to rebuild.

She had tried to talk to Marie and Josiah about Cole when they came for their visit, but both of them were vague and noncommittal. He was working. He was doing fine. He had gotten an apartment but dropped by and checked on them daily. He was deemed quite a catch in town. Several young women at church were showing a lot of interest.

It was surprising how much the thought of other women going after him stung.

They also mentioned that he had taken over teaching the teen class at church—a huge step for him. They said he was doing a good job with it. Hearing all these wonderful things made her happy, but she still missed seeing him.

She had written to him after Marie and Josiah left. A light, friendly note, asking how he was doing and giving him an update on what was going on in her life. He had responded by sending her a short two-sentence note folded in with a photo of the house he had just helped Vance Patterson finish.

They'd been through so much together that she had hoped they would be able to sustain a friendship. Now, she knew they would not.

At least he had been there when she really needed him and she was back on her feet now. No longer under any threats. Still, it would be nice to hear from him from time to time and know how he was doing.

A slight plume of dust rose into the air and vanished. It had not rained for several days, and the path up the mountainside was as dry and loose as talcum powder. It was probably one of her father's cousins, coming to pick up another load of honey or goat cheese, which Lindsey was also happily mastering at her grandfather's side.

Through the leaves she caught the figure of a man leading a horse. He emerged into the clearing and her heart leaped. It was Cole. Her foot stopped pushing the swing and she had to force herself to sit still, fighting the urge to run to him.

His hair was longer than she remembered. It now brushed the collar of his flannel work shirt. He was tanned and looked fit. His work with Vance had obviously agreed with him. She couldn't see his eyes because he was wearing sunglasses. As she watched him come toward her, she thought of Cole's sacrifices for her and Lindsey while they were hiking together, and a lump rose in her throat. She had missed him. More than she had wanted to admit.

The horse puzzled her. She had not known Cole to be a horse person, but then, she had not really known him all that well. At least, she had not known much about his likes and dislikes. Perhaps he had turned into an avid rider—but why would he bring his horse here?

⚬⚬⚬⚬

When he entered the yard, she rose and stood at the banister, looking down at him. Neither of them spoke. Neither of them smiled. There was an immediate emotional intensity between them. He took off his sunglasses, hooked them onto his pocket, and drank in the sight of her.

Being here on the mountain had obviously been good for her. She wore a simple cotton dress sprigged with small flowers. It looked cool and comfortable, and her hair was still wet from a recent bath. Her skin glowed from health. Her feet were bare. He had never found her as beautiful as he did at that moment.

"Are you, by any chance, the lady of the house?" he said.

"I am."

"Do you happen to know anyone who might want a good mare?"

"Depends. Does she have a name?"

"Yes, ma'am. Snowball. She's smart, gentle, and good with children, and I've heard from an excellent source that she's an especially good listener."

"I believe we might be in need of such a horse. How much do you want for her?"

"Oh, I thought we might work out a barter."

"A barter? What would this horse named Snowball be worth, do you think?"

"Well, I had to rent a horse van to get her here. And I brought along a few weeks' supply of feed and grain. And then there was the expense of purchasing her in the first place. The barter price would be steep."

"For a horse that's known as a good listener, I might be willing to pay a steep price."

The next thing he wanted to say was a gamble, but from what Marie had told him about the look on Erin's face when she'd said there were other women interested in him—a gross exaggeration on Marie's part, who wasn't above giving Cupid some help—he thought it was a gamble worth taking.

"I was thinking perhaps, I might be able to barter all that for one kiss from the lady of the house."

Erin came flying off the porch so fast he had to drop the reins just to catch her in his arms.

Their kiss was so intense it knocked him back a step and stole his breath. He bracketed her face with his hands. "Are you, by any chance, still single?"

"I am. Why did you stay away so long?"

"I figured once the bad guys were out of the way, you and Lindsey needed time to get settled and to sort out your life before I came and started upsetting everything."

"How would your coming to visit upset things? Lindsey adores you. Dad likes you—and that's saying a lot—and I've missed you."

"There's a contractor near here who's offered me a job based on Vance's recommendation. I can start the job next week if I want to, but there's one thing I need to know before I accept it. I can't live close to you and continue to pretend that I'm only a friend. If friendship is all you want from me, Erin,

I'll keep my job with Vance and build a life without you. It will be hard, but I've done hard things before."

"Before we talk about any of this, let's put the horse in the pasture out back," she said. "Lindsey and Dad will be home soon, and I'd like Snowball to be the first thing Lindsey sees."

It wasn't the answer he had hoped for, but he put the old horse in the pasture and locked the gate.

"Come and sit on the back porch with me," Erin said when he was finished. "There's so much I want to ask you. I don't get much news up here. Marie's so busy these days she seldom writes to me anymore."

They sat on the top steps of the back porch, watching Lindsey's favorite horse munch grass. He had laid his heart out, and if she chose to ignore it, that was her choice. He loved her, but he could live without her if he had to.

"What do you want to know?" he asked.

"How's Doc doing? I was pretty rough on him before I left. I don't know whether I did the right thing or not."

"He signed the farm over to a state agency. The grant came through, and more children are being helped than ever before. As an accessory to murder he should have gotten life in prison, but because of Doc's age and illness the judge was very lenient. Doc's being allowed to live in his home, but he'll be on a tether for the rest of his life."

"Can he still practice medicine?"

"No. A young doctor has taken over his practice, and people say that he's very good. Very "up-to-date" was the term Marie used. She and Josiah visit Doc frequently. When I went by to pay him for the horse, he was sitting under a shade tree and a Bible was open in his lap."

"Really? Did he say anything about why he was reading it?"

"Actually, I did ask him. He told me you'd said something that had made him rethink some positions he'd previously taken on Christianity. I guess Josiah's been studying with him too. What did you say to him, Erin?"

"That's not important." She looked a little guilty. "What about Sheriff Dempsey?"

"He's in prison and will be for a long time. The judge wasn't as lenient with him. The good news is that the fancy hospital he paid for by mortgaging his good name and clear conscience did help his wife. She's doing much better. She even came home and got a little job working at the telephone office. Marie and Josiah keep tabs on her too."

"Have there been any more mysterious jets landing in the middle of the night?"

"Marie says not. She almost sounded disappointed about it the last I talked to her. The DEA made a few arrests and the cartel have apparently moved their operations to another location. I doubt the arrests will do much good. I'm afraid we caused Dinah and Coyote to show their hand before they got all the information they needed."

A silence fell and lengthened between them. He knew Erin was wrestling with what to say to him. If she had to wrestle with it, he didn't want to wait around and hear her make excuses. He decided he would make it easy for her and for himself. The trip wasn't a total loss. At least Lindsey had her horse now.

"I guess I'd better be getting home."

Her hand slipped into his. "No."

"No?"

"Don't go." With her left hand, she turned his face toward her. "Take the job, Cole. Then come and sit on the porch and let me bake you a mulberry pie. Let Lindsey get to know you when things are normal instead of when we're running for our lives. Let us all get to know and appreciate who Cole Brady really is . . . and then I want you to ask my dad's permission to marry me. He likes you, and he'll like you even better when he finds out that you plan to stick around and aren't going to take his daughter and granddaughter off somewhere else. Can you do all that?"

"Easily." His hopes and spirits rose. "Vance is in between jobs right now. I can move here tomorrow if you want."

"The sooner, the better." She looked deep into his eyes, and his heart melted. "We are going to have *such* a good life together, Cole. I promise."

AUTHOR'S NOTE

To keep from accidentally pointing a finger at some innocent person living in a real town, I invented the small town of Fallen Oak and Stark County, Tennessee. Emory Mountain also does not exist. All the characters are based entirely upon my imagination.

I did, however, do a great deal of research on the Appalachian Trail. The culture of using made-up Trail names, the description and placement of the shelters on the Trail, the wild ponies, etc, are all as accurate as I could make them. Grandma Gatewood was a real person and a personal heroine of mine. One of FBI's most wanted did elude capture for several months by disappearing into the hundreds of hikers who walk the Trail each year.

The description of the country airport, church, and cemetery are an accurate portrayal of the parsonage where we lived in Ohio for many years. Sometimes private jets did land there. To my knowledge none were owned by drug cartels but those late night landings did set my mind to wondering about what if.

Like Marie, I'm an abysmal seamstress, a haphazard quilter, and the one afghan I managed to crochet was an embarrassment to my family. I discarded many hobbies until I found the one I loved with all my heart—spinning stories for readers. Oh, and my husband has finally learned to not use me for sermon illustrations without asking permission first.

Made in the USA
Monee, IL
02 May 2021

67528503R00184